Midge
& Decker

Also by Robert Mayer

The Execution
Superfolks

Midge
& Decker
ROBERT MAYER

A&W Publishers, Inc.
New York

Author's Note: Although this book is set in Santa Fe,
New Mexico, minor changes have been made
in several locations for fictional purposes.

The first chapter of this book originally appeared
in *Rocky Mountain Magazine.*

"Don't You Feel My Leg (Don't You Make Me
High) " © 1966 Popular Music Co. Used by
Permission.

Published by
A & W Publishers, Inc.
95 Madison Avenue
New York, New York 10016

Designed by Falcaro & Tiegreen Ltd.

Library of Congress Number: 81-66204

ISBN:0-89479-094-3

Printed in the United States of America

To
Vic Ziegel
and
Roberta Becker

There are so many faces in streets and bars and buses and stores that remind one of Original Sin, so few that carry permanently the sign of Original Innocence.

—Graham Greene,
Loser Takes All

CHAPTER 1

The System

LAND OF ENCHANTMENT
LAND OF ENCHANTMENT
LAND OF ENCHANTMENT
LIVE FREE OR DIE
LAND OF ENCHANTMENT
GRAND CANYON STATE
FAMOUS POTATOES
LAND OF ENCHANTMENT
LAND OF ENCHANTMENT

There were 1,628 cars in the parking lots. (Valet parking, $1.50. Preferred parking, $1. General parking, 50 cents.) That was not an exact count but Midge's best guess. She wished you could bet on the number of cars in the parking lots. It would be more scientific than betting on the races.

Only one car was occupied besides theirs. FAMOUS PO-TATOES, the car in front of them. Inside FAMOUS POTA-TOES a fat, sloppy brown-and-white St. Bernard was squeezed in the back seat, its huge head in the rear window pointed straight at Midge. Its eyes were closed and its tongue was hanging out, pale pink, spotted with saliva.

Across the parking lots the warm metal voice of the track announcer drifted fuzzily. "The horses are entering the track for the running of the ninth and feature race, the Fiesta Clas-

3

sic." The voice sounded as if it had its back turned. It sounded also as if it had taken a Fiesta drink.

The St. Bernard in FAMOUS POTATOES did not stir. The St. Bernard in FAMOUS POTATOES did not seem to hear the track announcer. The St. Bernard in FAMOUS POTATOES appeared to have died of heat stroke five minutes before.

"Decker?"

"What?"

"Can't we go in now?"

"You heard 'im."

Decker did not look at her as he spoke. He stared straight ahead through the fractured windshield with those crazy eyes of his.

Midge lifted the can of sugar-free Dr Pepper to her mouth and let the last warm drop sweeten her tongue. She set the can on the seat between them, alongside her tissues, and hunched forward against the steering wheel, raising herself slightly to unstick her purple pants from the pillow.

"Can't you sit still!" Decker said. His eyes flicked at her with annoyance.

"It's hot in here," she said.

He turned back to the windshield. The sun catching the edges of the cracks slashed at the eye like razors. Decker seemed to be staring the razors down. Then, without blinking, he drank from his can of Coors. It was his second can. He didn't seem to care that it was warm.

"Why don't you get a cooler?" she had said to him once, way back in July.

"With what money? The Frenchies drink warm beer all the time. That's what's wrong with you, you ain't got any class. Stick with me and maybe I'll teach ya some class."

She hadn't mentioned it again.

She hunched forward and adjusted the pillow. She was four feet eleven inches tall and needed the pillow to see over the dashboard, over the steering wheel. It was her car but Decker hardly ever let her drive. Driving was a man's job, he said. Except on the way to the race track. Then he insisted that she drive. On the way to the race track a man likes to have a chauffeur.

4

Perched high on her pillow—once solid pink, it was stained now in the shape of interesting butterflies by assorted fluids—she began to read the license plates again. Most were local, Santa Fe plates, or Albuquerque. But there were also in the row in front of them a SUNSHINE STATE, a FASTEN SEAT BELTS, and four different GRAND CANYON STATEs. Probably because of the big race tomorrow. The Arizona horse.

"Decker."

"What?"

"You see that dog up there?"

"What about it?"

"I think it's dead."

"I know."

He drank a slug of beer.

"Shouldn't we do something about it?"

"What do you want to do? It's dead."

She chewed her bottom lip. He was right. That's what she admired about Decker. His intellect.

She looked at his profile as he stared down the slits of sun: his black hair cut short, his flat nose, his strong jaw and protruding jaw muscles that never stopped working, bunching, committing some unseen task, as if he were chewing gum or tobacco, except that he rarely chewed gum and never tobacco. Her blouse—the lucky one, yellow with a green elephant on the pocket, the one she had been wearing the night he knocked on the door—was sticking to her back, was soaking wet under the arms, but Decker wasn't even sweating. He never sweated, he seemed incapable of it.

"How come you never sweat?" she had asked him once, in a tangle of twisted sheets, their second or third night together.

"My father was a snake," he said.

She had shivered, her sweat had turned cold, she had dried up instantly. She had cried with pain as he forced her nonetheless. Afterward he had taken off his T-shirt and shown her the tattoos on his upper arms. The word MOM on one arm. A spitting snake on the other.

Midge picked up the warm can of Dr Pepper and held it to her lips and leaned her head back as far as she could. All she got was warm air. She crossed her eyes on the can, her Adam's apple exposed. Decker, who thought he was a champion stud, could never make her reach any mountaintops. Not the kind she had read about in *Fury's Savage Sweetness*. She didn't know why she even stayed with him.

She put the can on the seat again. She knew why she stayed with him.

The slurred voice of the track announcer curled across the parking lots again: "It's post time."

"Now?" Midge said.

"Now."

She pushed open the door and, holding the pillow down with one hand, slid out of the car. The door creaked shut behind her. She had to wait while Decker uncoiled the twisted wire that held the passenger door closed, and got out, and lifted the door back into place, and wired it closed again, kicking it as he did. She crossed in front of the car, looking sadly at the huge head of the St. Bernard in the back window of FAMOUS POTATOES. The head didn't move but the two eyes blinked.

Decker hadn't waited for her. He was already ten steps toward the concrete walkway that split the dirt and gravel field that was general parking. Midge had to run to catch up to him.

She felt hurt. She had been crossing in front of the car to take his hand. She put it out of her mind. Feeling hurt would only cause trouble.

"Hey, Decker," she said, still two steps behind him, a bit breathless.

"What?"

"You know that dog?"

He didn't answer.

"It ain't dead."

"It's dead," he said, as she caught up beside him and took his hand.

"It ain't," she said. "I saw it blink."

"So what?"

"So nothing. It ain't dead, that's all."

Decker took his hand away and rubbed his jaw muscles. An

excuse, she knew. When he put his hand down again he didn't want it held.

As they walked in silence she looked at the cars broiling in every direction, like a drive-in movie with no picture playing. Endless cars from the concrete grandstand to the place where the track railing curved away, gleaming white. Behind the track across the pale desert she could see the state prison with its squat brown buildings and its tall steel water tower, set in the middle of nowhere. Just like the track was set. Far beyond the parking lots, at the end of the highway, the mountains rolled up like blue waves. Santa Fe was at the bottom of the mountains. She couldn't see it from here.

"One thousand six hundred and twenty-eight," she said.

"What?"

"Cars."

"Jesus H. Christ!"

"That's a lot, huh," she said. She was pleased by his rare enthusiasm.

Decker spat on the sidewalk.

"That's not what I meant," he said. "I meant Jesus H. Christ, can't you ever shut up."

She let him get a few steps ahead of her. From the track they could hear the crowd yelling at the ninth race.

Midget, he used to call her, when they first got together in June. Midget. Just because she was small. Eighty-seven and three-quarter pounds, to be exact. Four feet eleven inches exactly. She was happy with her size, she couldn't imagine herself being any other size. She had let him call her Midget for a week, afraid to tell him she didn't like it. Then one night, in bed, she had cried.

"Whatsa matter?" he said.

"I'm not a midget," she said. "I don't like being called a midget. My name is Beatrice."

He had stroked her hair, tender as he sometimes was back then.

"I know your name," he said. "I just say Midget 'cause I like you."

"I know," she said, sniffling through her tears. "But I'd rather be called Beatrice."

His tenderness had faded. He had swung his legs off the bed and sat on the edge in his Jockey shorts.

"I can't," he said. "I can't be seen with no Beatrice. I'd be a laughingstock. It's bad enough . . ."

He didn't finish the sentence.

A laughing stock with who, she wanted to say. We ain't never gone out with nobody but ourselves. But she didn't say it. She sniffled again, and turned over and rubbed her nose in the pillow.

For several minutes neither of them moved. Then he touched her back, her shoulder, and said: "Midge?"

With its own sweet will her whole body curved into a smile, cupped and joyous and waiting. She turned her head on the pillow to look at him.

"Is that okay?" he said.

She gazed at him with half-closed eyes, her best seductive look. And nodded.

"And nobody will know nothing else?"

She nodded again, could not stop her smile, turned in the bed to face him.

"No. Turn over," he said. "The way you was before— Midge."

The way he liked it.

It didn't matter. She understood.

As they crossed into the shadow of the grandstand she was sweating under her arms, in the small of her back, at the recollection of that night, of what had happened since, sweating in sympathy with the extended Santa Fe summer, still 81 degrees now at 4:57 P.M.(to be exact), Friday, September second, the start of the long Labor Day weekend when an estimated 512 people would be killed on the nation's highways, the radio had said in the morning.

"Four hundred ninety-eight," she said.

"What?"

"Nothing."

Sweating at the uncertain future that was growing inside her. At what Decker wanted her to do.

He pulled open the wooden door to the grandstand. The lobby was cool and dark. A roar went up from the crowd as the tote board posted the results of the photo finish in the ninth race. The track announcer's voice boomed like God over the roar: "The winner—number three, Fair Change. Second —number one, Go Lightly. Third—number four, Ampersand. Time of the race—one-oh-nine and two-fifths."

"Jeez," Midge said.

"Jeez what?"

"That's two-fifths off the track record."

Decker looked at her for the first time since they had left the car.

"How the hell do you know that?"

"Wanna bet?" she said.

"You and your numbers," he said, and turned away.

He looked toward the turnstiles. The two girls in their red blouses were still sitting there. He couldn't imagine what was wrong. The ninth race was over. Why didn't they leave? After the ninth race you didn't have to pay a dollar. After the ninth race you could get in free. See the last three races for free. Decker was no fool. Every Friday, Saturday, and Sunday, all summer long, they had come out after the ninth race. Without one cent wasted on admission.

But what was wrong now? Had they changed the policy because of the holiday weekend?

The bastards!

Then he saw the man from upstairs come by, the sleeves of his white shirt rolled up, wearing his bolo tie, and nod to the girls. The girls slid off their stools and walked away. The turnstiles were empty. The man from upstairs looked across, and smiled and waved at Decker and Midge. Decker's face burned. He cursed under his breath. He hated the man to see them, to know they came in free every time. Even though there was nothing wrong with it. That's why he insisted they sit in the parking lot till the last minute. So the man would be gone. It was the damn photo finish that had delayed him.

"C'mon," Decker said, after the man had left.

Midge didn't respond. He turned to look at her, and for a moment he didn't see her. Then he spotted her bending down near the far wall, picking up a betting ticket that someone had thrown away.

"A five," she said as she approached.

They pushed through the turnstiles. A Spanish couple, the

man small and tanned, the woman quite heavy in red slacks, were walking toward the exit. Decker confronted them with his needle eyes.

"You need your program?" he said.

The man shrugged, looked at his wife, and handed Decker the program.

"That, too," Decker said.

The man handed over his folded copy of the *Daily Racing Form*. Decker took it without a word and moved inside. A program cost seventy-five cents. A *Racing Form* cost a buck and a half.

"Thanks," Midge said to the couple, and she hurried after him into the grandstand. It was more crowded than usual for a Friday, because of the holiday weekend. The city would be jammed to bursting for Fiesta. Midge could hardly wait for the burning of Zozobra that night. The burning of Old Man Gloom. Her third favorite night of the year, after Christmas and Miss America. Much more exciting, certainly, than New Year's Eve.

She followed Decker to the bar, where he bought himself a paper container of beer, and followed him down an aisle between the crowded seats, to the sloping concrete area that led to the rail. People, men and women both, were standing about, talking or studying their racing forms, making marks on them with ball-point pens or pencils. Small children were running about, unnoticed. Decker had his program and his racing form sticking conspicuously out of the back pocket of his black pants, as if he had been up all night figuring out the winners, and had made his choices then, and could now relax with his beer.

"Well, whattaya waitin' for?" he said.

Midge was standing to the right and slightly in front of him, looking across the desert-dry infield. It would be nice, she thought, if they planted some flowers there.

"Get with it," Decker said.

He shoved her in the small of the back. She stumbled forward several steps, and caught her balance. She turned and looked back at him with anger and hurt. Then she turned again, and began to scan the ground. She saw a discarded betting ticket and picked it up, and she looked some more and found another ticket and picked it up. She moved across the concrete space that way, a small woman in and among the taller people, bending down, sometimes right beside their shoes, to pick up every ticket she could find. She wished she had never told Decker about the system.

It had been back in July, when things were going good. The welfare people had gotten her a job with the state for the summer months. The Health Services Department, it was called. After a few days—after he quit his week-old dishwashing job—Decker had asked how she liked it. They were drinking soda pop and eating bologna sandwiches in the kitchen of the trailer her brother let her use when he was busted.

"It's real interesting," Midge said. "We get the plague here every summer in New Mexico. From germs carried by fleas, which live on mice and squirrels and prayer dogs and such. If the flea bites a person, they could die. So they got to keep checkin' up, to see if the plague is around. They do that by settin' up traps out in the desert, and in the bushes and things. To catch squirrels and mice and rodents. Then they test them to see if they got the plague. To see where it's around. Me and some other people, we go and set the traps and catch the animals. We wear these rubber gloves so we don't get bit."

Decker had stopped eating, and was staring at her with disgust.

"You got to tell me that during dinner?"

"You asked me," she said, looking down at the table.

"Yeah," he said. "I guess I did." Then, as if to make up, he said, "How many animals you bring in? Every day, I mean."

Midge brightened. "Fifteen, sixteen. Sometimes twenty. It depends. They got other people doing it too."

Decker pointed his thumb and forefinger toward the counter near the sink, and pulled the trigger of an imaginary gun. "Fix me another sandwich," he said. Then he quickly stood up. "Never mind, I'll fix it myself."

Midge caught on right away. "What's the matter, you afraid I got the plague?"

Decker looked at her. Almost as if he was capable of being hurt himself. "Hey, what do you think I am?" he said.

Midge smiled. She felt as if she were married.

He came back with his sandwich and set it on the Formica table. "Thing I don't understand," he said. "There's thousands of little animals out there, right? Maybe millions. They catch fifteen, twenty a day that ain't got the plague, there could be a million more out there that do, and they wouldn't know nothing about it. Sounds like another one of them government moondoggles to me."

Midge finished chewing her last bite and wiped her mouth with a green paper towel. She was flattered by his interest. Most of the men her brother told to look her up, they didn't come back a second time.

"It's the law of averages," she said.

Decker squinted at her. She couldn't tell if it was admiration or disapproval. Decker disapproved of most laws.

"Go on," he said.

"They told us all about it when we started. Seems if you catch enough animals in the right places, it's called a scientific sample. If enough animals out in the desert has got the plague fleas, enough to make it a danger, then some of them will get caught in the traps. It's the law of averages."

She could tell he wasn't convinced.

"They told us it's like with a penny," she said. "You toss up heads or tails, maybe it comes up heads. You toss up again, it should come up tails. Fifty-fifty. Only it don't have to. It could be heads two times in a row. But you keep tossing up, maybe ten times, it's got to come up tails pretty soon. It's just got to. It's the law of averages."

Decker took a small, thoughtful bite of his second sandwich. They let the subject drop. But in the middle of the night, the lights of the trailer park squaring the darkness of the shade, he shook her awake. She became aroused almost instantly.

"Listen," he said. "About that law of averages. You think it could work at a race track?"

She rubbed her eyes, trying to wake herself up. Wondering how her breath smelled. Not that Decker seemed to care.

"What do you mean?"

He was sitting up in the bed, the sheet covering his middle. It seemed as if he'd been sitting that way for a while.

"If there's eight numbers," he said. "Post positions. And

12

the record shows they all come in about the same number of times every year. Then that should keep on happening, right? The law of averages?"

"Right," Midge said.

She couldn't see his eyes in the dark. She hiked up her nightgown and turned away from him. Ready.

They spent the next afternoon at The Downs, picking up all the discarded betting tickets they could find. Not looking for winning tickets that had been thrown away by mistake, as people must have assumed. There was no percentage in that. They got to the track after the ninth race, when admission was free, and picked up tickets that had been thrown away all day. Midge sorted them out, the ones, the twos, the threes, and so on. No matter which race they were from. When she counted them all up, they had more sixes than anything else. They had sixes from every race, which meant six hadn't won at all. Decker showed her the records in the program. It was just as he had said. Every number came up about the same number of times, the six as much as any other. So on the last race, the twelfth race, he bought a $2 win ticket on number six, Blue Lady.

The race was five and a half furlongs, which meant the starting gate was on the other side of the track. Midge had to stand on a bench to see it over the tote board. Number six was wearing yellow, the program said. A yellow shirt and a yellow cap. She could see it brightly as the horses broke from the gate, the red moving to the front, the green cutting across to second, then the white, the orange, the purple. The yellow had pulled to the rail, and was running last.

They watched as the horses moved into the turn, the red, the green, the white.

"The law of averages," she heard Decker mutter under his breath.

Then, as they came out of the turn, the yellow was moving up. It was fifth, then fourth. As they moved through the stretch it was third, and then it was alongside the leader, running neck and neck, the yellow and the red, the yellow and the red, and just as they reached the finish line the yellow seemed to leap ahead. A cute gray horse. Number six. Blue Lady.

The horse paid $14.20 to win. Decker leaned over and

kissed Midge on the top of the head. He bought her dinner at McDonald's, and that night, when she turned away, he told her to turn back. He told her that he wanted to look at her.

They had returned to the track every Friday, Saturday, and Sunday afternoon since. After they lost a few bets, Decker stopped picking up tickets. That became Midge's job alone. It was her system, he said. Her back ached, she wanted to stop doing it. But they won just often enough to keep him coming back.

Bending to pick up another ticket, Midge felt that she should hate Blue Lady. The filly who started it all. The pretty gray horse with the blue ribbon braided into its tail. Who had won five straight races since that day. Who would be in the big match race the next afternoon, the Unicorn Handicap. A filly against a colt. The best Santa Fe horse against the best Tucson Park horse. The last big feature of the Santa Fe season, which would be ending on Labor Day. But she knew she could never hate Blue Lady. She loved Blue Lady. Who started everything.

If she could own a horse of her own, she would braid a ribbon into its tail. A yellow ribbon, with a small green elephant attached. An elephant that didn't weigh too much.

She hurried over to Decker, to make sure he remembered. He was starting on another beer. An erratic breeze had come up and was swirling pale sand across the infield, like baby tornados. It blew globs of foam off Decker's beer. They splattered messily on the pavement.

"What you got?" he said.

"I didn't count them yet."

"Why not?"

"You remember about tomorrow?" she said.

"What about it?"

"You promised we could pay to get in."

"The hell I did," he said, and drank from the paper cup, as if to change the subject. Foam streaked his lips, oddly, like milk on a child.

"You promised."

He drank again.

"Why should we do a fool thing like that?"

"So we can watch Blue Lady against that Arizona horse."

He took a long drink of the beer, finishing it, and crumpled the cup and tossed it on the ground. It seemed to hesitate for a moment, then let itself be carried off by a gust of wind.

"Blue Lady don't got a chance in hell against that Arizona horse. He'll beat her going away. You'll see."

She kissed his arm, near the elbow. She shuffled through the tickets in her hand, counting how many of each number.

"Not enough for a scientific sample," she said. "Be right back."

She moved away, scanning the ground, picking up more discarded tickets, chasing some across the area among the people's feet as they tossed and tumbled in the spinning breeze. A five, a six, a nine, a nine, a two. More and more tickets, to get a big sample. To find Decker a winner. All the while thinking about watching Blue Lady run. Paying their way in like everyone else. Wondering if she would bet. She had $2 hidden away in her elephant bank, just in case. She had never bet on anything before. Not ever. It was a waste of money, and she didn't have money to waste. She . . .

Then she got the best idea of her life.

She stopped picking up tickets. She thought and thought about it. The more she thought, the more the feeling of excitement grew inside her.

She counted the tickets and ran back to Decker, who was standing near the rail, watching the horses parade for the last race.

"Number four," she said, breathless. "On the nose."

Decker hurried off to bet. She waited by the rail, trying to calm herself. Rehearsing how to say it. Till Decker came back, carrying another beer.

"Give me a sip," she said.

He looked at her with surprise, but held the cup to her mouth. She took a sip, and wiped her lips with her sleeve. Her heart was racing like the horses, her knees were starting to shake. You bet $50 on a horse, she thought, it must feel just like this.

Her mouth was dry already, but she forced herself to speak. "You don't think Blue Lady'll win tomorrow?"

A hint of little girl in her voice.

"No way," Decker said. "That Arizona horse will kill her.

Fillies just can't keep up with colts. It's the same as with people."

She hesitated. With the plague season over, her job would end in a week. It would be back on welfare. One eleven a month. Unless Decker took a dishwashing job again.

She plunged ahead anyway.

"You pretty certain about that?"

"Damn certain," he said.

Just like a man. Not even guessing what she was driving at.

"You wouldn't want to bet on it, would you?"

He looked at her over the rim of the paper cup. That strange light that was there sometimes shining from his eyes.

"With you? What you got to bet? Your brother's trailer? That ratty old car?"

It's more than you got, she wanted to say. What you got to bet? My brother's trailer? My car? Or maybe that torn old bedroll you brought on out? But she didn't say any of those things. Together, that's how they had something. Together.

"You want to bet or don't you?" she said.

"How much?"

"What's it matter how much? You're so sure Blue Lady's gonna lose."

"I'll bet your ass," he said. "You name it."

She reached up and took the container of beer from him and drank a full gulp. The cold was good but the taste was bitter. She handed it back to him. She looked around to see if anybody was listening. Nobody was. There was a wide circle of space around them. People always seemed to allow them a wide circle of space.

"We'll bet the baby," she said.

His eyelids closed halfway, focusing the light. His jaw muscles throbbed faster.

"What are you talking about?"

She was feeling braver, now that the worst had been spoken. "If Blue Lady loses, I get it done next week, like I'm supposed. Like you want. But if Blue Lady wins, I keep the baby. And we get hitched."

Married. Why hadn't she said married, as she meant? No matter, she thought. Words don't matter at all.

Decker looked away, at the desert beyond the infield, at

16

the penitentiary in the distance. He turned his back to her and looked up at the grandstand, at the upper deck, where the rich people sat in season boxes and ate sandwiches at tables with waitresses. The sun had sunk behind the grandstand, the breeze was starching his pants, and far down the highway the sky was gray. A storm was approaching.

"You're crazy," he said, turning to her again.

"What's the matter? You afraid you'll lose?"

He worked his jaw muscles, a pulsating nervousness building inside him. A thrilling kind of tension. The kind he used to feel driving the getaway.

"Well, yes or no?"

A bet for all time, Decker thought. To bet a life. Those rich people up in the box seats, they never made a bet like that. Even the owners of the horses. They never made a bet like that.

Besides. The Arizona horse couldn't lose.

"It's a deal," Decker said.

Midge licked the sweat on the edge of her harelip, to hide her smile. She stuck out her small hand.

"Shake," she said.

"Jesus H. Christ!"

The horses were entering the starting gate for the last race. Decker walked up toward the grandstand. A lot of people had left, to beat the traffic, to get a head start on Fiesta. He stood on a bench to have a better view of the race. To root home the four.

No need to worry about tomorrow, he told himself. The Arizona horse couldn't lose.

Besides. He could always skip town. It was getting about the time he should move along. It was getting about the time he should be alone.

Midge didn't follow him to the grandstand. She sat on the ground near the rail, her thin legs in her purple pants tucked under her. Across the dirt track the tote board loomed very large. She thought of saying a prayer, for Blue Lady. But she knew she didn't have to pray.

She had read the stories in the papers about Blue Lady. About that other big match race between a filly and a colt a few years ago. The filly was called Ruffian, and the colt was called Foolish Pleasure. Ruffian had broken a leg in the race, and had to be destroyed. Foolish Pleasure had won. That was the last such match race between a filly and a colt at a recognized track, the paper said. There had been nine such races in recorded racing history, the paper said, and the colt had beaten the filly every time. Nine times out of nine.

Midge untucked her legs and stretched out on the concrete. She extended her arms flat above her head and kicked off her sneakers and wiggled her toes. She looked up at the sky, at a bright patch of blue that was all she could see. She could tell people were watching her from a distance, giving her a wide circle of space, as always. She didn't care. She closed her eyes and let the wind and the dirt and the fading sun swirl over her, and kiss her face, her lips, again and again and again, as the pounding of the horses' hooves closed in.

＊

CHAPTER 2

Beer and Soda

The coach sped quickly through the Paris night. Neither of them spoke. The only sound was the clatter of the horses' hooves on the cobblestones. Count Gaston smiled at Evangelina, revealing his rotten teeth. She did not return his smile, but stared icily ahead. The lights of the city disappeared outside the windows of the coach, replaced by dark, brooding trees bending in a vicious wind. The count leaned toward her. His breath reeked of cognac. Without tenderness or charm he plunged his liver-spotted hand into the bodice of her dress. Evangelina, repelled by his very touch, tried not to flinch. She had hoped he would have the decency to wait till they reached the manor. But no, he must have her here, in the dark of the speeding coach. His coarse fingers enveloped her breast like scaly snakes. She fought to retain her composure, to hide her disgust. A bargain was a bargain. And found to her astonishment her nipples growing firm under his touch. She was horrified at herself, mortified at this signal of her own pleasure. She tried with all her being to will it away, to slacken herself with an effort of the mind. Instead she found herself mad with desire for this ugly creature beside her. Her face flushed in the night. Her orifice grew damp. She turned . . .

There was a knock, and then another, on the door of the trailer.

Her face flushed in the night. Her orifice grew damp. She

21

turned in the seat to face him, to plant her ruby lips on his face, his yellow teeth . . .

The knock was repeated.

Annoyed, Midge rolled over and looked at the alarm clock on the nightstand. It was almost 9:30. Nobody she wanted to see would be knocking on her door at this time of night. Nobody she wanted to see ever knocked on her door.

She rolled back onto her stomach to resume her reading, elbows propped beneath her, *Fury's Savage Sweetness* bent open on the yellow pillow.

She turned in the seat to face him, to plant her ruby lips on his face . . .

Another knock. Probably it was Old Man Peters, who managed the trailer park. Standing there with his fly open, making believe he had to tell her some new rule or something. Hoping she'd fall down dead in front of his open fly. Except that it couldn't be.

"Anybody home?"

It was a voice from outside the door, and it was young and strong. It wasn't Old Man Peters.

She squirmed off the bed, curious, and stuffed her elephant blouse back into her purple pants where it had come loose, and walked through the trailer toward the door in her pink socks, and then stopped. Who could it be? She knew of the stuff that could happen to single women. Broken bottles. Ax murders.

"Anybody home?" the voice said again. "I seen a shadow in there."

She leaned her cheek against the aluminum door. It felt cool, though the June night was warm. She had a feeling this very moment had happened before, but she didn't know where, or when. She had that sort of feeling six, maybe seven times a year.

"Who's there?" she said, through the door.

"That Beatrice Smith?"

"Who wants to know?"

He knew her name but it didn't prove anything. He could have got her name from the trailer-park office.

"Decker," the voice said. "My name is Decker. I'm a pal of your brother's. He told me to look you up."

She guessed he was telling the truth. Her brother had done that before. She opened the door a crack, but didn't unlatch the latch. She squinted one eye into the dark outside.

"My brother who?" she said.

"You sure are suspicious. Your brother, Jack. Jack Smith."

She couldn't see his face too well in the dark, but it looked kind of nice. Handsome, even. And he was tall. Five feet seven at least.

"When'd you see him last?"

"This afternoon."

"Well, that couldn't be, mister. So why not just shove off."

"Hey, wait, lady," he said. "It's the truth, cross my heart."

"My brother's in prison," she said.

Usually she said The New Mexico State Penitentiary, which made it sound sort of like a college. But this time it just slipped out.

"Yeah." He paused, and looked at his shoes. "So was other people."

Midge thought that one through.

"Oh," she said. Her voice was very small.

She reached up to unlatch the latch, then hesitated.

"You escape?"

"I wish."

"What you mean, you wish?"

"Parole," he said. "I got paroled this morning. Jake said he got this cute little sister. Said to look you up."

"Jake who?"

"Jake Jack, for Chrissake. There's two Jack Smith's inside. One's this big black motherf—— this big black gennleman. So they call your brother Jake. So's not to get mixed up."

"He really said that?"

"Said what?"

"About a cute little sister?"

"Sure he did," Decker said. "Now why would I be here if he didn't?"

"Yeah," Midge said. "I guess."

She stood on her tiptoes and unlatched the latch. She opened the door several more inches, then stopped.

"On your mother's Bible?"

"What?"

23

"Cross your heart on your mother's Bible that you're a friend of Jack's?"

"His best friend in the world," Decker said. "His best damn cellmate in the world."

The light from inside was on his face now. His skin was pale like Jack's but his eyes were dark and roving. She pulled the door open wide.

"Well, come on in then," she said. "Any cellmate of Jack's is a cellmate of mine."

It didn't sound quite right, but she let it go.

He picked up a navy blue rucksack from the ground beside him and stepped into the trailer. His deep eyes glanced around the living room at the two chairs and the Naugahyde sofa that had come with the trailer when Jack brought it secondhand five years ago, and the coffee table that looked like wood but was really only plastic, with a copy of *Woman's Day* on it that she had bought at the Safeway because it had a pattern in it for a nice heavy sweater she might knit for herself for the winter, and at the darkened doorway toward the kitchen where she hadn't done the dish or the pan from her hamburger sandwich yet—she wished she knew he was coming, she would have straightened up—and through the lighted doorway of the bedroom where he would see the rumpled spread and *Fury's Savage Sweetness* on the pillow. She hoped he couldn't read the title from here. She was pretty sure he couldn't. She was 20/20, and all she could tell was an *F*.

"Nice place you got here," he said.

"Nice and cozy," she said.

He put his rucksack on the floor. He was wearing black pants and black shoes, white socks and a white, short-sleeved shirt.

"You been readin'," he said. It sounded more like an accusation than a question.

"Oh, that." She felt her face flush, and she glanced toward the bedroom. "Just some work I brung home to catch up."

"What kinda work you do?"

"Science, I guess you'd call it."

Decker nodded absently, still looking around.

"Who for?"

"Department of Health Services. Just for the summer, right now."

"That's real interesting," he said.

She would have liked to tell him about the plague and the prayer dogs and how she helped catch them for tests, but he didn't seem real interested just then. No matter what he said.

They stood in the middle of the living room, about five feet apart, and looked at each other. She wasn't sure what to do. She wasn't too used to entertaining like this. She would have got some peanuts, if he had called ahead.

"You're real short," he said. "Just like your brother said."

She glanced down at her pink cotton socks.

"Don't got my shoes on," she said.

"I guess that's it," Decker said.

He glanced around the room. She couldn't think of a single thing to say. Why was you in jail, was all she could think of. But that wouldn't be very nice.

"Lookie," he said. "You got anything to drink in this place? I sure could use a drink."

"Sure I do," Midge said, embarrassed at her rudeness. "DDP. You want a DDP?"

"DDP bourbon?"

"DDP Diet Dr Pepper."

Decker made a face.

" 'That the extent?' as the queer said to the eunuch."

Midge didn't know what he was talking about.

"I beg your pardon?"

"Prison talk," he said. "It means is that all you got?"

"Wait a sec," she said, remembering, and she ran off to the kitchen in her socks, not certain why she was running. She didn't usually run about the house. She pulled open the fridge, the light popping on in its magical way, and way back down on the bottom shelf behind her blue pot of yesterday's macaroni and cheese she found two cans of beer left over from when Jack was there.

"Hey," she called out from the kitchen. She tried to remember his first name, but she couldn't remember it. "Hey you, Decker. You want a beer?"

"Now you're talkin'." His voice came back from the living room, sounding right at home. It sounded sort of nice. Like it had a compliment in it, and also a relaxation. It was a sound she had heard in a man's voice long ago, maybe in some other life. Certainly not in this one.

She carried a beer to the living room, and a Diet Dr Pepper for herself, and found Decker sitting on the sofa, leaning back, with his black shoes propped on the edge of the table and his hands clasped behind his head.

"Why not take off your shoes?" Midge said. "Make yourself at home."

Decker pursed his lips together and nodded, and leaned forward and pulled off his shoes without opening the laces, and dropped one and then the other noisily to the floor, and put his stocking feet back up on the table. The bottoms of his white wool socks were almost black.

For half a second the blackness made Midge feel bad. Then it made her feel good.

She handed him his beer, and in one quick motion he pulled the tab off the can and then bolted the top half of his body forward as the beer sprayed up at his face and his shirt and pants, and then wet the plastic coffee table as he tilted the can away and the foamy beer dribbled out.

"Goddamn son of a bitch!" he said.

Midge looked at the beer on his face and the wet on his pants and tried not to laugh, but she couldn't stop a smile. It was the kind of thing that Beatrice Audra Smith would do. She'd done it often enough with her DDPs.

"The soda pop fairy strikes again," Midge said.

"Who?"

"The soda pop fairy. She lives inside them cans. She makes them spray out sometimes."

Decker was looking at her kind of blank, and nodding his head up and down, but his eyes said he didn't believe her.

"This ain't soda pop," he said. "It's beer."

"Yeah," she said. "I guess it was the beer fairy then."

Decker's head motions switched, from up and down to side to side. He put down the dripping beer can in the wet of the table, and looked at his wet pants and wiped his wet face with his wet hands.

"You got a rag or somethin' I could use?" he said.

"Sure," Midge said, and she ran off into the kitchen, wondering why she hadn't gotten him a rag right away, wondering why all of a sudden she was running, running to catch up to what she should have done right away. This was the second time.

She reached up to pull some paper towels off the rack near the sink, but the rack was empty except for a few shreds of green. Damn, she thought. She knew she was out of paper towels and meant to buy some when she bought her hamburger on the way home from work, but she had clean forgot. Whenever she didn't make a list she forgot. She looked around for some other rag but she knew there wasn't any. She only used paper towels. For a second she thought she might cry. Then she saw the ironing board still open in the corner of the kitchen with the iron sitting up on it like a puppy begging and her yellow blouse that she had rinsed out in the morning and ironed when she came home from work, to wear to work tomorrow folded neatly on the board where she had left it. She didn't hesitate. Her elephant blouse didn't smell, she could wear it again tomorrow. She grabbed the folded yellow blouse off the ironing board and hurried on back into the living room and handed it to Decker.

"Here," she said.

"This ain't no rag," he said. "It's a nice new shirt."

"Just an old thing," she said. "Gonna be a rag anyway. Go ahead."

He looked at the blouse again—$12.98 at Penney's—and for the flicker of an instant she hoped he wouldn't use it—but she didn't know what else he should use—and then he shrugged, and wiped his face with the front of the blouse, squeezing his nose in it, and then shook it open and wiped his hands in it, squeezing the blouse real good, and then flecked it at his pants, but the wet had sunk in there, and wiped his hands again—the blouse still not in too bad shape, Midge thought—and then he dropped it on the plastic coffee table. Right in the pool of beer.

Midge dropped to her knees on the other side of the table and swished the blouse around in the beer, soaking it up. She picked up the can of beer and wiped it around, so it wouldn't drip anymore, and handed the can to him.

"Here's your beer," she said.

He took the can and drank a long drink, while Midge sat on the floor with her legs stretched out to the side. She thought of advertisements she had seen in magazines, where women entertained men with their legs stretched out to the side.

He leaned forward and set the beer on the table.

"Mind if I use your john?" he said.

"Right through there," she said, pointing to the door to the bedroom, and as he stood and she watched the worn back of his pants, the wrinkled back of his white shirt, moving away in the dim light, she thought: the john, dammit! the john had plenty of towels! Why hadn't she gone there, instead of to the kitchen? And she looked at her new yellow blouse, crumpled on the table in a wet ball of beer.

Not too bright, she thought. Which was something she already knew.

A scatterbrained scientist, you might say.

And she smiled, and touched the scar on her lip. A habit.

So far he hadn't mentioned it. So far it didn't seem to bother him at all.

She picked up her wet ball of blouse and went to the kitchen and dropped it with a plop into the aluminum sink. She heard the john flush, and when she went back into the living room Decker was emerging from the bedroom. *Fury's Savage Sweetness* was open in his hands.

"You're reading this for work?" he said.

She felt her face grow hot. She hoped he hadn't read the page she was up to, where the old man's hand was on her titties.

"The plague comes in the book," she said. "That's what we check the animals for at work. To see if there's plague around."

It wasn't really a fib. There was plague in the book. Only she hadn't known it till she was halfway through.

Decker sat back down on the couch and looked at the cover of the book—a black-haired girl with green eyes and a filmy nightgown was running away from a castle, while lightning crackled in the sky—and set it down on the floor.

"You read a lot?" he said.

"Most every night," Midge said. But she didn't like the sound of that. "When I don't have a date, or something."

"I like TV myself," Decker said.

"Me, too," Midge said. "Only not so much now in the summer. Now it's mostly reruns."

Decker nodded his head and leaned forward and picked up his half-empty beer and drank a swallow.

"They got TV over in the prison?" Midge said.

Decker nodded.

"What else you do there?" Midge said.

"Work."

"What sort of work they got?"

"Making license plates."

"That sounds like fun," Midge said. "Putting all them numbers on them plates. AGG646, AGG647, AGG648."

"Boring," Decker said. "Take a dumb moron to find it fun."

"Yeah," Midge allowed, after a while. "I guess."

Silence fell over them like a sheet. Midge noticed her unopened Dr Pepper, and pulled off the tab and took a drink.

"No whosis fairy," Decker said.

"Nope," Midge replied, and smiled.

There was silence again, but it was a different breed. A moment ago it was sort of embarrassed. Now it was sort of nice. A cozy silence.

"You got a car?" Decker said, when it had lasted just long enough.

"Yep. Aggravation, 646."

"How come you call it that?"

" 'Cause it's always breaking down. That's the license plate. AGG646."

"You mean AGR," Decker said.

"AGG. Aggravation."

"Only one g in aggravation," Decker said. "Should be an AGR."

"I thought there was two g's in aggravation."

"Now why would there be two?" Decker said. "Be a silly waste of a g."

Midge rubbed her eyes with her hand. She would have sworn, but now she wasn't sure. Decker seemed to know what he was talking about.

"I guess you're right," she said, and she guessed he was.

From somewhere outside she heard a car moving on the

gravel of the trailer park. She wished again that she had known he was coming, and could have bought some peanuts. Or maybe even cheese. Classy people served cheese. She thought of offering if he wanted to watch TV, but she didn't. She liked it, talking like this.

"So what you gonna do now?" she said.

"Look for someplace to sleep. Unless . . ."

"I mean now that you're out. You know, what kind of work and all?"

Decker leaned back and crossed his dirty white socks on the table.

"Guess I'll head back home," he said.

Midge felt a whooshing in her stomach, like when an elevator stops too quickly.

"Home?" she said. Her voice sounded sort of weak. With an effort she spoke louder. "Where's that?"

"New Jersey," Decker said.

"You got a wife there? And kids?"

"Nah, nothing like that. Just my dopey sister, and my folks."

The elevator had stopped. But it seemed to be stuck between floors.

"So when you thinking about going?" Midge said, and sipped from her DDP, but her eyes looked at his over the can.

"Got no money," Decker said. "Got to get a job first, and make some dough."

"What kind of job?" She felt altogether better. Also a little bit nervous.

"Restaurant, prob'ly."

So that's who he was! A famous European chef, who had studied in Paris. Who could char-broil steaks in the world's great bistros! Who would take her to special tables with white cloths, and roses, and set before her such feasts as only he could prepare. Who got sent to jail, most likely, for too much salt.

"Washing dishes?" she asked.

"What else?"

"Pays pretty good, I bet."

"Pays shit," Decker said.

"Why you do it then?"

"For the love of it."

30

"Oh."

"Just joking. A joke."

"Oh." Midge bit her lip. She was furious at herself for not having gotten the joke. It was a pretty good joke.

"When you come out of the clink," Decker said, "they don't make you vice president right away."

"I would."

"Would what?"

"Make you vice president right away."

Immediately she regretted the words.

Decker pursed his lips in that certain way he had a habit of doing, and drained the rest of his beer, and put the empty can on the table.

"That's nice," he said. "You let me know when they put you in charge."

I am in charge, Midge wanted to say—a joke for a joke—but she didn't say it. Instead she watched as Decker stood and looked at his wrist—as if there was a watch there, only there wasn't—and stretched his arms elaborately over his head. The sleeve of his white short-sleeved shirt was torn under one arm.

"Getting late," he said. "I guess I better hit the road. Go look for someplace to sleep in town."

Midge unstretched her legs and stood. Decker sat on the edge of the couch and made as if to put his shoes back on. Only he didn't unlace the laces first.

"Pretty late to find someplace," Midge said. She looked around as if surveying the room, and spoke a little quicker than she had planned. "You can sleep on that couch if you want. You being such a good friend of Jack's and all."

Decker bowed his head, and looked up at her from under his dark brows.

"You think that would be all right? It's kinda late to get a hitch."

"My coucha is your coucha," Midge said, and she couldn't help smiling. It was her best joke in weeks.

"Hey, you Italian?"

"No."

"My best friend as a kid was Italian. Angelo, his name was."

A joke, Midge wanted to scream. A joke. It's what the Spanish say. My *casa* is your *casa*. My house is your house. Only I said my coucha is your coucha. Get it?

Only it wasn't fair. How should he know what the Spanish say? Being from New Jersey and all.

"I'll get some sheets," Midge said. "It's no trouble."

She went to the bedroom and opened the closet and took out two white sheets and a matching pillowcase, and stood on tiptoe and managed to grab the corner of the extra pillow and pull it down. She stuffed the pillow into the case. She had trouble getting it to line up straight. She always did. She pulled out a blanket also, but then she put it back. It was pretty warm.

My coucha is your coucha, she said to herself, and she smiled again.

When she returned to the living room carrying the linens, Decker was reading in *Fury's Savage Sweetness*. Midge flushed.

"Pretty raunchy stuff," he said.

"Pretty bad," she agreed.

She dumped the linens on the couch, and stood there. Decker put down the book. Neither of them seemed to know what to say. In the distant night a car horn honked.

"I guess I'll go to bed now," Midge said.

"Yeah, I'm bushed," Decker said.

She picked up the beer can and the Dr Pepper and took them into the kitchen. On the way back through the living room she said, "Sleep tight, see ya in the morning," and then she went into the bedroom and closed the door.

She didn't get undressed right away. She sat on the edge of the double bed, and waited for him to knock. To say something. Two whole minutes passed. And then from the living room she heard him call, "Hey, this you?" and she hurried out to see. He was standing in the corner, looking at the picture she hated. She only left it there because it was Jack's favorite thing.

"This a picture of you?" he said.

She looked at the small oil painting, of her at four years old, in a red and white dress and white socks and black Mary

Janes, with a red ribbon in her hair and her old black rag doll in her arms.

"No," she lied.

"Looks just like you," he said. "Except for the . . . Where'd you get it, then?"

Except for the lip. The girl in the picture had nothing wrong with her lip.

"It's my sister," she said.

"Oh, yeah? Where's she live now?"

"She's dead," Midge said.

"Oh. Gee. I'm sorry."

"Yeah."

She waited for him to say something else, but the mood was wrong. A hundred dollars her mother had paid the artist to paint that. More money than her father made in a week. To paint her that way.

"I guess I'll go to bed," she said. She hesitated, and when he made no move to stop her she went back into the bedroom and closed the door. This time she went straight to the pillow and took out her pink pajamas that were folded neatly underneath. She shook them out and pulled her elephant blouse off over her head, glancing fleetingly at her small chest in the mirror over the dresser, and pulled on the tops of the pajamas. She unbuttoned her purple pants and sat on the edge of the bed and pulled them off, and was about to pull the pajama bottoms on over her panties, and then stopped. She slipped her hands into her panties and pulled them off, though she usually wore them to sleep, and half-naked tossed them into the bottom of the closet where the dirty laundry was, and remembered that *Fury's Savage Sweetness* was out in the living room and if she wanted to read in bed she would have to get it. Naked from the waist down she saw herself in the mirror, and then turned slowly and stared at the yellow shade on the window; at the inch of space at the side, where there was darkness and in the background one of the bright white lights of the trailer park, and then suddenly the dark leaves of the lilac bush outside waving black fingers in the space, making tapping noises on the screen.

Slowly, she sat on the bed, and pulled on the bottoms of the pajamas. Her heart was thumping in her chest. She peered again at the corner of the shade. Then she screamed.

Decker burst into the bedroom. He still had his pants on, and a white T-shirt turned yellow.

"What's going on!"

"A peeping Tom!" She pointed to the shade. "He was looking through the window at me!"

"Where? You think he's got a gun?"

She shook her head. "Old Man Peters. Who runs the trailer park. He's a pervert, I think."

"Son of a bitch!" Decker said. "I'll get him."

Sliding a little in his stocking feet he ran out of the bedroom, across the living room, and out into the dark. She heard him running around to the side of the trailer. There was silence for a moment and then he shouted, "Come back, you son of a bitch! You bother this lady again I'll break your pecker off!"

More silence, and Midge sat on the edge of the bed and waited, and heard the door close, and Decker, breathing heavily, came back into the bedroom.

"You don't have to worry. That creep won't bother you again."

Midge took his hand, and said, "Thanks," and then let it go.

"Was it him?" she said. "Old Man Peters?"

"What's he look like?"

"Sort of old. Gray hair. Sort of stooped over a bit."

"Yeah, that was him," Decker said.

Midge nodded, and stood from the edge of the bed where she'd been sitting. Decker was looking around the room.

"He won't bother you no more," he said.

"I hope not," Midge said.

They looked at one another, awkwardly, and took a step toward the door. Midge stopped first.

"In prison," she said, "them beds ain't too comfortable, are they?"

"Like boards," Decker said.

"That couch out there, it ain't too comfy neither. I was thinking, it being your first night out and all, you might like a nice soft bed. I mean there's plenty of room in here, just to sleep and all. If you like. It's up to you."

"It ain't the bed," Decker said. "My body's tough as nails. Feel that."

He flexed his bicep into a muscle, and held it out for Midge to squeeze. She squeezed it with her fingers.

"That's tough," she agreed, and her small hand lingered there a moment, and then she pulled it away.

"The thing is," he said, "you might feel better with me in here. In case that creep comes back."

"Yeah," Midge agreed. "I guess I would at that."

"Smart move," Decker agreed, and he went out to the living room and carried his rucksack back. "Thing is, I got no real pajamas."

"You can wear some of Jack's," she said, and she went to the bottom drawer and pulled out a pair. Brown with white curlicues. Decker took them and disappeared into the john. When he came out, Midge was under the covers, with all the lights turned out.

For a long time he didn't touch her. They lay side by side in the dark, breathing audibly. Pretending to try to sleep. Midge wishing she had changed the sheets that week.

Then he took her hand.

She thought of the oil painting in the living room. She thought of *Fury's Savage Sweetness*. She felt his weight on her, and it was good. She began to count to herself, because she had read in a book once that if you counted to yourself it made everything last longer. She counted all her fairies, lined up in a row.

Then, too soon, he shuddered onto her shoulder, and was still.

She held her arms tight around his sweaty back. Maybe next time, she thought.

Her cheeks were wet as she stared up at the dark. There never had been a next time. Not ever. But this time there would be a next time. She didn't know how she knew. But she knew.

She knew it as surely as she knew that Old Man Peters, his faded blue bathrobe dangling from the stretcher, had been rushed to the hospital for his gall bladder that morning.

CHAPTER 3

Gift Horses

"Look at that," Midge had said, sitting in the car in the parking lot, waiting for the ninth to be over.

Decker squinted past her at the black Lincoln Continental moving slowly on the access road. Moving like it owned the earth.

"Big fuckin' deal. I'll take a Jag anytime."

"You know who that is?"

"Some rich jerk, prob'ly."

"That's the Monsignor," Midge said.

"The who?"

"The Monsignor. From the church. The one who owns Blue Lady."

"That's bull," Decker said. "The trouble with you, you believe anything that anybody tells you."

"It ain't bull, it's true," Midge said.

Decker groaned, and twisted in his seat, and fished in the back of the car among old newspapers and discarded race programs and Kentucky Fried cartons and old shoeboxes that came from he knew not where. He grabbed a fistful of programs, and flipped the pages till he found one with Blue Lady.

"Look," he said. "Blue Lady. Owner. What does it say under owner?" He held the form under her nose, making her pull away. "Danny Roybal. That's what it says. No mon senior."

"Don't matter what it says," Midge said, refusing to look at the program. "It's the Monsignor what owns her. Why else would he be driving down to the stables?"

"Probably it wasn't no mon senior at all," Decker said. "Prob'ly just some rich guy that owns a Lincoln."

Midge blew breath through her lips, making them vibrate, like a horse nickering. Certain people were impossible to argue with. Certain people named Horace Decker.

"It was him," she said. "The vicar of Christ in New Mexico. Second in command."

Decker smacked his forehead with his hand, and said nothing.

Midge switched on the radio in the car, and dialed through the country music stations, hoping to catch some Maria Muldaur. They rarely played Maria Muldaur anymore. To hear Maria Muldaur she had to play her little phonograph at home, and she hardly ever got to play it, what with Decker watching TV all the time.

She zoomed back and forth across the dial. The best she could find was Dolly Parton, singing about some party she wasn't invited to.

"Fat chance song," Midge said.

"What?"

"Fat chance song. Dolly Parton not invited to some party, two doors down."

Decker smirked. "Double fat chance," he said.

Midge squinched her head behind him and looked toward the track. The horses weren't even near the starting gate yet.

She took her pink plastic wallet out of her bag, and looked at the things in the Clear-O-Phane folder: a picture of Jack in a crew cut before he went in stir the first time; a bent color snapshot, faded almost white, of her parents near a sign that said Carlsbad Caverns; her driver's license with the dumb picture; an empty space for a picture of Decker, which he would never let her take with her Instamatic. "Too many pictures around is askin' for trouble," he'd said when she tried, that time a month ago by Santa Cruz Lake.

In the wallet part, next to her $15, was a folded clipping from the newspaper. The edges had little cracks, like most of her fingernails. It was three weeks old. She opened it and read it through.

Match Race Set
At SF Downs

Officials of The Downs at Santa Fe announced yesterday the creation of the Unicorn Handicap, a two-horse race to be run Fiesta weekend. The race will be a challenge between the leading two-year-old at The Downs, Blue Lady, and the leading two-year-old at Tucson Park, a bay colt named Thunderbolt. A $25,000 purse will go to the winner.

Track officials hope the race will sustain local interest through the Labor Day weekend, when attention usually focuses on the All-American Futurity at Ruidoso.

As an added attraction, a spokesman said, the two top riders at The Downs will go head to head in the race. The leading jockey will ride the out-of-town horse and the second leading jockey will ride the local horse. Barring a sudden change in the standings, that would put Bobby Juarez, the young Mexican apprentice, on Thunderbolt, and Kathee Praline, a favorite of the local crowds, on Blue Lady.

C. J. Forman of Phoenix, owner of Thunderbolt, and Danny Roybal of Chimayo, owner of Blue Lady, have agreed to the terms of the race, the spokesman said.

Midge folded the clipping, neatly. She had another in her scrapbook at home, along with all the stories that had followed: stories about the two trainers, the two riders, the two horses. Some of them with pictures.

"Kathee and Blue will do it," she said aloud.

Decker pulled the top off his last beer, and tossed the tab out the window.

"What?"

"That race tomorrow."

He took the clipping and read it, and coolly took a long drink of beer, and swallowed it.

"Now what does it say right there?" he said, snapping the

clipping with his finger. " 'Danny Roybal of Chimayo, owner of Blue Lady.' No mon senior, is it?"

Midge shrugged her bony shoulders. She took the clipping from him and folded it twice and replaced it in her wallet.

"All the same," she said, "it's the Monsignor that owns her."

"You mean that newspaper is lying?"

"Yup."

"Now why would they do that, about a horse? About some cheatin' politician, maybe."

"So's not to embarrass the Archbishop," Midge said.

"Bullcock," Decker said, and drank more beer. "Who told you that?"

"Mrs. Gallegos."

"Who the hell is Mrs. Gallegos?"

"She works with me with the plague. She lives in Chimayo. She knows the whole story. Everybody in Chimayo knows the story."

"Knows what story, for Chrissake?"

"The story of how the Monsignor is who owns Blue Lady, for Chrissake!"

Decker smiled at the imitation. He reached for his crumpled pack of Camels on the dashboard, and pulled out one.

"You wanna smoke?" he said.

Midge smiled sheepishly. "It'll stunt my growth," she said. And squeezed his shoulder, and rubbed it.

It was an old routine, from their first night together. When Decker, straight from the pen, had knocked on the door of the trailer to look her up. She gave him a beer on the plastic table, left over from her brother. They made nooky in her bed. Afterward he offered her a Camel.

"I don't smoke," she said. "They say it stunts your growth."

He'd looked at her small body for a second, not sure if she was serious—thinking back on it, she wasn't sure, either—and then he'd laughed.

"You're a cutie," he said. "That's the way I like my women. With a good sense of humor."

Hot blood had coursed through her. His women.

"Okay," he said, turning in the seat to face her, leaning on the door with the wire on it, hooking one white-socked ankle over the steering column, almost in her lap. "Tell me the fairy tale."

"It ain't no fairy tale," Midge said. "It's the truth. There was this rich guy up in Espanola, name of Prescott. He used to raise race horses. One day he got sick, and the doctor told him he had cancer and was gonna die. He didn't want to die yet, so he started to pray to God. And to make his prayers better, he went to the church up there and donated the old priest, Father Archie-something, his best young future race horse. Name of Blue Lady."

"And the mon senior stole it?"

"Hold your horses," Midge said. "I'm telling ya the story, okay?"

"I ain't got all day," Decker said.

"Where you got to go?"

"Okay, okay, finish the stupid story."

"This father Archie-something didn't know what to do with the horse. He decided to hold a raffle. So the church would make some money. He told the Monsignor about it."

"And the mon senior won the raffle? The fix was in, if you ask me."

"C'mon, Deck, listen. The fix wasn't in. This guy Terry Blodgett, who was the trainer for old Prescott, he went to the Monsignor. He told him Blue Lady could be one terrific race horse. He said if the Monsignor kept the horse, he would train it for his regular price, and the church could make a lot of money. Provided it didn't break a leg or something. The Monsignor decided to do it. To put money away for his old age. Only he didn't want it in the papers that he was in the racing business. So they listed Danny Roybal as the owner."

"Who's he?"

"He's the caretaker of the church up there."

"It still sounds like a fairy tale to me," Decker said. He was trying to talk with his cigarette hanging from his mouth. "Next thing you're gonna tell me, that guy Prescott didn't die of the cancer."

"Right," Midge said.

"A fuckin' fairy tale."

"He got killed by a heart attack on the way home from the church."

Decker dropped his leg to the floor and began swatting with his hand at the seat between them.

"What's the matter?" Midge said.

"I dropped my butt."

Midge found it on the floor, and handed it to him. It was wet with spilled Dr Pepper.

"Damn," he said, and he tossed it out the window. It bounced off the Buick parked beside.

She remembered the day that Mrs. Gallegos told her about it. They were eating their lunch at a picnic table near Velarde, not far from the prayer-dog village, taking a break from the plague. Midge told how she went to the race track with her new boyfriend the day before, for the first time in her life, and that the first horse she picked had won. Number six, it was. A cute gray horse. Name of Blue Lady.

"Blue Lady?" Mrs. Gallegos said. "You bet on God's horse?"

"What do you mean, God's horse?" Midge said. "How can that be God's horse?"

Mrs. Gallegos' voice sounded sarcastic—but Midge wasn't sure—as she told Midge the story. When she was finished, Midge held up her red Thermos top that was filled with Bosco.

"A toast to Blue Lady," Midge said happily. "The Monsignor's horse."

Mrs. Gallegos touched the chocolate milk with her paper cup of coffee.

"To Blue Lady," she said. "The holy bank account."

The two women looked at one another. Then they drank.

The radio had faded away to static without them noticing. No Maria Muldaur. Midge turned it off.

"Look over there," Decker said.

She looked where he was pointing. A car was coming up from the barns, a white Mercedes, with a pretty, dark-haired girl behind the wheel.

"You know who that is?" Decker said.

"Who?"

"The Virgin Mary. The one who owns Thunderbolt."

"Smarty pants to you," Midge said. She turned her back to him, and sucked hard at her warm and mostly empty Dr Pepper.

44

And wondered who the pretty woman was.

Decker, grinding his jaw, stared straight ahead through the broken windshield. At the sun glinting off like razors.

She was four years old, or five.

"I don't want to go," she said.

"You have to go," her mama said. "So don't make a fuss. Just get in the truck."

Her mother was carrying a small suitcase, in which they would bury her.

"I don't want to go. I don't have to go to the hospital, do I, Daddy? I ain't even sick."

"Don't say *ain't*," her mother said.

Her father, with his boiled face and a large white blister on his neck, kneeled down and put his arm around her small shoulders. There was a faint hint of liquor on his breath.

"It's all right, precious," he said. "They're not going to hurt you. They're just gonna make you pretty."

They were standing in the summer sun, in the dirt front yard of the house on West Alameda. Her tricycle was on its side near the gate. Jack, eight years old, was sitting in the back of the pickup, shooting pebbles at a garbage can across the road with the clumsy slingshot he had made.

"But I'm pretty already," she said. "You always say I'm the prettiest little girl in the world. That the Lord God made me special."

"That he did," Bill Smith said. "That he did. Only . . ."

His voice broke off. She desperately needed him to finish the sentence. *Only what?*

"Get in the truck," her mother said, sharply. "Enough of this nonsense. We're supposed to be there already."

They were dressed up as if they were going to church, her father in his blue suit and the only tie he owned, her mother in a yellow dress with flowers on it that was tight around the middle. She herself in the white dress she had worn to Jack's birthday party the week before.

"Please, Daddy!" she said. "Don't make me go."

"See what you get for telling fairy tales," her mother said, pulling on white gloves. "It's time we spoke some truth around here. Your face isn't pretty, Beatrice. You've got a

45

harelip that people don't like to look at. God punished you for something—or punished your father and me, Lord knows—or maybe He just made a mistake. And now the doctor is going to fix His mistake. So you'll be nice and pretty for the boys. Don't you want to be pretty for the boys?"

Her mother's words made her feel terrible. She wasn't sure why.

"How could God make a mistake?" she said. "Maybe God likes me this way."

Her father at that moment turned his back on her. He walked to the truck, and climbed in behind the wheel. Her mother grabbed her hand.

"Enough of this chatter," her mother said, and pulled her around the front of the truck and half picked her up, half shoved her onto the seat, and climbed in beside her, her fat handbag on her lap, and shut the door, and her father started the engine and off they went, raising dust, a neighbor's Irish setter barking at the truck for half a block.

The hospital was downtown in those days. A pink brick building, happy on the outside. They dragged her down long corridors. What she remembered after that was hazy. A flannel nightgown. Her parents leaving, and she in a large, oversized crib, screaming.

"Early in the morning," a doctor saying.

And she in the darkness climbing out of the crib, and hiding underneath it, where even God couldn't find her.

And by the light of dawn a nurse finding her, dragging her out from under. Kicking and screaming she was placed on a cart with wheels. They strapped her hands at her sides. She kicked and kicked till someone held her feet. And then a room with bright lights in her eyes. Faces looked down at her. A big black something pressing toward her face.

To make her pretty.

Afterward she had tried to touch her lip, to press her finger in the space, as she always did, her mother if she saw her yelling, "Take your fingers away from your mouth!" But there was no lip left, she thought at first, and then realized it was a flat, smooth bandage.

"About a week," the doctor was telling her mother. "Then we'll take the stitches out."

It was a hot summer week and she spent it indoors, sitting on the floor, looking at pictures of actresses in her mother's magazines. Beneath the bandage it itched something awful. She scratched at the bandage, but it wouldn't come off.

"You're gonna be real pretty," Jack said, and looked at her with a wise, big-brotherly gaze, at the same time screwing up his eyes to picture what she would look like without the bandage.

She sipped malted through a straw, because to chew anything hard might tear the stitches loose. All the Bosco and all the chocolate malteds she could drink.

She looked at the pictures in her elephant book. She placed her small hand over an elephant's trunk, to see what it would look like without it. She wondered if it would still be an elephant without its trunk.

She tried to tear the bandage off, but it pulled at her skin and hurt too much to tear.

When a week had passed they got dressed up again. This time they went to the doctor's office instead of the hospital.

"How's the little princess?" a nurse in a white smock said.

It hurt when the doctor pulled off the bandage. If that was it she could have done that herself. She didn't need no doctor for that.

She looked at her mother's eyes. There were tears in her mother's eyes.

"Let me see in the mirror," she said.

"Let's get the stitches out first," the doctor said.

"Will it hurt?"

"It won't hurt a bit," he said.

He was a large doctor with thick, curly hair, and he was right. It didn't hurt at all.

She looked at her father's eyes. His face was shaking.

"How's that?" the doctor said. "Pretty as a picture, I'd say."

"It's still there," her father said, hoarsely.

"A scar, of course," the doctor said. "There has to be a small scar. But no separation. No more harelip. Just that little vertical scar that could have come from an accident. It still looks raw, of course, but that will fade in a few days. Nothing but a small, pale scar."

Her parents said nothing. The silence hung heavy.

"I told you that would be the case," the doctor said.

"Maybe we should see what Beatrice thinks," the nurse in the smock said. She lifted her down from the examining table and led her into a small undressing room, where a mirror was. "Just a teeny, weeny scar left," the nurse said. "Like a beauty mark. To lend mystery to a woman's face. It'll drive the little boys wild."

She looked at herself in the mirror.

She made faces, to see if it would pull apart. It didn't.

With her fingers she touched the small ridge of scar. She could hardly feel it, but it was there.

She grinned into the mirror. She smiled up at the nurse.

She had been afraid it would be gone altogether.

Midge imitating a vacuum cleaner sucked the last warm drop from her Diet Dr Pepper. To prove it to herself, she turned over the can, and held it upside down. A brown drop wet her purple pants.

"Damn!" she said.

She raised the can to her eye and peered into it, to see if there were any more drops. There weren't.

With her small hands she tried to squeeze the can, the way Decker did with his beers. The best she could manage was a small dent in the middle.

"Here," she said.

Decker dropped his eyes from the razor slits. He took the can and squeezed it easily in the center with one hand. Then, with both hands, straining, but trying not to show it, he squeezed it almost flat.

"That's pretty good," Midge said.

Without looking, Decker flipped the flattened can out the side window. It struck the Buick parked beside them, chipping a fleck of paint off the door.

"Hey, Deck, that ain't nice," Midge said.

"Tough titty," Decker replied.

He returned his eyes to the windshield. Something about the bright flaring sun-slits was hypnotic.

Midge rubbed at the spot on her pants with her thumb. She hoped that DDP didn't stain. She wrinkled her brow, and took Decker's beer from his hand.

"Hey," he said.

"Just a second."

She tilted the can, and poured more beer than she'd meant to onto the spot on her pants.

"What're you doing?" he said.

She gave him back the beer, and rubbed the wet of her pants with the palm of her hand. The wet spot, which had been the size of a dime, now sprawled larger than a fist.

"I'm washing my pants," she said.

"With beer?"

"People wash their hair with beer. Why not pants?"

"Women are nuts," Decker said.

He drank a slug from the can. Midge's thigh felt wet and clammy. She looked at the large blotch. She wondered if beer stained more than DDP.

Decker was in his windshield world again. She tried staring at the slits, but they hurt her eyes. Instead she began tapping rhythmically, with both hands, on the steering wheel, and then singing along. Her voice was high-pitched and cracking, but only slightly off-key.

"Don't you feel my leg,
"Don't you feel my leg,
" 'Cause if you feel my leg,
"You're gonna feel my thigh,
"And if you feel my thigh . . ."

"Cut it," Decker said.

Her palms continued tapping on the wheel.

"I'm singing," she sang.

"And if you feel my thigh,
"You're gonna go up high . . ."

"Cut it!" he said again.

She dropped her hands from the wheel.

"Why can't I sing?"

" 'Cause you're talking dirty. You know I don't like you talking dirty."

"I ain't talking dirty. It's a song. Maria Muldaur sings it all the time."

"I don't give a crap about your Chicano friends."

"She's not my Chicano friend. She's a singer, dummy. I play her records all the time. You've heard that song maybe thirty-seven times."

"I never heard that song."

"It was playing that night. The first night of Blue Lady. It got you all turned on."

"I don't remember nothing," Decker said.

He turned away and looked at the fleck in the Buick, where the orange undercoat showed through. Midge stared at her hands, folded in her lap. She was acting like a twerp, she knew. Doing anything she could think of to annoy him. And she knew why, too. Because he didn't want her to have the baby.

She didn't want it either. Not especially. She never gave it a thought before it happened. Lately she had been lying awake at night, thinking of what it would be like. When she slept, the same dream kept coming back, over and over. In the dream she was holding her baby, and it was crying. It wouldn't stop crying, no matter what she tried to do to comfort it. It screamed and screamed till it was bursting red in the face, and Midge woke up in a sweat.

So it wasn't really the baby she held against him, because probably he was right. Probably she shouldn't have it at all. She had loved her black rag doll as a child, but a real baby was different. She knew she would love her baby, but with a real baby love wasn't enough. With a real baby you had to be smart. You had to know psychology and stuff. It wasn't enough to read it fairy tales.

So it wasn't the baby itself she held against him, but the fact that he didn't at all want her to have it. She felt hurt, even though she knew he was right. And she didn't know what a person was supposed to do about that. Except to annoy the other one.

And annoying made her mad at herself.

She looked at his handsome profile. He was still staring wordless at his goddamn windshield cracks.

Which was all a twerp deserved.

She remembered when she got her black rag doll, the first present her brother ever gave her. They'd gone to the town dump one day with her father, to dump some garbage. There were tall piles of junk and refuse, old matresses, broken refrigerators, and a small fire in a pit at one end. Jack climbed on the piles, looking for things to salvage, things he could make something with, and found a black rag doll.

"Hey, look at this, Beatrice," he called, waving the doll in his hand. "Let's go watch it burn." And he ran off toward the pit with the burning trash.

"Let me see," she yelled, and she ran off after him, holding her nose against the smell.

When she caught up with him he was standing on the edge. Below them was a smoldering mound of newspapers, orange peels, paper bags.

"This'll be fun," he said.

"Let me see," she said.

He held up the doll, and she took it from him. It had a ragged black dress that was soiled with ashes, a gray rag for a face, red lips and a small nose and one white eye. There was a loose piece of thread where the other eye had fallen off.

"I want it," she said.

"We'll throw it in the fire," Jack said with enthusiasm, "and see how long it burns."

"I want to keep it," she said.

Jack looked at her, and made a face.

"It's dirty," he said. "It's junk. You've got lots of nice dolls at home."

"I want this one," she said.

Jack shrugged, and turned and ran off to the piles. "Merry Christmas," he called over his shoulder, though it was early spring, and he climbed the piles and picked up a baseball bat he found. He threw a rock up in the air and hit it with the bat. "It's cracked," he said, and he came over to the pit and threw it into the fire, and they stood side by side, she holding her new doll, and watched the broken baseball bat burn, till their father yelled that it was time to go home.

In the house she had lots of dolls: scrubbed ones with silky blonde hair and blue eyes and white or pink dresses that she had got for Christmas or her birthday. She put the black rag doll on the shelf beside them.

Sometimes, when she was alone in her room, she would tell stories to her dolls. Fairy tales, mostly, about frogs and handsome princes. The rag doll was the only one who listened.

Shifting position stickily in the seat, Midge wondered what happened to pretty scrubbed dolls, and tricycles, and all the other toys that children played with. What happened to them when the children grew up?

She didn't know. The only one she knew about was the black rag doll. She still had it. It was sitting on top of her dresser in the trailer, leaning against the wall.

She had never given it a name. She had never gotten around to fixing it.

She looked at Decker, still staring, and beyond him she saw the horses. They were nearing the gate for the ninth. She thought of Blue Lady, whom she loved. The gift horse.

Her gift man is what Decker was. A present from her brother in the pen.

She looked at his jaw muscles bunching, at the deepening sadness of his stare, and she felt bad about the way she was acting. She remembered what they said about horses. Don't look a gift horse in the eye.

The silence in the car was thick as Bosco. It was pressing on her chest. The silence and the trapped-in heat.

"What's the matter?" she said at last.

"I don't like you calling me dummy."

She protruded her lips, and blew a small wet bubble with her saliva. It burst very quickly.

"I know," she said, softly.

They both fell silent again. She knew she should say she was sorry. But she didn't feel like it.

She was about to take his hand when a hulking form beside him blotted out the track. It took up the whole side window: a belly in blue jeans and a chest in green shirt, and a brown belt with a silver buckle in the shape of a punching fist.

"You Decker?" a gruff voice said.

"Yeah," Decker said. He didn't even look at the man. He seemed to know what it was.

"We got to talk," the gruff voice said.

"Not now."

"Now!" the voice said. A large hand yanked at the door. It didn't open, because it was wired shut.

Decker looked at Midge. He didn't say anything. He twisted in the seat and unwrapped the wire, and pushed open the door and got out. Midge sprawled across the seat for a glimpse of the large man's face. The slamming door almost hit her nose before it bounced open again and hung loose.

CHAPTER 4

Three
Blue Ladies

While Midge was scurrying about gathering discarded tickets, Decker stood near the paddock, drinking his beer, watching the horses being saddled for the eleventh. He liked especially to watch the jocks. He admired the way they acted so cocky, for little men.

His favorite was Perfecto Baca, who was wearing a purple shirt, standing beside the eight. Baca was a tough hombre. The leading rider two years running, till that Mex kid came along this year. And the female beating him out too. That was a real pisser.

Decker could do without female jocks. They ought to be home cleaning house. This Kathee Praline, she was a good looker, he had to admit that. But as for riding, forget it.

"Isn't she beautiful?" Midge said, coming up beside him, looking at Kathee Praline.

"I've seen better," Decker said.

"You always seen better," Midge replied.

The starter in the center of the paddock checked his watch. "Okay riders," he yelled from beneath his brown Stetson.

Midge watched with something like pride as Kathee Praline in a royal blue cap and blouse above her white satin pants bent her left leg behind her, and a trainer cupped his hands and held her leg as she swung up into the saddle. With her left hand tight on the reins she moved a big brown horse called Executioner out behind the others. Midge liked all the girl riders, Marie Irigaray with her dark ponytail flying, Tomey Swan who was best on the quarter horses. But her favorite was Kathee, because Kathee rode Blue Lady.

The parade moved around the oval toward the dirt ramp and the track. The jockey shook her head to free a pulling curl that was caught under her helmet. The two-horse in front of her balked at the ramp, and Kathee pulled up Executioner and used the moment to lift off her helmet and settle it on again.

"Hey, Kathee, win this one!" Midge yelled.

The jockey looked to her right and found Midge's face.

"Come on up here and help me," she called, and she patted the rear of her saddle.

Midge giggled. The jockey smiled. The smile lit up her face like an angel's.

I'd like to help you, Decker thought. I'd fill your saddle real good.

Executioner pranced up the ramp in the wake of the shitting two.

"Bet that two," Midge said, tugging at Decker's elbow. "He's lighter now."

She wanted Kathee to win. She always wanted Kathee to win. But you couldn't ignore science.

Decker turned and gave her a dirty look.

"D'you run faster every time *you* shit?"

Midge, convinced of her logic, shrugged, and walked away, keeping her eyes on Kathee Praline. Except in the movies she had never seen anyone so pretty: blue eyes, blonde curls tumbling from under her helmet, a face all cream and pink. She wondered if Kathee was really that pretty, or if sitting on top of a horse made you pretty, and wearing white satin pants, and silk shirts and caps that were bright red or blue or green. She had never done any of those things.

She looked around for Decker. He was still standing by the paddock. She walked over and nuzzled against him.

"Look at the fatso," he said.

She followed his gaze to the jockey-room ramp, where a large woman was standing with her hands in her pockets in a tight yellow pinafore, looking out at the track. Two hundred sixty-seven pounds at least.

"Who's that?" Midge said.

"A rider. A new girl jockey."

"Come on," Midge said. "Who is it?"

"I told you. A new girl jock. They brung her out special from New York. She's gonna ride Blue Lady tomorrow."

Midge jabbed Decker in the ribs, hard, with her pointy elbow. Decker danced away, laughing, and did a little jig, and scooted away toward the rail.

"Kathee's gonna ride Blue Lady!" Midge yelled.

"You wait and see," Decker said.

She let him go and stayed by the paddock, looking up at the woman. She was bigger than two Midges. Maybe bigger than three. You ought to be pretty important to be that big, Midge was thinking, and then the woman turned and went into the jockey room, where no one was allowed, the signs said, which proved she was pretty important at that.

With the horses out on the track the paddock was empty. Midge was alone near the rail. A security guard in a gray uniform stood, bored, at the bottom of some stone steps. Midge walked down to where the guard was gazing at the track, a gun in a holster on his belt.

"Hey," she said.

The guard didn't seem to hear her.

"Hey," she said again, and she tugged at his sleeve.

The guard looked down at her. He had a large, pink face. He was pretty big himself.

"Yeah?"

"Who was that lady up there?"

The guard looked up the ramp where she was pointing. There was nobody there.

"Who?"

"That fat lady in the yellow dress. Who was there a minute ago."

"You mean Nita? She's the jockey-room laundress."

"That ain't so important," Midge said.

"It is if you're a jock," the guard said, "and you want clean pants."

"I suppose that's very true," Midge said.

She looked up the ramp toward the jockey room, hoping to get a glimpse of the forbidden inside. The door was open but all she could see was dark. A head poked through the door and a voice called down: "Bill, got a minute?" The guard looked around and saw nobody there but Midge, and with heavy steps walked slowly up the ramp.

Midge looked around for Decker. She could see the back of his head down by the rail, with just the beginning of a bald spot which got him furious if she ever mentioned it. She looked up the ramp. The guard had disappeared into the room. Five feet away was an open gate that led behind the paddock. She hesitated. Then she walked through the gate, expecting to be called back at any moment. When nobody called she kept on walking.

A rocky dirt path sloped away from the grandstand and the paddock. Alongside the path was a chain link fence, and behind the fence a wider, smoother path along which they brought the horses on up. She kept on walking, as if following a stream to its source. At the end of the fence was a sentry box in which two men were talking. She thought of asking for directions, but was afraid they would send her back. Instead she walked on by. The men didn't seem to notice.

The path continued to the top of an embankment. From there she could see the barns spread below: rows of long silver roofs stretching in every direction. There were 1,268 horses registered at the track, she had read. They were all down in those barns, except for the eight up running in the eleventh.

She looked around guiltily, expecting some giant paw to crash down on her shoulder and yank her back. Some giant paw as belonged to the man with the fist on his buckle. Some giant paw as had practically yanked Decker from the car.

"Who was that?" she'd said, when they had finished talking out of her earshot and the man had walked away and Decker had climbed back into the car.

"Business," Decker said.

"What kinda business?"

He turned to her with a look in his eyes that scared her. A look of pain, or fear. Or both.

"My business," he said.

There was anger in the look, too. It was a look she saw every day, and couldn't think where.

She didn't ask him again. She was hurt that he didn't trust her.

"My business!" she mimicked now, aloud, in a throaty voice, and looked around again, and seeing no one there she scrambled down the embankment to a wide dirt road that led to the barns.

She thought there might be a sign at the bottom that said BARNS, or something. Like the sign in an arc over the entrance to the trailer park, that said ENCHANTMENT TRAILER PARK. It was made out of metal letters, and from the inside looking out it said KRAP RELIART TNEMTNAHCNE. Every time she drove out under the sign she read it aloud, for good luck.

The first morning she drove out with Decker, she read it as usual. "KRAP RELIART TNEMTNAHCNE."

"What?" Decker said.

"It's good luck," she said. "It's an old Indian saying. I say it whenever I'm leaving home. It means, 'I hope I come back happy.'"

She was sure he would catch on right away. But he didn't. She had said it every day since then, and he hadn't caught on yet. By now she was afraid to tell him, afraid he might get mad.

At the bottom of the embankment, there wasn't any sign. Just the barns. The first barn had a large red A on it. Horse heads poked from most of the stalls, and two horses were walking in circles with their halters tied to some contraption. There were no people about that she could see. The second barn had a bright blue B. In addition to the horses in the stalls, a goat was tied to a pole, and two chickens were poking at the ground. As Midge watched, a woman came out of one of the stalls. She was wearing jeans and a western shirt, and her graying hair was pulled in a pony tail.

"Looking for somebody?" she said.

"Nope," Midge said, shaking her head, and only then realized that she was.

"Ma'am?" Midge said.

The woman had turned to go about her business. She turned back to Midge, waiting.

"Could you tell me where's Blue Lady?"

"That's Terry Blodgett's horse. Barn X. Second barn from the end." And she pointed down the road.

Third, Midge wanted to say. Third barn from the end. But if the lady didn't know her alphabet it was no business of hers.

"Thanks," she said, and she walked off down the road, trying to walk a little bowlegged, like the lady did, as if there was a fat pony between her legs. She counted off the letters on the barns as she walked, and hooked her thumbs into the top of her pants, and said, "Howdy, podner," to the air, the way they did in the movies. Till she came to barn X, and saw a tall blond boy in front of it, raking straw, and she got all shy again. Behind him the barn stretched thirty stalls long, with a horse head poking from each.

"Hi," she said, and she approached with hesitation. The boy didn't seem to hear her. He kept on with his raking.

"Hi," she said again, and stepped closer. Still the boy didn't hear.

She looked about. There was no one else around. She shrugged, and decided to give it one more try. She moved still closer to him. This time the boy saw her feet, and stopped raking and looked at her face. He was fair and young. Sixteen, maybe. Seventeen the most.

"Hi," Midge said.

The boy smiled, and waited.

"My name's Midge," she said, and she stuck out her small hand. The boy reached down and shook it, but he didn't say his name.

She looked around, still fearful some giant fist would yank her away from where she didn't belong.

"D'ya think I could meet Blue Lady?" she said.

She looked back at the boy but he didn't answer. She said it again. "D'ya think I could see Blue Lady?"

This time the boy, watching her face, smiled, and nodded, and leaned his rake against a pole, and pointed over his shoulder.

"Whatsamatter, can't you talk?" Midge said.

The boy shook his head no.

Midge's eyes widened. She cupped her hand over her mouth, horrified at what she had done.

Gently the boy reached with his long arm and pulled her hand from her mouth. He formed words with his lips, but she didn't understand. She felt awful. Like a dummy, she thought. And then felt even worse.

The boy took her wrist, and opened her palm. With the index finger of his other hand he wrote something on her palm.

"It's . . ." Midge read aloud.

". . . o kay. It's okay."

She looked up at the boy's face, and smiled. The boy smiled back.

He motioned for her to follow, and he climbed a slope to the long side of the barn. The bottoms of the stalls were closed. Horse heads poked from the tops, shaded by a long orange canvas. Neat stacks of feed were piled on one side. She counted the horses' heads as they walked by. Six, seven, eight, all brown. Then came three gray faces in a row. The boy stopped. She looked on down the stalls. All the rest were brown.

"Which one is Blue Lady?" Midge said.

She was sure she would know, but up close it was hard to tell. There was no yellow ribbon, no saddle cloth, no number like in the programs. She thought she knew but she wasn't really sure.

Before the boy could show her, a cloud of dust blew across them as a white pickup braked to a stop and a man climbed down. He was dressed like the woman in jeans and a western shirt except that his hair was brown over a ruddy face, and on his head was a blue baseball cap with white letters that said The Downs. Over his shirt was a leather vest.

"Fool," he said, nodding a greeting as he approached. "Who's this?"

The boy made a motion with his hand, between them, as if Midge should talk to the man. Then he walked away, and took his rake, and started raking again. His hair looked pure white in the sun.

"Why'd you call him that?" Midge said.

"Who? Fool?"

"Yeah."

"Because that's his name."

"That's his name? Fool?"

The man took off his baseball cap, and scratched his head, and put it on again.

"I guess he's got some other name. David, Danny, something like that. But everyone calls him Fool."

"You his friend?"

The man nodded. "Terry Blodgett," he said. "Fool there works for me."

She liked Terry Blodgett, in spite of things. She guessed it was all right. Maybe Fool was like Midge. A nickname that didn't hurt.

"My name's Beatrice," she said. "Beatrice Smith."

Blodgett found another rake that Midge hadn't seen against a pole, and began to rake the straw near the stalls, just like Fool was doing. His grip on the rake was strong. She could see the veins in his fist.

"Well," he said, continuing with his raking, "what can I do for you, Beatrice Smith?"

Midge hooked her thumbs into the top of her pants, then took them out again.

"Which one is Blue Lady?" she said.

"The gray one," Blodgett said, without looking.

Midge made a face. There were three gray ones. She turned around and looked to be sure. They were all still there.

"There's three gray ones," she said.

"That's right."

"So which is her? Blue Lady?"

"All three," Blodgett said.

"All three?" She looked at the horses again. "Now that can't be. You think I'm dumb or something?"

Blodgett leaned on his rake and looked at her face.

"It's just a precaution," he said.

"How do you mean?"

"Suppose you wanted to hurt the horse "

"I wouldn't!"

"Maybe not. But suppose you did. You wanted to hurt Blue

Lady so she couldn't win the race tomorrow. Which horse would you hurt?"

Midge looked behind her uncertainly.

"I don't know," she said.

"Exactly."

"Exactly what?"

"All three are Blue Lady."

"You mean they take turns racing? So if one gets hurt you've still got two Blue Ladies left?"

Blodgett couldn't help smiling. "Something like that," he said.

Midge looked at the horses with wonder. She knew that's how it had been with Lassie. There had been lots of Lassies.

"Can I pet them?" she said.

"Suit yourself," Blodgett said.

She moved up closer to the stalls. The one on the left looked the most like Blue Lady. She reached up and rubbed its face, just below its eyes.

"Hello Blue Lady," she whispered. "You gonna win that race tomorrow? I'll bet you are!"

The horse looked very intelligent with its big gray eyes, and she waited for it to answer, to give some sign. But it didn't. Maybe she had the wrong one, she thought. On second look the one in the middle looked realer. She moved over and petted that one, and then she still wasn't sure, and she petted the one on the right. And then she thought it was the first one again. She couldn't be sure at all.

She turned back to Blodgett, who'd been watching.

"Three Blue Ladies!" she said. "Imagine!"

Blodgett winked. Midge walked past him, out into the sunlight beyond the overhang. She shaded her eyes with her hand.

"You got any chocolate cake?" she said.

"Chocolate cake?"

"It said in the paper, chocolate cake is Blue Lady's favorite."

"Paper's wrong," Blodgett said. He took a tin of chewing tobacco from the pocket of his vest. "Green chili is what she likes best."

"Green chili? You got some you could feed her now?"

"Not the day before a race," Blodgett said.

Midge understood. She had once got the runs from too much green chili. Right out there with the prayer dogs. It was embarrassing. She'd had to use pages from her manual, which wasn't very respectful. And none too soft, neither.

"But two of them won't be running tomorrow. Two of them Blue Ladies."

"You've got a point," Blodgett said.

He unwrapped a plug of tobacco. Midge bent down and picked up a piece of straw and put it between her teeth. The way they did in the movies.

"Only one's gonna run tomorrow has got a certain tattoo inside her lip," Midge said. "625230"

Blodgett looked at her with amazement.

"How in hell do you know that?"

"They showed her registration and Thunderbolt's in *The Reporter* once. I got a way with numbers."

"You sure do," Blodgett said.

He shoved a plug of tobacco into his mouth. Midge flushed happily at the praise. From high above at the track there came a roar from the crowd. Then it was quiet again. Quiet as night.

The lingering silence made her nervous.

"625230 gonna win tomorrow?" she said.

"She'll try her best," Blodgett said.

Again there was only silence. It seemed that horse people didn't talk much.

"So, how's the Monsignor?" Midge said.

"Who?"

"You know. The Monsignor." And she screwed her face into a wink.

Blodgett replaced the tin in his pocket.

"You a friend of the Monsignor's?"

"Nah. A long time ago we was lovers."

Blodgett, who'd been about to spit tobacco juice, began to choke on it. He expectorated the whole plug and still couldn't catch his breath.

"You . . . and the Monsignor?"

"All three of them," Midge said.

The trainer was coughing, choking on his laughter.

"At the same time!" Midge added.

Blodgett grabbed a pole to keep from falling. He held on till he caught his breath. His face was red from the choking. Decker never laughed quite like that.

"What'd you say your name was?"

"Midge."

She flushed, suddenly self-conscious and all shy again. She couldn't believe the jokes she'd been making up. Especially about a man of the cloth. Though she wasn't sure what that meant, either. She never knew what particular cloth they were referring to.

Tobacco juice had stained Blodgett's shirt. He wiped it with his sleeve. "My hat's off," he said. He grinned at her, and then he removed his The Downs baseball cap and stepped forward and put it on her head.

"Why'd you do that for?" she said. She tried to peer up at the peak from underneath.

"It's a present. From Blue Lady."

"For me? I can keep it?"

Blodgett nodded. Midge took off the cap and looked at it, and put it back on her head, pulling it tight. It was much too big, it touched her ears on the sides. Immediately it was her favorite thing.

"Thanks," she said.

It sounded feeble, it wasn't thanks enough, but she didn't know what else to say.

"One thing, though."

"What's that?" Blodgett said.

She stood on the toes of her sneakers and whispered in his ear as he leaned down. He looked around, then whispered back in hers.

"I knew it!" Midge said, and she jumped up and down on her toes. "I knew right off that was her!"

She looked at the three gray horses. At one in particular. The one she thought was the beautifulest by far.

"You don't have to worry," she said. "I won't tell a soul. On my mother's Bible."

"I'm sure you won't," Blodgett said.

She turned to go and took two steps away, then turned back.

"You won't tell that Monsignor what I said?"

"On my mother's Bible," Blodgett replied.

She stuck out her hand to shake. Blodgett looked puzzled for a moment. Then he shook hands with her.

She was struck again by how quiet it was by the barns. She couldn't hear a sound, except for the soft scratching of Fool's rake and a fly that was buzzing by her ear. It was like being out in the country on a summer's day. As quiet as it was by Santa Cruz lake. Also it smelled of manure. As if all the horses ate too much green chili this morning.

"Hey, listen," she said, and was startled by the sound of her own voice. She lowered it to just above a whisper. "If some guy comes around with a fist on his belt, watch out. He's trouble."

"Who is he?"

"I ain't really sure. But he's mean."

"I'll keep my eye out," Blodgett said. "A fist."

"Right. A fist. Right there on his buckle."

Blodgett turned, as if he had work to do now, and Midge walked off and said good-bye to Fool, who waved, and she started to walk up the road with the cap on her head. She heard another roar from the crowd above, and she started to run, past the barns, the alphabet moving by in reverse, and she scrambled up the embankment and ran along the rocky path toward the white concrete rear of the grandstand. She had so much good stuff to tell Decker! Sometimes she worried they would run out of things to talk about. But not today.

But she couldn't find him. Not by the rail and not at the paddock and not at the bar buying beer. He must be in the john, she decided. She pulled her The Downs cap low on her head and began to move about the concrete slope, doing her job, picking up all the losing tickets, remembering them in her head: a two, a six, a four, another six, a nine. Thinking all the while about Blue Lady.

"Beatrice!"

She was startled by the familiar voice. She stood up quickly.

"Mrs. Gallegos! What are you doing here?"

"We're staying in town for Fiesta. John figured we might as well kill some time at the track. They let you in free after the ninth race."

"Yes," Midge said. "I heard that."

"Did you lose something?" Mrs. Gallegos said, with a nod toward the pavement.

Midge flushed and shoved her pack of tickets into the pocket of her pants.

"Just dropped a dime," she said. "It don't matter. It must've rolled on down. It don't matter. What can you buy with a dime now, anyway? Not even a pack of Jujubes anymore."

"Will you be here tomorrow, for the big race?"

"You bet," Midge said, hopeful that Decker would keep his promise. "How about you?"

"We wouldn't miss it for the world. Most of the whole village is coming down. Even Father Archuletta."

"That funny old priest? Are they . . . I mean . . . allowed? In them jackets and collars and all? Them that ain't the Monsignors, I mean."

"I don't think the Father will actually bet," Mrs. Gallegos said. "But who knows?"

"He sounds like a nice man."

"Well, he's a man, anyway. . . . John! Over here!"

Mrs. Gallegos waved to a stocky, dark-haired man, who walked toward them in Levi's and a sport shirt, a program in his hand. He looked like a man who worked hard all day for his family.

"This is my husband, John Gallegos. This is Beatrice Smith, who I've told you about. Who works with me."

"Nice to meet you," John Gallegos said.

"Pleased, I'm sure," Midge said.

She looked around, embarrassed. She spotted Decker standing by the rail. "I have to go now," she said.

"Maybe we'll see you tomorrow," Mrs. Gallegos said. "When we come to boo Blue Lady."

"Ain't no way Blue Lady will lose," Midge said. "It's the law. The law of averages."

She noticed their puzzled looks, and she wanted to explain.

But she decided it would be too hard. John Gallegos didn't work with the plague. Mathematics was something that not just anyone could grasp.

Blodgett would have understood. She should have told Terry Blodgett not to worry.

"Pleased, I'm sure," she said again, and she hurried away toward the rail. Halfway down she waved again, then continued on.

She wondered what Mrs. Gallegos had told her husband about her.

She wondered, too, how they could come to boo Blue Lady. If they didn't like it that the Monsignor owned her, it wasn't Blue Lady's fault.

The nicest people could act strange and cruel sometimes.

When she got to the rail, Decker was mad as hell.

"Where you been?" he said.

She wanted to tell him everything: about Fool, and Blodgett, and the three Blue Ladies. But this clearly wasn't the time.

"I said where you been? I been looking all over for you."

"Business," Midge said.

"Business? What kinda business you got?"

"My business."

Decker turned away. She couldn't leave it like that.

"Hey, Deck, I'll tell ya all about it." She slipped her arm through his. "But first I got to get more tickets. Got to find you a winner in the twelfth."

He turned to look at her. He took off the baseball cap and examined it, and put it back on her head, a little crooked.

"Be about time, too," he said.

She scooted away and did as she always did: she gathered up tickets, moving among the legs of the larger people. She sipped his beer, and a little bit later they had bet. She had bet her unborn baby on Blue Lady. On the law of averages. It was her The Downs cap that gave her the idea. It was a thinking cap. Handmade by the thinking-cap fairy.

She gave Decker the winner in the twelfth. When he went off to bet she lay on the ground and kicked her sneakers off, and looked up at a bright patch of blue, which was all she could see, and she pulled the peak of the cap over her eyes as the sound of the horses' hooves closed in.

She remembered Decker's face when the fist man came. Remembered where that look was every day. It was the very same look the prayer dogs had when she found them caught in the traps.

She jumped up and pulled on her sneakers and without tying the laces she scurried off to find him. He was just leaving the cashier's window. Together they walked in the crowd toward the exit.

"What you gonna do with the money?" Midge said.

She was determined to take his mind off whatever.

"The twelve bucks?"

"And twenty cents."

"Yeah. Be terrible if we forgot the twenny cents."

"What you gonna do with it?"

"Maybe I'll buy a house."

"That's a good one! One of them great big mansions out near Bishop's Lodge."

"Or in New Jersey," Decker said.

A tremor of anxiety ran through her. She looked up at his face. All she noticed was a speck of dried blood, where he had cut himself in the morning.

"Maybe a car would be better," she said. "A Jag, like you always wanted."

"Or a big black limo, like that mon senior of yours."

"Or a white Mercedes, like the Virgin Mary drives!"

She squeezed his arm tight as they moved through the parking lot. She loved it when he would kid with her like this.

With his free hand he took his crumpled pack of Camels from his shirt pocket and flipped up a cigarette and pulled it out with his lips. He freed his other hand and lit up.

"Give me a puff," she said.

"You? It'll stunt your growth."

"I guess I'll risk it," she said.

She wanted to share everything with him. Everything.

She took the cigarette and brought it near her lips. Then she thought of the bet. The baby. She didn't puff. Instead she gave it back.

"You didn't even take a puff," he said.

"I know. It'll only make me cough."

They walked on quietly, till they neared the car. Many spaces were empty already, but FAMOUS POTATOES was still parked in front of them.

"Looks like they came for that dead dog," Decker said.

She went close and peered at the empty back seat. She moved up and looked at the front seat. She stuck her hand in through the small wing window that was open. Decker was busy at their own car, unwrapping the coiled wire on the door.

"You know that dead dog?" she said. "He's licking my fingers right now."

"Prob'ly he's got the plague," Decker said. He pulled open the creaking door and slid in, and pulled it shut behind him. "Prob'ly he'll be dead in the morning."

She slipped into the car and found the key in her purse, and switched on the ignition and gave her gas. As the car shook to life and warmed up, she took off her smart new cap and looked inside it.

"Thinking-cap fairy's got a place in Hong Kong," she said.

CHAPTER 5

The Virgin

It was Jack who always wore a baseball cap when they were kids. A black one, with no letters. He wore it at breakfast eating his Rice Crispies, listening to them snap, crackle, and croak, while Beatrice ate the raisins out of her Raisin Bran with her fingers, counting how many, trying to leave over the rest of her soggy cereal, saying it didn't have no taste without the raisins, till her mother threatened to force it down her throat with a spoon and she mushed it around and ate a little till it was time for the school bus and she managed to leave at least half of it in the bowl. He wore the cap as they waited on the corner for the bus in the morning light, she still sleepy many times from staying up telling stories to her dolls. He must not have worn it in school because the teachers wouldn't let him, but he was in different classes three grades ahead and she never really saw him without it. It was always on his head again when they met in the schoolyard at three o'clock and waited for the bus to take them home.

He wore it playing in the street after school. Their parents asked him not to wear it at dinner, but when he wouldn't listen they stopped bothering about it after a while. He wore it watching TV, and he still was wearing it when they shooed her off to her room to go to sleep. It was not so much a baseball cap as Jack's cap. Part of being a boy.

"I want a cap like Jack's," she told her mother once.

"Girls don't wear baseball hats," her mother said.

75

"Why not, if I want to?" she said.

"Because it isn't ladylike." And on Saturday morning her mother in a good mood took her to Penney's on the Plaza and put nine hats on her head till they came to a roundish pink one with a pink cardboard rose on the side that her mother liked the best.

"That one looks precious," her mother said, and led her to a mirror. "Don't you like that one, Beatrice?"

"Yes," she said, because her mother was in a good mood and she didn't want to upset her. They bought the hat and her mother had the salesgirl snip off the price tag with a scissors, and her mother put the hat on her head and they went down the block to the Capital Pharmacy and had lunch there, just her and her mother, which they hardly ever did, a hamburger each and her mother drinking coffee and she drinking milk with chocolate syrup, Mr. Reynolds behind the counter saying how pretty she looked today and her mama saying it must be the new pink hat.

When they got home she wanted to go out and play, and her mother said to put her nice new hat in her closet, which she did, only instead of on the shelf she dropped it on the floor next to her torn old sneakers and her socks. She went in the backyard to play, her shoes getting muddy because it had rained the night before, and when they were good and muddy she slipped back to her room and went into her closet and jumped up and down on the hat.

Her father, who was a mailman, worked Saturdays. When he came home that afternoon her mother told her to show him her new hat.

"I don't know where it is," she said. She couldn't think of anything else to say.

"It's in your closet," her mother said. "Go get it."

She shook her head no, and her mother started to get angry and then went to get it herself, and found it there on the floor all muddy and smashed. Her mother's eyes were tiny as she carried it into the living room, holding it out like a dead skunk. Before Beatrice could say anything her mother slapped her across the face with the filthy hat. Then she pulled her into the bathroom by her ear and sat on the side of the tub and took her pants down and spanked her behind till it hurt with the flat, hard side of her father's brush. Beatrice screaming to God for her to stop, God not hearing too good. He rarely ever did.

When it was over and she was finished sobbing on her bed, and supper was almost ready—spaghetti, her favorite—her mother came and sat on her bed beside her.

"You know why I hit you?" she said.

Beatrice rubbed her nose in the pillow, but didn't answer.

"Why?"

"Because I jumped up and down on the hat."

"That's only part of the reason. You know why else?"

She shook her head, wiping away some tears that arrived late.

"Because you lied to me. You said you liked the hat. It cost me four dollars. If you told me you didn't like it I wouldn't have bought it."

She didn't know what to say. She had only said she liked it to make her mama happy.

"If there's one thing I want you to learn in life, it's never to lie. The truth will keep you out of trouble. You understand?"

She said she did, and she promised to tell the truth from now on, and her mother kissed her hair and said come inside now and eat some spaghetti, which she did, only she really didn't understand. There at the table was Jack with his hat on. Jack was smarter than she was, and Jack kept out of trouble by telling lies.

Eventually she decided that her mother was right, but that was later on, after she discovered other things such as jokes and make-believe. Ways to change the truth without lying.

It was that way in books, for instance. Her father was Catholic and her mother was Protestant and they didn't go to church very often except sometimes on Easter or Christmas, but her father's favorite book was about the church. It was called *Death Comes for the Archbishop*, by a writer name of Willie Cather, and it was about an archbishop a hundred years ago who come to Santa Fe and built the great big church down by the Plaza on Cathedral Place. His name was Bishop Lamy, her father said, but when he read her a story from the book it was about some Bishop Latour.

"How come Willie Cather changed his name?" Beatrice asked.

"It's done that way in books," her father said, "so you can make up stories about people without giving offense."

Beatrice thought about that. It seemed like a fine system. If it was good enough for smart men like Willie Cather who wrote books it surely was good enough for Beatrice A. Smith. No need for writers to keep it all to theirselves.

It sure came in handy the next summer, when Jack took her with him to steal the virgin.

She didn't remember why he wanted to do it. Just to stir up some excitement, she supposed. Stealing things was Jack's favorite thing. At first he would steal candy bars from Safeway, and then peaches or apples or pears. Then he took things he didn't even like to eat, such as avocados, and hid behind a tree on Alameda and threw them at passing trucks. One time when someone rang their doorbell and complained to their mother, Jack looked her right in the eye and said he didn't do it. And her mother believed him, because if there was one thing she was doing in life it was bringing up her children not to lie.

After a time he got tired of stealing things that could fit in his pocket. It was much too easy, he said. He said this one day when he was shooting baskets with his friend Eddie into the rusted rim of a peach basket nailed to a telephone pole across the street, and Beatrice was sitting on a rock making circles in the dirt with a stick. His basketball was old and had a hole in it, and used to go flat every day.

"Oh yeah?" said Eddie, who wanted to go steal some candy. "Why not go steal a brand new basketball then?"

Beatrice giggled at the picture of Jack trying to stuff a basketball into his pocket. But Jack said, "Maybe I will."

"You and what army?" Eddie said, which was something Eddie used to say all the time.

"Me and my little sister," Jack said.

"Beatrice?" Eddie said. "What's she gonna do, hide it in her thing?"

Jack dropped the soft basketball and ran over and grabbed Eddie's shirt collar in his fist and pulled back his other fist and threatened to punch Eddie square in the face. Eddie's face was growing pink from being choked by the collar.

"Take it back!" Jack said.

"I was only kidding," Eddie blurted.

"Take it back," Jack said again.

"I take it back," Eddie said.

Jack dropped his fist but he still held Eddie by the shirt.

"Now you tell her you're sorry."

"Crap no," Eddie said, "I ain't 'pologizin' to no kid."

Jack raised his squared fist again.

"I'm sorry," Eddie said. "I'm sorry, Beatrice, for what I said."

"That's okay," Beatrice said magnanimously, and squinted up from her stick and the dirt. She had no idea what it was he had said.

Jack left go of Eddie's shirt. Eddie stuffed it back into his pants. Slowly his face returned to normal.

"Now, me and Beatrice is going to steal a basketball," Jack said, "and you can come along and watch if you're not too chicken."

"How you gonna do it?" Eddie said.

"Simple as pie," Jack replied.

Their father was not home from work yet and their mother had gone to Albuquerque to help Aunt Vanilla pick out a sofa, so they didn't have to stay at home. Jack picked up the soft basketball that could hardly bounce anymore, and his bicycle pump that was laying at the side of the yard to pump up the ball again every few minutes, and he put them under his arm, and he took Beatrice's hand with his other, and together with Eddie tagging behind they walked the four blocks to Kahn's Sporting Goods on Galisteo. They stopped across the street from the store. Jack left go of Beatrice's hand and took the bicycle pump and stuck it in the flat basketball and blew it up. He bounced it on the ground and it bounced.

"You stay here," he told Eddie, "and hold this," and he handed him the bicycle pump, and with the basketball under his arm he took Beatrice with him across the street. He opened the door and they went in, and as they walked in the aisle in front of the cash register he began to bounce the ball.

"No ball playing in the store," a man behind the counter said.

"Oh," Jack said, and he handed the ball to Beatrice, who had to cradle it like a baby in both arms, and they walked toward the back of the store.

When they came to a wire basket filled with new basketballs, Jack stopped and looked around. The store was practically empty. No one was looking. He took the old basketball from Beatrice and put it in the barrel, and took a new one out and gave it to her. Together they walked toward the front.

"You want to buy something?" the man at the register said.

"I'm waiting for my friend," Jack said, and he took the basketball from Beatrice and began to bounce it.

"No playing in here," the man said. "Take that thing and wait for your friend outside."

Jack shrugged his shoulders and stopped bouncing the ball, and took the ball and Beatrice outside. They stood there a few seconds. Then they walked away and crossed the street.

Eddie was waiting where they had left him. Jack handed him the ball.

"Son of a gun," Eddie said. "You did it."

He handed the ball back to Jack, but Jack wouldn't take it.

"It's yours," Jack said. "Let's go." And he hurried away, Eddie and then Beatrice running to catch up to him.

"What do you mean it's mine?" Eddie said, when they got back to their own block.

"You keep it," Jack said. "Maybe next time you'll believe what I say."

"Hey," Eddie said, "thanks."

"Only you got to let me use it when I want," Jack said.

"Anytime you want," Eddie said.

They shot a few baskets with the brand-new ball and then Jack said that was enough, and Eddie took the ball home and she and Jack went on into the house.

"How come you give him your ball?" Beatrice said.

"So mom and dad won't see it and ask no questions."

"Oh." Jack was as smart as they come.

"Too bad, though," she said.

"What's too bad?"

"That you don't like stealing candy no more."

Jack put his hand on top of her head in a funny way. Then he went into his room and rummaged around somewhere. When he came out he was holding two Baby Ruths, and he handed her one.

"Just for me and you," he said.

They went out back and ate up the candy, which their mother always said would ruin their teeth. When they were done Jack went into the kitchen and came out back with matches. One at a time he lit the wrappers and held onto them till his fingers almost burned, and then he watched the ashes blow away.

"I know why you did that," Beatrice said.

"You do? Then why?"

"I guess they was 'tomic secrets," she said. "So the Russians and the Japs won't find 'em."

Jack grinned at her and rubbed her hair.

"You're a good little agent," he said.

Beatrice felt nice all over. She picked up a stick and started drawing circles in the dirt. Jack leaned back in the dirt, with his hands behind his hat, looking up at the clear blue sky. Beatrice watched a sparrow that had landed in the yard hop about poking the dirt for worms.

"Could be," Jack said after a time.

"Could be what?" Beatrice said.

"Could be you're ready for a new assignment," he said.

Absently she threw the stick into the yard. The sparrow flew away.

"What kind of 'signment you mean?"

He didn't answer right away. As if he was thinking it over. In a little while they heard a car pull up in front. They stood, Jack dusting his cap on his pants, and they ran around to the front of the house to see.

"Mum's the word," Jack said as they ran.

"Aunt Vanilla too," Beatrice said.

There were 27.5 churches in Santa Fe, Midge knew, and there must have been about 18.5 back then. (The .5 was the Jewish church on Barcelona, which someone told her wasn't even open on Sundays.) She had been inside two of them in her life: the big cathedral on Cathedral Place, from which she

figured the church got its name, where they used to go sometimes on Christmas Eve with music playing in the Plaza a
block away and farolitos lining the streets and houses nearby
and everybody's noses all red from blowing cold white breath
in the Christmas spirit of forgiving, and she wondering what
presents Santa Claus would bring her from Woolworth's or
Penney's in the morning; or sometimes on Easter Dawn when
spring was coming and birds were chirping in the fuzzy green
trees just starting to grow new leaves. The cathedral could
hold 2,024 people at one time without collapsing, and was
built in 1848 by Bishop Lamy or Bishop Latour, depending if
you believed the sign they wrote outside or Willie Cather.
The other one she'd been inside was the Church of Santa
Anna on Guadalupe, just three blocks from their house, from
where they stole the virgin of Santa Anna. It was the only
church wherein she'd spent the night, although that wasn't
part of the plan. Jack done better off planning basketballs.

He told her about it first, before he showed it to her, and
that was his first mistake. He told her that when the time was
ripe they was gonna steal the virgin from the church. She said
that sounded like fun, though she didn't know what he meant,
and the next day when she was alone in the kitchen with her
mama who was peeling the potatoes for supper she said,
"Mama, what's a virgin?"

Her mama got all red, like she had something in her eye,
and said, "Who told you a word like that?"

She realized right away she shouldn't have asked, so she
quick made up an answer: "One of the kids at school." It
wasn't a lie 'cause Jack was a kid at school too.

Her mama went on peeling potatoes with her knife and for
a time she didn't think she would answer. Then her mama
said, "A virgin is a good little girl."

It didn't seem right somehow: stealing a good little girl.
But her mama never lied.

"Am I a virgin, then?"

Again her mama got red. "Of course you are," she said.
"But it's not a word you should use. It's a word that's better
left unsaid."

She couldn't figure that out at all. Why make up a word if it was better left unsaid? It'd be like making up a number that didn't count. But she didn't bother her mama about it no more. One thing was sure. After she stole the little girl she wouldn't be a virgin anymore. Especially if they got caught.

Things got more confused when a few days later Jack took her and Eddie to the church. It was a flat old building, older even than the cathedral, with mud cracking in places on the outside that let the adobe bricks show through. There was some scraggly bushes and trees around it, and a cross and a bell on the top, and a dark wooden door in the front and a smaller one on the side, and one little stained-glass window on the other side toward the back. A sign outside said this church of Santa Anna was a historically preserved church, the second oldest church in the country, second only to the Oldest Church over on Santa Fe Trail. Which was still the oldest, even today.

Jack looked around. There was nobody much coming on the street. He pulled open the big wooden door, which wasn't locked, and they went on inside. Outside it was a sunny Wednesday afternoon in June, and pretty hot, too. Inside it was cold and dark.

They stood around in the back and waited. Nobody turned on the lights, but after a while it got lighter by itself. There was a little stream of daylight coming in from the one small window near the front, and along both sides there was tables with candles on them, hundreds, maybe even thousands of candles. Turned out there was 868, to be exact, but she wouldn't have the time to count them till Friday night. Even with all them it was pretty dark.

Jack pointed straight down the center aisle and said, "There she is. The virgin of Santa Anna."

Beatrice looked where he was pointing but all she could see from here was a platform with more tables on it and as-sorted statues of saints and martins and such, all lit by more candles burning below. There was no little girl at all, only some old lady dressed all in black with a black man's tia on her head, kneeling near a bench in the front. She was sure Jack had got it wrong.

"You mean that bending old lady over there?"

Jack looked where she was pointing. "Shit!" he said, and then he covered his mouth as if to take it back, and then he whispered it. "Shit."

"We better scram," Eddie said. Neither of them had noticed the praying old lady before.

Eddie turned to go but Jack grabbed his shoulder.

"Hold on," he said. "We got just as much right here as she does. She's just an old lady, she won't know what we're doing."

Eddie shook his head.

"Go play chicken then," Jack said. "Me and Beatrice'll go have a look ourselves." Which Beatrice didn't mind at all. There was no harm in lookin'. The stealing wouldn't be till Friday.

Jack led the way down the aisle, with Beatrice following, holding onto the back of his belt, like an elephant in the circus holding onto the tail in front, and Eddie tagging after. They got to the front, near the platform with the saints and martins, and Jack looked at the old lady on the side, who wasn't paying them no mind, being too busy crossing herself. He kneeled down the same way she was, and Beatrice copied it beside him, and Eddie beside her. Their hands clasped in front of them the way they all had seen in pictures, Jack's holding his baseball cap.

They were quiet for a minute, hoping the old lady would leave, but she didn't. The quiet made Beatrice nervous, kneeling there like that, and she started to giggle. Jack poked her shoulder to stop it, and she did.

Jack looked at the old lady. She still wasn't paying no mind. He nudged Beatrice's arm.

"You see up there?" he whispered.

She looked up at the table above them. There was three statues. Two of Jesus and Christ on the Cross, and a smaller of a lady in the middle.

"Yeah," she whispered back.

"The one in the middle."

"What about it?"

"That's her. That's the virgin. The one you got to take."

"Oh."

It's not, she wanted to say. Mama said it was a little girl.

But she knew Jack would be angry if she mentioned mama. She shut her mouth.

"It's worth priceless," Jack whispered. "It'll drive them nuts when it's gone. Especially with her feast day coming up."

"It sure will," she agreed. It usually made people feel good if she agreed.

He nudged her arm again.

"See that window over there?"

"Yeah."

They were still whispering. Eddie was looking around, getting nervous. The old lady's eyes were closed.

"They never lock it. I tried three times. It's so small they figure no one can get in."

"Yeah."

"But you're small enough to squeeze through."

"Yeah."

"There's a table under the window, see? You'll step on that table. Then all you got to do is jump down, and come take the virgin, and hand it to me through the window, and climb on out. You think you can do all that?"

"Easy as pie," she said.

She had forgot to whisper. She said it aloud, and her voice in the darkness spooked them.

"Okay," Jack whispered. "Let's go. Slowly." And they all stood and walked down the aisle on their tiptoes, so as not to disturb the lady, till they got near the door and Eddie ran to it, and pushed it open and ran into the sunlight, she and Jack close behind. They didn't run but walked as quick as they could away from the church, and crossed the street and walked that way the whole three blocks to Alameda.

On Friday their parents were driving to Denver for someone's daughter's wedding, which was why Jack had chosen Friday. They were supposed to spend the night at Aunt Vanilla's, but Jack called her up after school and told her they'd be eating dinner and sleeping over at Eddie's house instead. Which was fine with Vanilla. She had some man she'd just as soon entertain. Vanilla was always entertaining men, but when Beatrice asked her she'd never sing for them. It was a wonder she could sing for anyone, without no piano.

"You ready?" Jack said.

"I didn't finish my sandwich," Beatrice said.

They were sitting on the floor of the kitchen, she and Jack and Eddie, eating tuna fish and jelly sandwiches. Eddie's parents thought he was staying with them.

"Let's move it," Eddie said.

"Leave her eat," Jack said. "We got to wait till it's dark anyway."

Beatrice stood up and went over and dropped most of her sandwich in the garbage. It was something you were allowed to do when someone was getting married up in Denver. When she got married herself, Beatrice figured, she'd throw her sandwich away every day.

"I'm done," Beatrice said.

"So I noticed," Jack said. "Let's have a drink first."

"A drink?" Eddie said.

"One for the road," Jack said.

He went to the refrigerator and poured three glasses of milk, and got down the Oreos from the closet. Jack ate them straight, crunching away. Eddie dipped them in the milk till they were soft. Beatrice twisted them apart and licked the icing off the inside before she would eat the cookie part.

When they were through they put the glasses in the sink and went to the living room and looked out. It was almost dark outside. The street lights were just going on.

"Sweaters on," Jack said. "We may be gone for a while."

"I don't need no sweater," Beatrice said.

"Sweaters *on*," Jack said, barking it this time. Beatrice went to her room and got her sweater.

She had a hard time closing the buttons. She was beginning to get a little nervous.

"Okay," Jack said, and they went out into the yard and he closed the door behind them. It was night. There was no one around. "Let's go." He was whispering, though the block was empty. "Act natural," he whispered as they moved through the gate into the street. They did their best to act natural as they walked the three blocks to the church, Jack on one side and Eddie on the other, Beatrice in the middle. None of them said a word. Beatrice giggled twice along the way.

They stopped across the street from the church, and flattened their backs against a wall. For five whole minutes they stayed that way, Jack making sure there was no sign of life at the church. It looked deserted, a squat low fortress in the night.

Jack looked up and down the street. There were no cars coming.

"When I say go," he said, "we'll dash across the street to those bushes. Okay?"

"Okay," Eddie said.

"Jack?" Beatrice said.

"What?"

"I got to make a sissy."

"Oh, Christ. Didn't you go at home?"

"No."

"Why not?"

"I forgot."

"Some army," Eddie said.

"Listen," Jack whispered. "You'll go in those bushes. Okay?"

"Okay."

"Okay. When I say go, we run across." He looked up and down the street. There were still no cars. "Okay. Go!"

Together they ran across the street and in among the bushes outside the church, Jack arriving first, then Eddie, then Beatrice.

"Nobody saw us," Jack said. "So far so good."

The bushes screened the whole side of the church. They couldn't be seen from the street. Quickly they worked their way toward the back.

"Okay," Jack said. "Go around and make. We'll wait here."

"I don't got to anymore," Beatrice said.

"What do you mean you don't got to? You said you did."

"I already did it," Beatrice whispered.

"When?"

"Running across the street."

"Holy cow," Eddie said.

"Okay," Jack said. "Knock it off. We got work to do."

He led them a few steps further, to a clearing in the bushes. In front of them was the dark, looming side of the church. Above them was the small window. Jack stood on his toes and reached up, and pulled at the window. It was stuck for a minute. Then he pulled it open.

"See. Just like I said."

He kneeled in the dirt beside them. "Okay. Ready?"

"Ready," Eddie whispered.

"Ready," Beatrice said.

They moved under the window. Jack put his hands on Beatrice's hips, and lifted her. She reached up but couldn't grab the adobe where it jutted in to the window. "Help me," Jack said.

Eddie put his hands on Beatrice's legs, and pushed. Together they got her higher.

"Christ, her pants are wet," Eddie said.

"Never mind. Higher."

They pushed harder and Beatrice got both hands on the bottom of the windowsill. They bent their shoulders, and she was able to scramble higher, till she got one leg inside and sat on the sill.

They stopped and didn't move, all three catching their breath. Beatrice peered inside.

"What do you see?" Eddie said.

"Dark."

"Sit there till you can see," Jack said.

In a minute she could see: candles, benches, the platform in the middle where the saints and the martins were.

In the street they heard a truck go by. None of them breathed while the bushes flared with light and then went dark again.

"Okay," Beatrice said. "I'm goin' in."

"Make it snappy," Eddie said.

"Just be careful," Jack said. "We'll be waiting right here."

She swung her left leg over, and reached down with her toe. For a second she thought the table wasn't there. But it was. Slowly she sat down on it, and she moved to the edge. She put her arms at her sides, and she pushed herself off. Just as she did the table broke beneath her. She fell to the floor and the table fell beside her.

"What happened?"

She heard Jack trying to whisper loud from outside.

"The table broke," she said.

"You okay?"

"Yeah."

"Okay. Go get the virgin. Make it quick in case somebody heard."

She scrambled to her feet. Her behind was a little sore from where she landed. She looked around. She was glad the black old lady wasn't there. She wouldn't like to see her in the dark.

She went to the front and stepped up onto the platform. In the light of the burning candles the two men looked sad, hanging from crosses like that. With their long beards they looked like the Smith Brothers, no relation, who invented the cough drop. She wondered what Jesus and Christ had done that was bad. Prob'ly they had cursed all the time, calling each other by name.

"Beatrice?"

She heard Jack's loud whisper from outside. She stepped off the platform and ran on over to the window, and looked up. The candles seemed brighter now in the dark.

"What?"

"You got it?"

"Not yet."

"What's taking so long?"

"Nothing. Be right back."

She ran back over to the platform, and stepped up. Between Jesus and Christ was the smaller statue of the lady. She hadn't got a good look Wednesday. Now she could see it better. It was a lady with a pretty face, and a white nightgown, and a gold circle attached to her head. Her hands were together, praying. She looked maybe twenty years old. No little girl at all. If Jack was right, then her mama made a mistake.

"Beatrice?"

Jack was calling again. She reached up to take the statue. It was heavier than it looked. She reached up with both hands, and took it off the table. Carefully she stepped down, and walked on over to the window.

"Jack?"

There was no answer.

"Jack?" She said it louder this time. Her voice had an echo in the church.

"Yeah?"

"I got it."

"Great! Okay, hand it through the window."

She moved to the wall but she couldn't reach that high.

"I can't."

"Why not?"

"It's too high."

"Climb up on the table."

"I can't. The table's broke."

"Oh. Hold on." She heard them whispering outside. "Okay, Eddie's gonna boost me up. I'll stick my hand through the window. You put it in my hand."

"Okay."

She heard scraping on the wall, and grunting. She saw a hand near the window. Then it fell away and there were noises.

"Jack?"

"Hang on," she heard him say. "I fell. I'm coming back."

She waited. The wall scraped again. Then Jack's dark face was in the wondow.

"It's Satan the Devil," he said, in a drawn-out voice.

"It's Jack Smith," Beatrice said. "Don't tease."

He wriggled around by the window, and stuck his hand though.

"Okay," he grunted. "Hand her over."

Beatrice reached the statue up as high as she could. It just about reached Jack's hand.

"You got it?" she said.

"Wait."

He wriggled around and got his arm further down, and closed his hand on the statue.

"Okay," he said. "Let go."

She left go of the statue. Slowly Jack raised it up toward the window, and out. Then his face disappeared.

"Lemme down," she heard him say, and then a thump.

"Jack?"

"Yeah?"

"You okay?"

"Yeah."

"And the virgin, too? She didn't break, did she?"

"No. She's fine. Come on out."

"How?"

"Through the window, like we planned. Climb back up on the table."

She stood there for a moment, looking up at the window. Only then did she get scared.

"I can't. The table's broke."

There was silence from outside.

"Jack, you there?"

"Yeah. I'm thinking. You sure it's broke?"

"Yeah."

"Try it again."

She pushed the slanting table against the wall. It was still slanting. She leaned her weight on it with both hands. The leg collapsed altogether.

Suddenly she started to cry.

"It's broke," she said. "I can't get out of here."

"Listen," Jack said. "Try the doors. Maybe they're not locked from inside."

She wiped her tears with the back of her hand, and ran down the aisle to the big front door, and turned the handle and pushed. It didn't move. It was locked tight. She looked around and saw a smaller door on the side. She ran and tried it. It, too, was locked.

She turned to go back, and she saw the lady all in black coming toward her. She screamed, and ran behind a pole, making herself as small as she could.

"Beatrice?"

It was Jack again, whispering from outside. She peered around the pole. There was no old lady. Just the candles making shadows on the wall. Slowly, looking all around, she moved through the benches to the window.

"Jack?"

"What happened?"

"Nothing. I got scared. The doors is locked. What am I gonna do?"

"The benches," Jack said. "See if you can pull a bench to the wall."

She moved to the front bench, and pulled it. Nothing happened. She leaned her body behind it, and pushed with all her might. It didn't move. She went back to the window.

"The benches is nailed down. I can't move them."

There was no sound from outside.

"Jack?"

"Yeah."

"Go get Mommy and Daddy."

"Mom and Dad are in Denver."

She didn't answer. She'd forgot.

"Get the priest, then. The priest will let me out."

"There's nobody around. The church is closed for the night."

"Get somebody, then. Call the police. The police will get me out."

"We'd all be arrested. For stealing the virgin."

"Give it back to me then. I'll put it back first."

"Don't matter. They'll know you was stealing something. What'd you be doing in there? What would you tell them?"

"Tell them I lost something."

"We can't," Jack said. "They wouldn't believe it."

Her tears were pouring down. Her nose got full with sniffles.

"Jack?"

"What?"

"I'm scared."

"I know. Now listen to me. You're a big girl, right?"

"No. I'm a little girl."

"You've got to be brave. Here's what you have to do. Go to sleep on them benches. In the morning they'll open the church. Real early. You tell them you fell asleep and got locked in. And then you go away. Don't give them your name or nothing. Okay?"

"I'm scared to sleep in here," she blurted through her tears.

"There's nothing else to do, Bea. There's no way out."

She couldn't think of a way. All she could do was sniffle.

"It's all locked up," Jack said. "Nobody can get in. Nobody is gonna hurt you."

"You gonna stay close by?"

"We can't. Somebody might see us. We gotta go hide the virgin someplace good."

"Then you'll come back?"

"We can't. They'll see us. Anyway, you'll be asleep by

then. Just go to sleep. When you wake up it'll be morning. We'll come back then and make sure you got out. Okay?"

She didn't answer.

"Okay?"

She looked around the church. There was nothing moving. Only the candles flickering, and the saints and the martins looking down. Maybe God would protect her, here in a church.

"Okay," she said through her tears.

She might have said something else. But she could hear their footsteps running away outside.

She sat on the floor with her back against the wall, and cried. The floor of the church was cold where her pants were wet. She cried till there were no tears left.

She needed to blow her nose. She thought of using a white tablecloth on a table covered with candles, but decided that wouldn't be nice. She blew it in her sweater instead, and got it on her hand, and wiped it on her pants.

Still sitting on the floor with her back against the wall, she closed her eyes. A pretty lady appeared dressed all in white, with a circle attached to her head.

"Who are you?" the lady said to her.

"I am a virgin," she said. "I am a good little girl."

The pretty lady smiled. Stars fell out of her head. One of them landed on her lip. When she brushed it away like a crumb of bread, a small scar remained.

"What's it you want with me?" Beatrice said.

The lady's voice was scary now, like a ghost:

"I have lost my name."

"I didn't take it!" Beatrice said. "I swear I didn't!"

She woke up shivering. She stood and went to a table with candles on it. It was warmer standing near the table.

She decided to count the candles in the church, those on this table and those across the way, and those in front where the virgin used to be. All the candles by all the saints and martins. Turned out there was 868, if you only counted the ones that was lit. She didn't feel much like counting all the others.

She walked to the broken table and looked up. Through the

narrow window she could see dark sky, darker than the church inside. Just a slice of it. And looking down from the slice was a single star.

She knew at once what it was.

"It's the harelip fairy!" she said.

Looking down in the night to protect a girl like her.

It was the very first fairy that ever came to her.

She looked at the star till her eyes began to shut. She went to the benches and in the flickering light of the candles she found one with padding on it, and she stretched out. She knew she wouldn't sleep. She would just stretch out and rest. The way her father liked to do after work.

A sound near the door awakened her. Like a key, and something rattling. At first she didn't know where she was. Then she remembered, and she lay very still. Through the window high up the sky was blue.

Footsteps moved by toward the front. She peeked over the bench. The back of a priest disappeared through a door she never saw, behind the saints and martins in the front. When he was gone she sat up and ran to the side door where the priest came in. She leaned and pushed it open, and it opened, and she ran out into the air.

She ran behind the church and then walked slowly to the other side. She hid behind a bush, till she was sure that there was no one around. She saw something black in the dirt below the window. It was a cap that was just like Jack's.

It's a present for me, she thought. A present sent down from a star.

She picked it up and turned it over and looked inside. There in ink on the peak his name was printed: Jack Smith. It was his, not hers.

She put it on her head and walked home.

When she got there Jack and Eddie had just woke up. They were still wearing pajamas at the door.

"Did anyone see you?" Jack said.

Beatrice shook her head no. The lady dressed in white didn't count.

She took off the hat and handed it to him.

"I found it in the dirt by the church."

Jack took the hat, and he hugged her tight, and he kissed

her hard on the cheek. He had never done that before in all her life.

On Sunday it was in the paper. The front page.

"HISTORIC STATUE STOLEN . . . Virgin of Santa Anna Missing from Church . . . Priceless icon 400 years old . . . Thieves Entered Church Through Unlocked Window . . . Police Suspect Teen Prank. . . ."

There was a picture of the virgin before she was stole, and a picture of her empty space among the saints and martins.

Nobody in the whole city knew where the virgin was hid, except Jack and Eddie and her. Jack took her down and showed her that afternoon. She was wrapped up tight in plastic, stuck far back in a hole in the rocks under a bridge across the Santa Fe River. The Delgado Street Bridge, it was.

Nobody knew a thing about it. After a few days it wasn't in the paper anymore. Life was like before.

Then the dreams started. The pretty lady in white, prowling through the dark. Looking for her name.

"I didn't take it," she said. And woke up sweating.

Three weeks passed. The missing virgin was forgotten by everyone but her. Her and the lady in white.

"She must be cold there, wrapped up only in plastic," she said to Jack.

"It's only a piece of wood," Jack said.

One night on the local news they showed Father Joseph Brown, of Santa Anna Church. The Feast of the Virgin of Santa Anna was coming up next week, he said. If anyone had information about where the statue was, they would be very grateful.

He looked like a nice man, Father Joseph Brown, with brown hair and thin wire glasses. And Jack didn't care anymore. It was only a piece of wood.

The next afternoon she went over to the church by herself. It was dark inside, as always. The broken table was fixed, she noticed. But it wasn't by the window anymore.

There was no one in the church. Not even the lady in black. She went to the door behind the saints and martins, and knocked.

"Come in," a man's voice said.

She pushed open the door. Father Joseph Brown was sitting at a desk, writing. She recognized him from off the TV set.

"Yes?" he said. "What can I do for you, little girl?"

The walls were covered with books. More books than she had ever seen.

"I think I seen the missing statue," she said.

Father Brown stood up from his desk, and came around.

"What do you mean, you think?"

"It was her," she said. "She's wrapped up all in plastic to keep warm. But it was her."

"Where did you see it?"

"In a hole in the rocks. By the river."

"Do you think you could take me there?"

She nodded her head.

The priest locked up his office. He had his car outside. They got in and drove to the river. It was only a low trickle, with most of the mountain water gone.

"Up there," she said, and they drove to Delgado Street.

She got out and scrambled down the bank, the priest climbing down after. Under the bridge she pointed up at the rocks. The priest climbed up, and looked in the hole. He dropped a pebble in, to see if there were snakes. Then he stuck his hand deep in, and pulled out the wrapped plastic, and slowly and carefully took the wrapping off.

With his other hand he crossed himself on his chest.

"Blessed be the Lord, and the Virgin Mother," he said.

He took them back to his office, her and the virgin both. He sat her on a chair, and asked her her name, and made some telephone calls, and hung up.

"How did you happen to find it?" the priest said.

"I was playing down by the rocks."

"That was pretty high up," the priest said.

Beatrice looked at her shoes.

He didn't ask her anything else. She got up and walked around his office, looking at all the books.

"I guess you put too many books on that table," she said.

"Books on what table?" the priest said.

"That table out there that was broke."

The priest looked at her kind of funny. He started to say something, then stopped.

"Yes, I guess we did," he said.

A minute later the office was crowded with people. Her mother, who hugged her, and a policeman in his uniform and a detective who wasn't and some men from the newspaper. One of them had a camera. He took pictures of the virgin, and of her holding it, and pictures of her and Father Brown. Father Brown kissed her on the cheek and the flashbulb popped again.

"I'd like to ask Beatrice some questions," the detective said.

"She found it while playing by the river," the priest said.

"Still . . . ," the detective said.

"It's a miracle," the priest said. "The Lord has restored the Virgin to us in time for the day of her feast. We are very grateful. I think the case should be closed."

The detective shrugged his shoulders, and he put his notebook away. "Whatever you think is best, Father," he said.

The next day it was in the paper again. Right on the front page. Her holding the virgin, and Father Brown kissing her cheek.

TYKE FINDS STOLEN STATUE, it said.

"What's a tyke?" she asked Jack.

"I guess that's you," he said.

At first he seemed angry about it. Then he went around smiling.

He never mentioned it again.

He never asked her to help him again, either.

Now, twenty-three years later, he still doesn't ask her help. But she goes to see him, unbidden, on visiting days, bringing cookies or fruit or whatever she can afford.

She never went back to the Church of Santa Anna. There was no reason to. Though it was odd, Midge thought, thinking back, that in all the years since then, in a town so small— 48,241, to be exact—she had never again set eyes on Father Brown. Not till this very afternoon, at the track.

CHAPTER 6

Also-Rans

Horses, 798.2; also 636.1. Dogs, 636.7. Elephants, 568.19. For whatever animal Beatrice wanted to read about, there was a card in the file of the Santa Fe Public Library, and on the card a number. All she had to do was follow the numbers written in white ink on the spines of the books, follow them from stack to stack, her small hand trailing along the books like a boy's running a stick along a fence, until she came to the correct number—798.2—and presto, there was a book—or three books, or ten books—about horses. Or dogs. Or whatever. After the crash that killed her parents she took to going to the library straight from school, five days a week, and staying till dinner time, so she would have to spend as little time as possible at home with Aunt Vanilla. (Her name was Vanessa, but she colored her mousy brown hair such a bright blonde that behind her back Beatrice and Jack called her Vanilla. They felt she didn't want them, had taken them in only grudgingly after the death of their parents, and they returned her hostility in kind.) Perhaps it was there in the library during the long afternoons that she ritualized her fondness for numbers, and imbued them with the power of magic: know the right number and you could escape into any sort of world you desired. She memorized the numbers of all the books she read, and then, without making a conscious decision to do so, she expanded this to encompass just about every number she encountered: the numbers of the houses they passed on the

101

way to school (she was particularly intrigued by 814½ Galisteo; she did not understand how you could have half a house) and the price of every item at Safeway when she accompanied Aunt Vanilla to the market. People she met, such as the men Vanessa was always dating, did not know what to make of her. When she spouted numbers they tended to think she was a very bright little girl, but this conflicted with the gut impression they formed upon first seeing her face and her scarred lip, which was that she must be below normal in intelligence. This impression was fostered by Aunt Vanilla, who called her fascination with numbers a stupid waste of time, and lamented the fact that her sister had left her with a ten-year-old juvenile delinquent and a seven-going-on-eight-year-old retard. Her dumbness became almost laughable when visitors asked Beatrice—at the sly urging of Vanessa—what she wanted to be when she grew up. A teacher? A nurse? At first Beatrice would give the answer straight out, looking right at them, but after the smiles and the laughter and the looks that were even worse, she took to staring at her brown-and-white saddle shoes while responding. She didn't change her answer, because it was the truth about what she wanted to be, and her mother had taught her always to tell the truth, but her face would grow hot and she would stare at the floor before giving her response:

"Miss America."

And then, when they tried to hold in their laughter, she would run away to her room.

Midge smiled, looking in the mirror of the small bathroom, pulling at the sleeves of her Fiesta dress, smiling at her childhood stupidity, smiling, too, at how pretty she looked. The dress was black with a white lace collar. The skirt was pleated and full, and when she twirled her hips it would swirl up around the tops of her maroon boots. From the closed toilet seat she lifted her black Navajo hat that Jack had bought for her the year before, and she put it on her head. It was too big and too flat, it made her look squashed and dumb, but when she slipped it down onto her back, with the black cord chin strap around her neck, it gave her the desired effect: of a cowgirl of the Wild West.

"Fifty-five," she said into the mirror.

There had been fifty-four Miss Americas since Miss America began. Five from California. Five from Ohio. Five from Pennsylvania. None from New Mexico.

"What's taking so long in there?" Decker yelled.

None with a scar on her lip.

Decker was stretched out on the bed, in his black chino pants and his white T-shirt, his newly polished black shoes soiling the quilt. His head was propped on the two pillows and he was watching some kids' program on the TV, drinking warm Schlitz from a can.

Midge ignored him and combed her hair, which had become mussed when she put on the hat. She could tell that Decker was nervous, and when he was nervous he was irritable. The truth was, he was always irritable, but sometimes he was more irritable than others. He was nervous, she supposed, because she had asked him to take her dancing at the Jockey Club after they watched Zozobra burn, and Decker hated dancing like he hated going to the dentist. And he was nervous, too, she thought, about the bet. If Blue Lady won they would set the date, and most men, it was her experience, got nervous about things like that. 99.999 percent.

Her belly in the mirror revealed nothing. There was still seven months to go. But she would choose a date early on.

"I gotta use the john," Decker yelled. "Let's move it."

She put her comb in her red plastic purse and opened the narrow door and swept into the small bedroom, twirling around once so that her skirt would swirl the way Loretta Young's used to do in the reruns, so Decker would notice how pretty she looked tonight. Her swirling skirt hit the corner of the bed and stopped swirling. It bunched up instead. Decker swung his legs off the bed.

"Can't a guy take a crap around here?" he said, and he stalked into the bathroom and slammed the door.

She knew what Vanessa thought. And the others. Poor Midge, who has to settle for any man she can get.

"Nuts to them," she said.

She straightened the bedspread and arranged the pillows side by side. Decker had taken the sports section of the newspaper into the john. The front section had slipped to the floor. She picked it up and saw on the front page a large picture of a beautiful young Spanish girl, smiling with bright teeth between curtains of jet-black hair.

"Fiesta Queen Abigail Ruiz," the caption said, "who will be installed by the Archbishop on her throne in the Plaza after the burning of Zozobra tonight."

Midge looked at the picture. The prettiness of the girl made her feel good. Two things always sent her spirits soaring. One was animals, which were loyal and innocent, and always needed someone to take care of them. The other was prettiness, prettiness in all things.

The toilet flushed and the john door opened and Decker came out, buckling his belt, and tossed the sports pages on the bed she had just straightened.

"Blue Lady!" he said. "This jerk writes as if she's God's gift to racing. Wait till tomorrow. They'll be singing a different tune."

Midge smiled inside. Decker was getting worried about the race.

She felt like teasing him about it. But she decided she better not.

"You ready?" Decker said. "I'm starved."

"Ready as I'll ever be," Midge replied.

She put down the newspaper with the picture of the Fiesta queen on it and grabbed her purse. She followed Decker through the cluttered living room as he put on his white shirt but didn't tuck it in, and out into the warm dusk, and she locked the door behind them. She liked living in the trailer park, except for one thing: they didn't allow pets.

"Who's driving?" she said cheerfully, taking the car keys from her purse.

Decker looked at her with his look. "Whattaya mean, who's driving?" he said. "I'm driving." And he took the keys from her. He strode toward the driver's side, then stopped and looked at her again. "Why'd you even ask?"

"Just 'cause we're going to the track."

"We ain't going to the track," Decker said. "We're going to see that dumb puppet burn."

"At the track," Midge said.

"Get in," Decker commanded. "It ain't the same thing."

He slid behind the wheel and tossed Midge's pillow onto

the back seat. Midge, walking around the back of the car, formed words with her mouth through the rear window: "It is the same thing." But she didn't say the words. Instead she stuck her tongue out at the car, and continued around to the passenger side, and uncoiled the wire and got in, and coiled the wire shut again.

Decker started the ignition. It was the one act that always flooded him with a feeling of power: the way a car—even this dumb car—responded to his wishes. He looked at Midge expansively. She thought for a moment that he was admiring her outfit. But he wasn't.

"You sure you don't want to eat at McDonald's?" he said.

"The food booths are fun," Midge said. "Navajo tacos. *Carne adovada* burritos. You'll see. You got your beer?"

"In the trunk. You sure? For old times' sake?"

She reached over and squeezed his hand. "That's nice," she said. "How about tomorrow night? Tomorrow we'll go to McDonald's. My treat."

He said nothing. It was always her treat.

Decker gunned the engine and released the brake. "That dumb Mex food gives me heartburn," he said. He backed up and turned the car onto the macadam road that led out of the trailer park. Old Man Peters, home from the hospital, watched them go but didn't wave as they passed.

"They got burgers there, too," Midge said. "You don't gotta eat Spanish if you don't want to."

"That ain't the point," Decker said, and he zipped the car into the heavy, slow-moving traffic on Cerrillos Road, heading out toward the track.

"KRAP RELIART TNEMTNAHCNE," Midge intoned.

She waited for him to say what the point was. But he didn't say. Instead he cursed and honked at a car in front of them that was slow keeping up with the traffic.

Dusk was dying quickly. The sun shot down by purple clouds had sunk behind the Jemez Mountains, and darkness was being drawn over them from the rear, like a blanket. Some of the cars had their headlights on already, others their parking lights. Decker, saving the battery, was using neither.

Midge looked idly at the roadside franchises passing on her

right: Kentucky Fried, Baja Tacos, Blimpies, Burger Chef, Dairy Queen, Long John Silver's, Dunkin' Donuts, Village Inn. She had been in every one of them at one time or another, she figured, except for Long John Silver's. She didn't care much for seafood.

As the restaurants passed, she told herself that she was feeling good. Very good. They would have fun at the food booths, and at the burning, and then they would go dancing at the Jockey Club, and then tomorrow they would come out early. They would pay to get in and watch all the races, and then would come the Unicorn Handicap, with Blue Lady. She had felt a strange calm ever since they made the bet. Killing the baby had been worrying her more than she admitted, even to herself, and now it was as if that worry was gone. She had cast her bread upon the horses, as the Bible said. Blue Lady would decide, and she and Decker would be honor-bound by it.

So she was feeling good, she told herself again. Very good. Except that it was not entirely true. Beneath the good feelings there was an unpleasantness, something that had happened in the past few hours, some upsetting incident that she had not been able to put entirely out of her mind. It was not the man with the fist. She had decided that was nothing after all. It was something else, something less personal. She looked straight ahead, at the traffic backed up ahead of them, bumper to bumper for .7 miles to the track. And then she remembered. The van.

It had been less than two hours ago, as they left the track after the last race. Decker in a good mood because the four had come in, paying $12.20. The cars bumper-to-bumper leaving the parking lot, four lanes converging into two. When a large horse van moved alongside and slightly ahead of them, the rumps of four horses visible through the slatted gate.

"Hey, Decker," she said. "Where you think they're taking them horses? Moving them out to some other track already?"

Decker had leaned forward, squinting through the creamy glare of the dirty windshield, and then leaned back again.

"Not them horsies," he said.

"What do ya mean not them? Where they goin' then?"

"Read the sign," he said.

They were almost beside the van. She looked up at the

106

lettering on the door. It said: MOUNTAIN PACKING COM-
PANY INC.

"So?" she said. "What's it mean?"

"It means them horsies have had it. It means they're
headed for the glue factory."

For a moment she didn't understand. She thought he was
making a joke she didn't get. Then, suddenly, she understood.

"You mean they're gonna kill them?"

"Dead as a doorknob," Decker said. "They're gonna
chop . . ."

He was about to describe in detail the methods of Mountain Packing. But he saw how upset she was, and he stopped.

"Them's horses that can't run for beans," he said. "It's
horses that run last every time, or next to last. Horses that
never won a race, and never could. After a while they get
tired of that. They sell 'em off for dog food. Or to be ate in
Paris, France, where horses is just like snails, only bigger."

"But how can they do that?" Midge said. "Them's race
horses. It's not like cows or chickens and stuff. Them horses
got names. Like Blue Lady. And numbers. People bet on them
horses, thinkin' they can win this time. They can't just kill
'em like that."

"Sure they can," Decker said. 'Them that owns 'em."

"But that'd be like killing your pet dog. Killing Benjy. Or
Snoopy. What kind of a person could do something like that?"

"These is slow horses," Decker said. "It ain't right to keep
making them race. They'd get laughed right off the track. You
take a kid who can't play ball too good. It wouldn't be right to
make him keep playing, would it? With the other kids laughing at him?"

"I guess," Midge said.

She thought about that for a while as the car stopped and
started in the traffic and dark gray took over the sky.

"You know that kid who couldn't play ball good?" she said
after a time.

"What kid?"

"The kid you just said. Who couldn't play ball too good."

"What about him?"

"It wouldn't be right to kill him, would it? To chop him up
into Gainesburgers, just 'cause he couldn't play ball?"

"It ain't the same thing," Decker said. "A kid grows up and becomes a man."

"Or a woman."

"Right. A kid grows up and becomes a man. He can do a million things. Playing ball isn't everything. A horse, there ain't nothing he can do but run. And if he can't run fast, he ain't worth a damn to nobody. Ain't nobody gonna give 'em room and board till they die of old age. It just ain't worth it."

"Yeah," Midge said. "I guess."

"It's just like with people," Decker said. "Ain't nobody gets a free ride."

"Yeah," Midge said. "I guess."

She wouldn't want to be a horse, she decided. Certainly not a horse nobody loved.

It had upset her plenty at first. Waking up nauseous every morning, wanting to throw up but not being able to, and not knowing what it was. Feeling tired all the time, thinking she had the flu except that her throat wasn't sore, which it always was with the flu. And then one day Mrs. Gallegos saying to her: "You know what it sounds like to me? It sounds like you might be pregnant, Beatrice."

The two of them in the Plaguemobile, driving home in the late afternoon.

"Me? Prego? Now that's a good one!"

"You don't think it's possible? You do have a boyfriend, don't you?"

"Course I do. But I never thought a jit about getting pregnant."

"It's not thinking that does it," Mrs. Gallegos said.

Which was a pretty smart joke for a nice Spanish lady to say, she had to admit. And sure enough, at the end of the week she missed her time of the month.

"That's not proof, of course," Mrs. Gallegos said. "You ought to get a test."

"From a doctor?"

"You can do it yourself. You buy it in a drugstore."

Which seemed what a scientist should do. She bought one of the tests and read the instructions, about putting your early morning urine in a test tube, and waiting maybe two hours to see if a red ring formed in the gook on the bottom. The only problem was how to do it without Decker finding out. The next morning she did it and put the tube on the windowsill in the bathroom with the curtain half-closed, hoping he wouldn't look. But when he went in to shave he pulled the curtain open for better light.

"What the hell's that thing on the window?" he said, standing in the doorway with his face all lathered white and his razor in his hand.

"Nothing, Deck," she called back from the kitchen, where she was fixing his corn flakes. "I'm just growing a mushroom, is all."

"A mushroom?"

"A special kind."

He went back into the bathroom, but when he was finished shaving he came on out with the blue box in his hand that he found in the wastebasket with the picture of Snoopy on it.

"Some fuckin' mushroom," he said. "What's going on?"

She had no choice. She told him. Together they went into the bathroom, to look at the tube. A red ring was starting to form.

"That means yes?" he said.

"That's what it says."

"Dammit! How could you go and do something like that?"

"It wasn't me alone."

"Yeah, I know, I know. It takes two to screw. When do you think it was?"

"I guess it was that time you turned me around. The first night of Blue Lady."

"Yeah," Decker said. "That's what I get for being sentimental."

They went back into the kitchen. She peeled him a banana. He couldn't stand his corn flakes without a banana.

"You angry?" she said.

"I guess it was an accident." He wiped his neck with his towel. "You'll just go to that clinic and get rid of it. I think they don't even charge if you don't got no money."

She turned away from him and fumbled with the packets of sugar that he stole from restaurants for his coffee. Sugar with birds on it.

"That's what I hear," she said. "You don't have to pay at all if you got no money."

Twice that afternoon she telephoned the clinic to make an appointment. Dr. Grauer, it was, on Don Gaspar. Both times she hung up when they answered.

On Saturday she went into town and walked past the clinic. A plain adobe, in a residential neighborhood. A nice little house, without even an embarrassing sign or a picture of a baby. Just a small wooden one that said Henry Grauer, M.D. It was across the street from a two-story building that said Catholic Maternity Home, for unwed mothers. That wasn't used anymore. That had stood empty now for years.

She walked up the block and crossed the street and sat on the curb in the shade. She wasn't planning to go in, she hadn't even gotten dressed up—just her pink pants and a yellow blouse and sneakers. She watched the house from across the street, but she didn't know what for. Perhaps to see women going in fat and coming out skinny. But no one went in or out.

It must be closed, she thought, and she crossed the street and went through the gate in the wall and up to the door of the clinic, to prove to herself it was closed. Hesitantly she tried the handle. The door swung open in her hand, as if it was waiting for her.

She wanted to turn and leave. Instead she followed the opening door into a room. A girl was sitting on a metal chair near one wall. She was black-haired, Spanish, with a figure like a movie star's, dressed tight in jeans and a sweater. She was sixteen at the most. Her chest was thirty-seven. At the other side was a desk with a lady behind it, who had a white smock on, and glasses.

Midge looked around. There was nothing else in the room except some more metal chairs, and a table with magazines, and a small tree in a pot in the corner. The lady at the desk looked up from a fat hardback book she was reading.

"Can I help you?"

Midge wasn't sure. She closed the door and walked softly to the desk, as if she were in the library.

301.5. Abortions.

She had looked it up.

"I need to make an appointment."

The lady put a marker in her book and closed it and told Midge to sit in the chair beside the desk. She sat and looked at the pretty Spanish girl. The girl was looking down at her lap.

A telephone on the lady's desk buzzed. She picked up the receiver. "Yes," she said, and she hung up again. She got up and walked toward the girl.

"You can go in now, Miss Smith," she said.

The girl seemed nervous. She got up and walked behind a partition and down a corridor. The lady sat down at her desk and opened a drawer and pulled out a large white card and picked up a pen.

"Your name?"

"Midge . . . I mean Beatrice."

"Beatrice?"

"Yes."

The lady wrote it down.

"Beatrice what?"

"Smith."

The lady held her pen over the card, but didn't write. She looked Midge in the eyes.

"Beatrice Smith?"

"Yes."

The lady shrugged her shoulders and wrote it down. Then she looked up again.

"If you have health insurance, we need your real name," she said.

"I don't got insurance," Midge said.

State workers like Mrs. Gallegos got insurance, she knew. But not the temporaries like her.

The lady wrote on the card. Midge felt something was wrong.

"That's my real name," she said. "Beatrice Audra Smith. I have this nickname called Midge. But that ain't my real name."

"It doesn't matter," the lady said. "Don't worry about it."

Midge looked toward the chair where the girl had been sitting. She looked sort of like the pictures of that Abigail something who'd been elected Fiesta queen. But it couldn't be. Lots of the girls in town were dark and pretty.

Still, it did matter to tell the truth. No matter what the lady said.

"It's a common name," she said.

"What is?"

"Smith."

"Yes," the lady said. "We get a lot of them. Are you married?"

"No . . . I mean, not yet."

The lady made a check on the card. In the not-yet box, Midge hoped.

"How old are you?"

"Thirty and a quarter."

The lady's eyes flicked up at Midge, then down. Probably she looked younger than that, Midge figured. All the lady wrote on the card was thirty.

"How old is the fetus?"

Midge squinted at the lady with one eye. Till now the lady didn't seem dumb.

"It's a minus," she said. "It ain't been born yet."

"Yes, I understand that. What I mean is, how long have you been pregnant? Do you know?"

Midge crossed her legs at the knee, the way sophisticated women did. There was a hole in the corner of her sneaker.

"Since the night of Blue Lady."

The lady took off her glasses and rubbed her eyes with her hand. "I don't understand. I mean, how long ago was that?"

Midge counted up in her head, with her lips moving.

"Forty-three days."

"You're sure?"

"Not counting today."

The lady wrote it down on the card.

"How do you know you're pregnant?"

"The mushroom."

"The what?"

"That test Mrs. Gallegos said. From the drugstore."

"A self-administered test came up positive?"

Midge nodded uncertainly. "And I missed my time."

The lady wrote it down.

"They spelled it wrong," Midge said.

"Who spelled what wrong?"

112

"Your book," she said, reading the title upside down. *The Female Unicorn.*

The lady smiled faintly. "It's not 'unicorn.' *The Female Eunuch.*"

"Oh."

She didn't ask what it meant. It was prison talk.

"When do you want it done?" the lady said.

"What done?"

"The abortion."

Midge flushed. She realized she was sweating. She didn't like doctor stuff. Even being a scientist herself.

"After work ends."

"When is that?"

"One week from Labor Day."

The lady checked the calendar on her desk.

"How about September thirteenth? At eight A.M. That will be for a test. If it comes up positive, they'll do it the same week."

The thirteenth is unlucky, Midge wanted to say, but that was being silly. She said it was okay.

"The fee is three hundred dollars."

Midge uncrossed her legs and put both her sneakers on the floor Sometimes you could look too sophisticated for your own good.

"I heard it was free," she said.

"It's only free to those who can't afford it."

"I don't have any money. Decker don't neither."

"Do you work?"

"Yes. With the plague. The bubonic."

The lady wrinkled her face, the way people often did when they heard, and seemed to lean back away from the desk.

"It's important work," Midge said.

"I'm sure it is. How much do you get paid?"

"A hundred ten a week," Midge said with pride.

But it ends in two weeks, she was about to say, but the lady had already wrote it down.

"The doctor will work something out," the lady said.

Midge looked around the room, not knowing what else to say. They could have used some pictures on the walls. Elephants, horses, Mother Goose. Something.

"If you have any questions, any doubts, ask about them now," the lady said.

Midge tilted her head to the side, but she couldn't see past the partition. She leaned over further and almost fell off the chair. She grabbed her balance just in time.

"Where do they do it?" she said.

"In the doctor's office. In the back."

"Why not in the hospital?"

"St. Vincent doesn't permit abortions. But it's not necessary. It's a simple procedure. You just lie down and rest for a few hours afterward, and then you're fine. It's as if nothing happened."

"So I heard," Midge said. "It's nothing to it."

"Do you have any other questions?"

Midge didn't respond. She was disappointed, somehow. She had expected more. She had expected the lady to ask her about her baby. To ask her why she didn't want it. Perhaps to tell her she should have it after all. Lying in bed at night with Decker sleeping she had rehearsed a whole set of answers to the question. There was Decker, of course, and a baby should be wanted by its father. But there was also her. She just wasn't —she didn't know what the right word was—she just wasn't fit to be a mother. Not old enough yet, somehow, and never would be. Not nearly smart enough, neither. She wouldn't know how to raise it up correct.

Thinking of the reasons again, she was glad the lady hadn't asked. Things that seemed true in the middle of the night were impossible to say in the day. She couldn't have told this lady any of that.

Still, she wished she'd been asked. She wanted the lady to care.

The lady wrote on a small appointment card and gave it to her. Midge stood mechanically and followed the lady to the door.

"We'll see you on the thirteenth, Miss Smith," she said.

You can call me Midge, Midge thought of saying, but she didn't say it. Then she was out in the sun and the door was closed behind her. She put the card in her purse without looking at it.

She walked down the block to the car. In front of every

house she noticed dark green garbage bags waiting for the garbage men to come and haul them away. She looked back at the clinic and saw none.

She wondered where they put them. What they did with them.

She sat on her pillow and drove out Cerrillos Road to the trailer park. All she could think along the way was what did they do with them.

She parked and got out of the car. From inside the trailer she could hear the TV on. Kids' programs. Decker prob'ly still in bed, watching.

She opened the door and stepped into the living room. Suddenly she felt sick. She ran to the kitchen. She managed to get most of the vomit into the sink, where Decker had left the cereal bowls from breakfast.

She leaned against the fridge until she felt better. Then she drank some water and cleaned up. Decker never heard a sound, with the door to the bedroom closed and the TV on.

He honked the horn again, a long, nasty blast. The car inched forward in the slow traffic, around a bend. In the distance now she could see the back of Zozobra, all white except for his belt, spotlighted in the twilight in front of the track grandstand. Excitement kindled inside her.

They used to burn Zozobra at Mager's Field, not far from the Plaza. But the streets were narrow and there was too much traffic and last year a man in a traffic jam had got out of his car and pulled out a pistol and shot the man in the car in front of him. So this year they'd moved the burning out to the track, where there was parking and a lot more room. Some people didn't like it, though. Already there was talk about moving it back next year.

With an effort she was putting the baby out of her mind. But not the horses in the van. They made her think of something else.

"A goddamn monkey!" she said.

"What?"

She rolled down the window and let the breeze blow on her face. It was heavy with exhaust.

"A play I was in back in school. I keep on thinking of it."

115

"What kinda play?" Decker said.

The exhaust made her face feel dirty. She rolled the window to the top, shutting out the noise.

"It took place in a zoo. All the pupils was supposed to be different animals. The teacher asked who wanted to be what kind of animal to raise their hand. I raised my hand and said I wanted to be an elephant. But the teacher said I couldn't. She said elephants was big, and I was much too small."

"She had a point there," Decker said.

Midge's eyes flickered across his face.

"So then I said I wanted to be a giraffe."

"That's even bigger," Decker said.

"Yeah," Midge said. "That's what the teacher said."

She lifted her black Navajo hat from the seat between them, and placed it on her lap, fingering the bead on the chin cord.

"So then I said I wanted to be a lion, because lions are strong and proud. But all the boys wanted to be lions, and the teacher said that was only right."

"What's right is right," Decker said.

"You think that's right? You don't think I could of been a lion?"

"I suppose, in make-believe."

"Anyways, I had one last pick. And I said I would be a peacock. A beautiful peacock, with bright shiny feathers."

She looked at the side of his face, her own face growing hot. Daring him to say the wrong thing. Decker turned his head to look at her, then turned back to the traffic.

"You think I should of been a peacock?"

"You'da been a terrific peacock," he said. "One hell of a peacock."

"Darn right I would," Midge said. "Only the teacher said no. She picked somebody else. And then, when all the animals was given out, I still didn't have one yet. And she said that everybody who didn't have an animal yet would be a monkey. I had to be a monkey with all the others. Standing in the corner the whole play, picking fleas off Sally Montoya."

"How long ago was that?" Decker said.

"Second grade."

"And you're still mad about it?"

"When I think of it."

They drove forward in silence, stopping and starting, watching the taillights of the car in front of them flare from dim to bright, from dim to bright. Made fiery by the cracks.

"My momma and poppa came to see the play in the afternoon. On the way home, in the rain, their car was hit by a semi. When me and Jack got home on the school bus nobody was there. Aunt Vanessa came to get us that night."

A respectful, long silence. Midge set the Navajo hat flat on top of her head. The way that made her feel squashed, and dumb.

Decker tried to think of what to say. He couldn't think of a thing. All he could feel was guilt. But it was the only thing to do. He was not meant to be a father. To fondle a little Decker on his knee. If Midge couldn't see that, forget it. They were two of a kind, he'd thought. Free spirits in wide circles. Till this baby thing came, and gave her fancy ideas.

He didn't want to hurt her. To tell her to her face—her poor face—that he was going. Better to leave in the night, as he had come. Let her wake up and find he wasn't there. Free to cry—if she wanted to cry—in the privacy of her own trailer.

A getaway driver is what he was. And though he had sworn off breaking the law—he'd go crazy back in the pen, a stud like him—that's what he would always be: a getaway.

He would take her dancing tonight, like she wanted. He would do anything she wanted tonight. And then good-bye.

He hit the brake hard, and then the horn. Midge shook the monkeys from her head. Zozobra loomed large on the right.

"Thar she blows!" she said. She had heard them say that once, in a TV movie.

"A big mother, ain't he?" Decker said.

She took off the hat, and breathed deeply. There were only good times ahead. The food booths and the burning and the dancing tonight, and Blue Lady tomorrow. And a week from tomorrow was Miss America. The Saturday after Labor Day, as always. They would stretch out on the bed and watch the show, the girls in their beautiful dresses, and Decker no doubt would make clever remarks about how stupid the whole thing was, but his eyes would be glued to them girls in bathing suits on the screen, which was all right with her, so long as the bed he was watching from was hers. The music would play and they would introduce the ten finalists, the master of ceremonies with his slicked-down hair and his rolling eyes, and the girls again in swimsuits and evening gowns, and then he would ask for the envelopes please, and one by one he would open them up, the fourth runner-up, the third runner-up, the tension building now, the second runner-up, and then it was the moment, the big moment, six of them left to choose from, and then he would open the last envelope, the band playing, the crowd cheering, and he would say it, yell it almost: "The winner is"—a pause—"Beatrice Audra Smith, Miss New Mexico!" And the band striking up, "Here She Is, Miss America," and the crowd clapping and tears running down her cheeks, and them putting the crown on her head and a bouquet of roses in her arms, and out the ramp she would walk, with the perfect walk she had learned, out into the lights above the audience, the tears running down, and when she got back the other girls all crowding around her, hugging her, saying how glad they were that she had won. She crooking the roses in one arm, waving to the crowd, the tears still running down. Everyone in the audience thinking how nice it was. Some of them crying, too. Remembering the speech she had made:

"I would like to free the world from the plague. The terrible, spreading plague of unhappiness."

And the flash bulbs popping in her eyes, making her blink.

Her very last chance, this year. Next year this time she might be a Mrs. A mama, too.

"Hey, Midge, you crying?" Decker said. He felt a clutch of remorse. As if she could read his thoughts.

"Who, me? Why would I be crying?"

"I don't know. It looked like you was crying."

Decker swung his hands on the wheel. She wiped her face with her sleeve. The car moved onto the frontage road, following the winking taillights, toward the track, and the puppet, and the night.

CHAPTER 7

Friends

From the old neighborhood in Hoboken they used to go on Friday nights to the Palisades, to eat hot dogs and say dirty things to older girls, and listen to the squealing of the teen-agers on the roller coaster and the dippy-doopy fairies wheel and the Whip. United by fear, they pretended an insufficient number of dimes, and avoided all rides. Their mission was to stuff their bellies, and to deride the courage of the screamers. Till one sad Friday, Angelo, who was ten years old and their leader, announced that he would brave the Spinning Wheel.

"You'll fall off and break your head," Joey said, watching with large eyes the wire mesh wheel spinning above them, the blurred people upside down, almost, and not even held by straps.

"You can't fall off, dummy," Angelo said. "The centrigial force holds you in place."

Angelo bought his ticket for 30 cents and, pausing at the turnstile, announced that anyone who didn't ride was out of the gang.

One by one they followed. Bought their tickets and climbed onto the horizontal wheel and pressed their backs against the wire mesh and wished they were at home, doing homework or being sick. All except the smallest one, who held back, hiding his face behind a large puff of pink cotton candy.

"What's the matter, Whore-Ass?" Joey said. "You afraid?"

Horace shook his head no, and dropped his cotton candy on the ground, and terrified, with sticky fingers, bought his ticket and climbed aboard. His hands pressed at his sides clutched tight to the wire mesh.

A bell rang. Music started. The wheel began to turn, slowly, all of them in a circle, backs against the mesh, looking in toward the middle. Faster and faster the wheel spun, like a merry-go-round, only faster still, till the whole world was turning. Then the wheel began to rise, to tilt, to turn over. He was convinced he would fall out and break his head. He tried to cry out. But the same force that was jamming his back against the mesh refused to let him scream. It forced his cries back into his throat. Around and around went the wheel, the lights, his head a spinning top. Till at last it leveled off, and slowed. The others jumped down, Angelo in the lead, before it even stopped. Horace waited but it didn't stop for him. Shakily he stepped out of the wheel. The world was still spinning. He walked stiff-legged, like he would years later after especially bad drunks, until the ground rose up and struck him in the face. He found himself on his hands and knees, vomiting up the hot dogs and the mustard and the pink liquid coating and the ride.

"What's the matter, Whore-Ass? Can't take it?" Joey said.

"Whore-Ass is a sissy," Mickey said.

They didn't wait for him. He took the bus home alone, in the dark.

The terrible nickname clung. He pretended that it didn't bother him. What they meant, he knew, was hooer. Hooer-ass. And that wasn't close at all.

One day years later a teacher in his dumb high school English class set him straight, while he was struggling to read Shakespeare aloud. The Immortal Bird.

"It's *whore*," the teacher said, amid the giggles of the class. "Like *oar*."

From that day on the only name he used was Decker.

He slammed the door of the car and walked around to the other side, where Midge in her Fiesta costume was struggling with the wire. He turned his back to her and scanned the horizon. There was the puppet glowing white against the night sky, the grandstand with its yellow lights, half-filled already, the long double row of canvas booths with naked bulbs overhead and blue flames heating large corn pots, and grills. The ominous forms he was looking for weren't there.

"Where's the rides?" he said.

"What rides?"

Midge, having solved the twisted wire, had slid out of the car and closed the door and, lifting it into place with her thin hands, was wiring it shut again.

"The carny rides. The roller coaster. The fairies wheel."

"There ain't no carny rides," Midge said. "This ain't no carnival. This is Fiesta. Two hundred sixty-eight years they been having this. Two sixty-nine, if you count a shortened one they had once during the war."

"Shit," Decker said. Exulting. "They ain't even got no rides? What kind of half-ass place they running here?"

"I thought you didn't like no carny rides."

"Who told you that?"

"You did," she said, but he pretended not to hear amid the noise of other cars parking on the gravel, of people joking and laughing as they passed, of music wheezing from uncertain speakers mounted on the parking-lot poles. He squeezed her elbow and guided her in the footprints of the crowd, across wooden planking, to what was barely recognizable as the infield of the track. On a platform at the base of the puppet near the three-eighths pole a mariachi band in bright blue uniforms and fringed Mexican hats was blaring trumpets and sawing violins into a microphone. The sight and the sound were out of sync, the music trailing the eye by at least a beat.

As they searched for a good spot to sit on the patchy dirt, Midge looked at him with concern.

"You forgot your beer!" she said.

"Shit."

"It's only there in the trunk. I'll walk you back."

"You stay here," Decker said. "I'll go get the beer."

"Don't forget where I am! Straight out from the end of the scoreboard. That's the best way to remember."

"You think I'm dumb or something?"

Midge hunched her shoulders, widened her eyes, pressed her lips together, in an expression of innocent guilt.

"You just don't move," Decker said. "I'll find you." And he left her there and walked away, across the wooden planking, into the thickening crowd.

And thought: Now I could do it. Get a hitch back to town, clear my stuff out of the trailer, and be gone. With no messy scenes.

But he couldn't do it. Not after promising her a good time tonight. She had earned that much, she was counting on it. He was no kind of creep. Only a creep would do that.

Time enough later. After tonight.

Twisting and turning against the flow of the crowd pouring in, he thought of Tempest Storm. Perhaps because of the spotlight on the puppet. He recalled how on Saturday nights they would take the yellow bus to Union City. To the Hudson Burlesk. Holding their breaths till they were inside the theater in the dark, because to get in you had to be eighteen years old and they were just barely fourteen then. But the man at the door in his maroon uniform with gold braids on the shoulders never stopped them. Didn't even wink, or smile.

"As long as you hold your head up tall and don't look at the ground," Angelo had told them, and he had been right.

A small band playing below the stage. Dirty comedians in silly suits. The prelims, to get you in the mood, younger ladies, mostly, who didn't even take it all off. Except for one who did. Cherry Paprika. The ushers in the intermission selling binoculars that you could hardly see through, and dirty books that weren't dirty at all. And then the main attraction. Tempest Storm. Her long hair jet black, her smooth skin milky white against a bright red sequined dress. Or violet. Or green. With the biggest set of jugs he had ever seen. Twirling them in opposite directions like two tanks just barely not colliding. And at the end of her act, slinging them over her shoulders. First one, then the other. Actually making the purple nipples, or purple in the purple spotlight anyway, disappear over her shoulders and down her back. That's how big they were.

"Mother of God," Angelo would say every time, on the bus on the way home. "Ain't nobody got jugs like that."

The others would agree, and they would speculate about what they would do if they could have one night alone with Tempest Storm.

124

Decker would contribute to the remarks—no more Whore-Ass now—but at home alone in his basement bedroom afterward with his parents asleep upstairs it was not Tempest Storm but Cherry Paprika who nightly dampened his sheets. A redhead, she was, a natural redhead all over. With the brightest pink set of nipples he ever did see. She didn't have the jugs of Tempest Storm, but you didn't have to be a cow, for Christ's sake. Cherry's were smaller, maybe, but better. They stood up firm and perky and spit in your eye. And how she could dance, with come-to-me-honey legs that did everything! And she talked to the men in the audience while she stripped.

"Come on up and help me, honey! Come do it to me, daddy, do it NOW!"

The NOW with a little yipping squeak that made him die.

Her green eyes sparkling and these little oohs and yips from her working mouth, right while she was taking it off. These noises making her not a stripper at all. Making her real. Hauling her over the footlights, into his lap.

The following winter Tempest Storm was gone. Replaced as the main attraction by Miss Paprika. Proving to Decker what he always knew: that he was really smarter than the rest. A person of rare judgment, of mature taste.

When the gang lost interest in the Hudson Burlesk, and began to cruise the nighttime streets in Angelo's car to pick up girls, Decker broke from them. He remained loyal to Cherry. He went alone to the Hudson, all bones and slicked-down hair, even on weekday nights. Hardly anybody was there except Cherry Paprika and him. Nothing but the ever-purpling footlights in between. One night, he used to think, one night, as she is about to pull off her G-string, they will forget to purple the lights, and POW!

He tripped on a log divider in the parking lot, stumbled, barely caught his balance against a man who was walking by.

"Excuse me," he said.

Elaborately polite.

Not wanting one of these Chicanos to pull a knife on him in the dark.

The man looked at him, half-annoyed, half-understanding,

125

and walked on. Decker found the car after getting lost twice. He took the six-pack of Schlitz from the trunk and slammed it shut and tried it to make sure it was locked, though the trunk was empty now except for the jack handle and the spare. Satisfied, he walked back amid the crowd still streaming in toward the infield. Holding the six-pack at his side.

Remembering Cherry Paprika. Cherry was what they jiggled in front of your eyes when you were a kid. When you grew up what you got was Midge.

He found her where he had left her, on a straight line down from the board. Like she said.

"You got your beer?"

"Of course I got my beer. Whattaya think I got?"

He put the six-pack on the ground and sat on the dirt beside her. Midge looked away, at the silhouette heads stretching in front of them. Expectation was building in the crowd as the time for the burning neared.

Upset, but not knowing why, she turned to him.

"You mad at me, or something?"

"No," he said. Softer than he usually spoke. Looking straight ahead, instead of at her, his thoughts far off in the dark. "I ain't mad at you."

She took his hand and placed it on her knee. She squeezed her fingers between his. But she was not sure that she believed him. Not a decimal-free 100 percent.

Fist.

The fucker.

It was only a matter of time. He knew they'd show up, one sunny day or the next.

He'd told himself they wouldn't bother. They'd let it go. What was a lousy 500 bucks to them? But he knew it wasn't true. This wasn't Jersey. This was piker country.

He could have split this goddamn burg right from the slammer. But he was damned if he was gonna run with his tail between his teeth for a lousy 500. And then there was Midge. A good, one-night lay. A good, two-night lay.

Whose dumb ways kind of grew on you.

Who made you feel comfortable, somehow.

Washing dishes had been a drag. He could never make

enough that way. And Midge with her nice salary. It would get him through the summer, at least.

As each week passed, he'd allowed himself to hope. They'd forgotten about it. They'd let it go. But he knew it wasn't true. It wasn't just the money. It was the principle.

Today they'd come. As if they could read his mind. As if they knew he was planning to split tonight.

"You owe us money," Fist said.

"Yeah."

"Let's have it."

"I ain't got it."

"Why not?"

"I been in the slammer."

"Old news," Fist said.

"How's I supposed to raise it in the slammer?"

"You been out three months."

Decker didn't answer. They kept their tabs.

"You'd wouldn't be planning to skip town this weekend, would you?"

"For a lousy five hundred bucks?"

"Eight hundred," Fist said.

"What do you mean, eight? Five hundred."

"Interest. A hundred a month. Not counting the time you was inside. The boys is being nice."

"Yeah," Decker said.

"You don't have it?"

"No."

"Well, you got till tomorrow night to get it."

"How'm I supposed to do that?"

"What the fuck do I care how? Pull a job. Bet on a horse. Just get it."

"I ain't going back inside."

"Play me hearts and flowers. That's your sweat, not mine."

"Hey, listen," Decker said. "Gimme a break. It's the principle, right? Not the money. I mean, you guys are big time."

"Go on."

"Two weeks. Gimme two weeks to raise the money."

Fist looked past him, at the cars in the parking lot.

"It's your lucky day. You got two weeks. You caught me in the Fiesta spirit."

"Thanks," Decker said, sullenly.

Thanks for nothing. Where'm I gonna get $800 in two weeks?

"With new interest," Fist said. "A second mortgage, so to speak. A hundred more a week. In two weeks you owe us a thousand."

"You ought to work for Exxon," Decker said.

"If you don't have it in two weeks, we break your arms. No more charity."

"I'll get it. Don't lose no beauty sleep."

"If you should happen to leave town instead, we'll take it out on your friend."

"What friend?"

"Little Orphan Annie there in the car. Beatrice Audra Smith, called Midge."

Decker's face grew hot. The fuckers kept their tabs.

"Make sure I see you around," Fist said.

Decker turned and walked toward the car.

"Viva la Fiesta!" the fucker called after him.

A thou in two weeks! If he left town they might come after him. But they'd have to find him first. By then he could raise the money, somehow. He didn't think they'd really touch Midge. It was a phony threat. They weren't as mean as all that.

He felt her hand on his. Bet on a horse, Fist had said. A hundred on a five-to-one, it would have took. On a ten-to-one, now. Only he'd never do it, even if he had the dough. It was lousy odds.

And here was Midge, betting her goddamn baby on a race.

A weird, unwelcome thought lit up his brain, like the TILT on a pinball game: *You're the one ain't good enough for her!*

It was the other way round, of course.

No it ain't, stupid.

He drank a slug of beer, and he belched. There was no doubt about it. He had to split this fuckin' town tonight.

"How dumb can we get?" Midge said.

"What's your problem now?"

Decker switched his beer can from one hand to the other and wiped his lips with the back part of his wrist.

"We didn't get any food!"

On the platform far in front of them, at the hem of the puppet's white skirt, the mariachis were still playing. Assorted dignitaries were seated on folding chairs, heads bent together. One of them, Midge could see, was the Monsignor.

"Ain't nobody lighting no matches yet," Decker said. "Let's go get some now."

"We'll lose our seats. We got this nice place to sit and all."

On all sides dark silhouettes of people, couples, families were moving about, looking for room enough to spread blankets. The spotlight on Zozobra seemed to be growing brighter as the darkness became solid.

"Is that puppet a queer?" Decker said.

"A queer? What do you mean, a queer?"

"Look at him. Why's he wearing a skirt?"

Midge squinted at the puppet. It was obviously a man: a big nose, big lips, a black bow tie, and black buttons, like on a suit. And a skirt! She had never noticed that before. She had come or been taken to see Zozobra burn every year since she was a child, and she had never noticed that he didn't wear pants. He always wore a skirt.

"Course he ain't no queer," she said. "That's just the way they made him, is all."

"Who? Who made him that way?"

"A long time ago. Some artist."

"It figures," Decker said.

He lifted his beer to his lips and drank. Midge uncrossed her legs and spread the pleats of her skirt across her boots, like a cowgirl.

"How come they burn it?" Decker said.

"He's Old Man Gloom. That's what "Zozobra" says, in Spanish. They burn him to start off Fiesta, and it makes gloom vanish and everybody happy."

"Just like that," Decker said.

She looked at his sad eyes. She wished she could reach inside somehow and scrub the sadness out. But she didn't know how.

"I know," she said. "I'll go and get some food. You stay and keep our place."

She stood, straightening the dress. She had put on small

white gloves against the evening chill. She took them off and put them in the pocket of the skirt, so as not to soil them with food.

"What'll you have? Some tacos? A *carne adovada* burrito? Those are usually the best."

"A cheeseburger," Decker said.

"Don't you want to try something new? Some local color?"

Decker looked at her sourly, lines around his lips.

"I knew we should have gone to McDonald's."

"Okay, okay. A cheeseburger. But you wait. You'll want to eat some of mine."

"Fat chance," Decker said, and he drank at his beer.

Midge checked to make sure she had her purse. She stepped gingerly around a blanket spread by a couple behind them. The couple was passing a tiny cigarette back and forth. The air stank with the stuff.

"Hey, Midge?"

"What?"

"Don't get lost!"

"I won't," she said. "We're right down from the end of the score. . . ."

Decker was grinning at her, making a funny face.

"You get lost!" she said.

She whirled, the black skirt twirling effectively this time, like Loretta Young's, and she stalked away, as best she could stalk while picking among the blankets, the people's feet, the children squirming about in the darkness.

Behind the tote board was the wooden planking, like a low bridge, so people wouldn't walk on the turf of the track where the horses ran. But some people were. They would have to rake it smooth in the morning. She crossed the planks to the grandstand area, which towered high now with people who had paid for reserved seats, and she moved among the throngs behind it to valet parking. Instead of cars, the close-in lot was lined with a double row of food booths. Canvas tops and flaps had been stretched over wooden frames. Water pipes and gas pipes had been run along the pavement to feed the booths. Painted signs on each booth advertised tacos, corn, burritos, hamburgers, fried bread, corn dogs, tamales. Some booths had long lines of people in front of them. Others had only small clusters. Speakers on poles carried the tinny mariachi music into this area as well. Mexican music wouldn't be bad, Midge figured, if only they had wrote more than one song.

She found a booth that advertised both cheeseburgers and *carne adovada* burritos, and she got on the end of the line. She took her $5 bill from her purse and clutched it in her hand to have it ready.

The line of people was hardly moving. Three feet away was another line, for the next booth. It, too, was hardly moving. Midge decided to make a race of it, her line against the adjacent line. But the movement was so slow that she soon lost interest and called it a tie. She decided instead to stand on one foot for as long as she could, then hop her weight over to the other foot, counting off the seconds as she did.

"Forty-six, forty-seven, forty-eight . . ."

"How ya doin'?" a hoarse voice said.

"Forty-nine, fifty . . ."

Wavering on one leg, she looked at the line across, to see if the voice was addressing her, though she couldn't imagine that it would. Sometimes she talked to strangers, but strangers hardly ever talked to her.

"How ya doin'?" the man said again.

It was a black man, three feet away on the adjacent line, and he was looking right at her. He was short, not much taller than she was, but he must've outweighed her five times. He was built like a bunch of basketballs pasted together: a brown basketball for a head, other basketballs for biceps, arms, thighs, legs. A bunch of them for his belly. She had seen him somewhere before.

Around the track! He hung out at the track.

"Okay," she said, uncertainly.

"Where's your man?" he said.

The question put her at ease.

"Decker? He's over there, down by the puppet. Mindin' our seats."

She flashed the man one of her friendly smiles that showed her two front teeth.

"You know Decker?" she said.

The man shook his head. He was wearing fat white pants and a fat blue shirt. His hair was black and fuzzy.

"Not to talk to," he said. "I just seen you folks at the track all the time." He extended his short arm across the space between the lines. "My name's Short Bread," he said.

Midge switched her purse from her right hand to her left, and shook his hand.

"Pleased, I'm sure," she said.

Their hands fell to their sides. She didn't know what more to say.

"And you?"

"And me what?"

"What's your name?"

"Oh. Bea . . . I mean Midge. My name is Midge. And Decker down there is . . ." She stopped. Consternation flickered across her face. She didn't know how to finish the sentence. ". . . is Decker," she said, shrugging.

Both lines moved a little. The two of them inched forward. A shifting breeze blew barbecued smoke their way.

"That sure smells good," Midge said.

"It sure does, Little Lady."

She smiled again. She liked that name. Little Lady.

They inched forward again on their respective lines, almost side by side.

"You find many tickets?" Short Bread said.

"I beg your pardon?"

"Live ones. I seen you pickin' up tickets all the time at the races. You find many live ones that the dumbos throw away?"

"You mean winning tickets?"

"Yeah."

"I ain't lookin' for winners. It's the losers I want."

Short Bread seemed surprised. "Now why would you want them?"

She looked around, embarrassed. She reached into the pocket of her skirt, took out her white gloves, pulled on first one then the other, with her purse stuck under her arm. The gloves gave her a feeling of dignity.

"It's scientific," she said. "It's a system."

"Now that's what I thought," Short Bread said. "Every time I seen you doin' that, I said to myself: 'Now that little lady's got a system.' "

"You did?"

"I did. But I'll be danged if I could figure it out. How's it work, that system of yours?"

Midge looked around, to make sure no one was listening in.

"You promise you won't tell?"

"Cross my heart," Short Bread said, and with a fat black finger that was sort of pink on the inside he made a cross on one of the basketballs of his chest, in the vague vicinity of his heart.

Midge inched slightly out of line, closer to him. In as few words as she could, because they were getting near the food booths now, she explained the system. The flat, tinny music covered her words.

"And it works?"

"Lots of the time. It's what all us scientists use."

"I'll give you this much. It's a cheaper system than mine."

"You got a system too?" Midge said.

"Every sucker born's got a system."

"Oh yeah?" She didn't like being called a sucker. If that's what he meant. She much preferred Little Lady. "What's yours?"

"I spread the bread," he said.

"The bread?"

"The dough. The money. The moolah." He flipped his fat fingers like a magician and produced as if out of the air a crisp new $50 bill. "The long green."

"That why they call you Short Bread?"

"Right you are, Little Lady. 'Cause I'm short, and I spread the bread. Also I'm partial to cake of the same name."

She was still doubtful.

"What kind of a system is that? Who you spread it to?"

"I got me some friends in the jockey room," he said.

"I know who! The Fatso!"

"Who?"

"The Fatso. That lady."

"No lady, man. The riders. The jocks. I made myself some friends. They tell me who's gonna win. When I make a killing, I lay a bundle on 'em."

"The riders know who's gonna win?"

"Often enough."

"It's the horses who I'd like to ask," Midge said.

"Maybe. Only I ain't seen a horse yet that would tell you. Or would take a bribe, for that matter."

"No, I don't suppose."

"That's why it's the men that ride, and the horses that run."

She wasn't sure what he meant, but there was no time to figure it out. The man in front of her stepped away and she was eye level with the counter. A lady in a soiled apron was looking down at her. Midge removed her gloves and put them in her pocket.

"One *carne adovada* burrito and two cheeseburgers," she said.

"Anything to drink?"

"No. Decker's got his beer. At first he forgot it in the trunk, but then he went and got it. We'll drink that."

The woman was looking at her the way people often did: sort of friendly and not at the same time. Then the woman turned and peeled two flat chopped meats off of wax paper and put them to sizzling on the grill, and turned back and folded a tortilla in her hand and began to scoop the *carne adovada* into it with a spoon.

Midge looked at Short Bread. He had just reached the other booth and was ordering his own food: two corn dogs, French fries, a Coke.

"We got beer," Midge said toward him, but he was facing the booth and didn't hear her over the tinny music and the crowd. Immediately she was relieved, and she wondered why she had said it—Decker would kill her—and then she grew angry at the thought. What right would Decker have to kill her? It wasn't as if she hand't paid for the beer!

Besides, if they were going to have a life together, it was past time they started to socialize.

The woman placed three wrapped wax papers in front of her.

"Three dollars," the woman said.

Midge gave her the $5 bill and put the change in her purse. She took the waxy packages and turned to go and almost bumped into Short Bread, who was turning with his food. He had the sticks of his corn dogs stuck between two different fingers and was balancing his Coke with that hand and carrying his fries in the other. Together they walked beyond the lines of the food booths, toward the track. As they did, the music stopped, and after noisy, crackling static a man's voice came through on the speakers, welcoming this grand and glorious crowd.

"You got a girl friend?" Midge said as they walked.

Short Bread looked askance at her and winked.

"Not right now," he said. "Used to. But not right now."

"You're here alone, then?"

He rolled his eyes over his own round bulk.

"Person built like me is never alone."

Midge laughed loud in appreciation.

"That's a good one. The thing I mean is, if you're here to watch Zozobra burn . . . if you don't want to sit alone, I mean . . . we got plenty of room down front, where Decker's holding our place. If you'd like to, I mean."

"Well, that's nice of you to ask. I'd like that very much. If you're sure it's all right."

" 'Course it is," Midge said, and she bit her tongue over what Decker was going to say.

Over the loudspeakers the boring speeches continued. They moved through the crowds to the wooden planking, and crossed to the infield. Midge was about to begin picking her way through the people seated tightly on the ground, but Short Bread pointed to an aisle, where it would be easier, and they walked over there.

"You live in Santa Fe?" she said.

"Albuquerque. I work in a bar at night. Come up to the races by day. Took my vacation now, though, got me a little motel room for the weekend. Gonna see all the races and take in the Fiesta. Not have to drive back and forth."

"You ever been to Fiesta before?"

"Nope. Always been working."

"You mean you never saw Zozobra burn?"

"Nope."

"It's real fun. I think you're gonna like it."

"I think so," Short Bread said.

"How you likin' Fiesta so far?"

"So far I especially likes the company."

Midge gave him a look, but he wasn't teasing. She flooded

with warm feelings all over. Decker could learn some lessons from Short Bread. On how to make a person feel good.

Embarrassed, she changed the subject.

"Who you betting in the big race tomorrow?"

"The big race?"

"You know. Blue Lady and Thunderbolt."

"Oh, that. I won't be betting that race."

"How come?" Midge said.

"Whoever wins'll pay two twenty. I like the long shots myself."

"Oh."

Short Bread sensed that something was wrong.

"You planning to bet that race?" he said.

"I already did."

"Now how could you already have? The windows don't open till tomorrow."

"It's a separate bet. Between me and Decker."

"Oh, a side bet."

"Right."

"Who'd you take?"

"Blue Lady."

Short Bread nodded his head several times, like Jack's soft basketball bouncing. "How much did you bet?"

Midge paused in the aisle and looked around, trying to spot Decker in the dim lights that had been lit on the poles when the music stopped and the boring speeches began. At first she couldn't find him. She felt herself go red as she replied.

"It's not how much we bet. We didn't bet money."

"What you bet, then?"

"There he is," she said, spotting Decker, pointing to a clearing in the crowd.

She began to inch her way through, Short Bread following. She stopped. She was going to touch his arm. But she pulled her hand away.

"Don't be mad," she said. "I can't tell about the bet. It's a secret."

"Well, that's fine then," Short Bread said. "Every lady's entitled to have a secret."

Right, Midge thought. Every lady's entitled.

"It's the ones that can't keep a secret that get you into trouble."

Midge agreed, though she wasn't quite sure what he meant. She had lost her concentration.

"There's Decker," she said again, and she began to thread her way toward him among the blankets and the feet, Short Bread following behind. She felt a moment of apprehension about what she had done. About bringing Short Bread along. But there was no turning back.

Twelve and a half feet before they reach Decker she stopped again.

"Mr. Short Bread?"

"Yeah?"

"What's your real name? Underneath Short Bread. The one you was born with, I mean."

He didn't answer at first. He seemed to be thinking about it.

"You got to think about it?"

Short Bread laughed. "Just recollecting things," he said. "A name is like a box of memories." He tried to shift all his food into one hand, to shake, and then he recalled they had shaken hands already.

"My given name is Marvin," he said. "Marvin Kimberly."

"Well, hello then, Marvin Kimberly. My name before it was given Midge was given Beatrice. Beatrice Audra Smith."

She looked into his round face. He was one of those people that had a twinkle in their eyes, even here in the dark. There was light bouncing off his cheeks.

"I guess right now," she said, "we should all go over and meet Horace Decker."

They walked on over to where he was sitting on the ground. In the dark he didn't seem angry. Not yet.

"This here is Decker," Midge said. "This here is Marvin Kimberly. Also known to his friends as Short Bread."

Decker didn't reach up to shake hands. Nobody noticed, because Short Bread's hands were full.

"Short Bread is a big fish at the track," Midge said.

"What kind of a big fish?" There weren't no blacks in New Mexico was big fish.

"A race track trout," Midge said.

"A tout!" Decker said. "The word is 'tout!' Not 'trout!' " He looked up at Short Bread and shook his head. "Do you believe her? Here, have a seat. Sit down and eat with us."

"Don't mind if I do," Short Bread said, and he sank his fat body to his knees and sat on the ground near Decker.

It's a joke, Midge wanted to scream. I know he's a goddamn tout, for Chrissake!

But, all things considered, she said nothing.

CHAPTER 8

Prayer Dogs

"You come to the track often?" Short Bread asked.

"Whenever work permits," Decker replied.

He stuffed his mouth with cheeseburger and Short Bread bit into his corn dog and Decker said, "What's that sissy stuff you're drinkin'?" and reached to the side and twisted another Schlitz out of the six-pack, saying. "Here, have a beer—on me" and even went so far as to pull off the tab before handing it over to Marvin. Midge watching it all with non-belief, like some miracle before her eyes. Decker who called them niggers in the trailer and Short Bread Marvin Kimberly who was a gentleperson sitting there on the dirt in the dark the best of friends, playing kissy-facey like a couple of prayer dogs. Who would have thought it? Certainly not Midge B. A. Smith.

"If you're gonna drink his beer I'll drink your sissy Coke," she said, and Short Bread with his mouth full took it from beside his knee and handed it across to her without ever taking his eyes off Decker, who was gabbing beyond belief about the track, telling how you couldn't believe everything you read, not even in the race track program. How, for instance, with this Blue Lady, for instance. How the program said the owner was Danny Roybal, but Decker had it on good authority that the true and real owner was the mon senior from the church. Midge's mouth fell open when she heard him say that, her jaw hung loose, red chili ran down her chin.

"Is that a fact?" Short Bread said.

"The one and only truth," Decker said.

Midge wiped her chin with her hand but in a minute it would be her eyes that needed wiping. Short Bread, being a race track trout, knew all about the Monsignor, she figured. He was only putting on like he didn't. The two of them gabbing away, ignoring her completely, as if she was the wife of one of them who didn't know a thing about sports.

She took another bite of her burrito. It made her eyes water. She wasn't really sure why this was happening. It felt so damn good it hurt.

"Blue Lady is a fine filly," Short Bread said.

"She sure is," Decker said. "She sure is. A'course, that Thunderbolt is a promising colt, too."

"You get no argument there," Short Bread said. "I hear that's who you bet."

Midge, watching the two of them, saw Decker's eyes flicker across her face with pain.

"Who told you that?" he said.

"Your lady did happen to mention it," Short Bread said, catching himself up. "She wouldn't say how much you bet, though, or what. 'That part's a secret,' she said."

"Yeah, well," Decker said, his eyes on Short Bread again. "She wanted to bet this Blue Lady. Her female intuition. So I took the other horse. I figured I'd give her some action."

"Action's the name of the game," Short Bread said.

Her female *what?* It was science, for Chrissake! It was the law of averages.

Midge, her eyes wide, was speechless. But it was just as well. There wasn't nobody gonna listen to her just then. A couple of jabbering prayer dogs, they were.

After elephants, prayer dogs were her favorite thing.

(That wasn't their scientific name, of course. It was a nickname she had made up, from the way they held their hands together when they was eating. Their scientific Latin name was prairie dogs.)

Midge knew all about them.

She knew, too, that in some vague way that she would never comprehend, they were even responsible for Decker.

Until that summer the only work she had done was cleaning rooms in local motels: the Western, the Adobe, the dilapidated Pueblo Lodge, the even more dilapidated Sunset
Court. She could make a bed as neat as was necessary and
scrub a sink pretty good and pick up wet towels and wash out
toilets without flinching and put those paper rings on them
with hardly any trouble at all to indicate they were nice and
clean for the next tourist *tush*. She would be hired in June
when the tourist season began and the motels needed extra
maids, and she would be let go in September when the tour-
ists went home and her scrubbing wasn't needed anymore.
She had heard that in other cities it was blacks who were let
go first, but in Santa Fe there were hardly any blacks. In Santa
Fe it was Midge was the first to go. She'd go on the Unemployment or the Welfare, and then in December she would
ask around again, and sometimes she'd be hired for the
Christmas-week rush, or if she was lucky and the mountains
were covered with snow she might scrub sinks and push
around a cart piled high with clean sheets and rolls of toilet
paper the whole of the skiing season. Till the skiers with their
lift tickets dangling from their jackets like they were for sale
melted away in March, and she'd be out of work again till
June.

Year after year her twenties had passed that way. Most of
the other maids were young Spanish girls, and though she
tried to be friendly sometimes, mostly they were too busy to
talk. After work they'd rush on home to young Spanish hus-
bands and things, so she would go home too. Home to the
room-with-hot-plate she rented by the month downtown if
Jack was out of the clinker, or to his trailer out in the Enchantment Trailer Park if he'd been caught. Between times she'd
busy herself by visiting the animals in the dog pound, or looking things up in the library, or reading her paperbacks with
the pretty, frightened girls on the cover.

She didn't expect this summer to be any different from the
rest until one morning in May the lady at Unemployment said
a job was open with the state.

"It just came in this morning," Mrs. Knickerbocker said, for
that was the lady's name on a sign on her desk. "It might be a

bit more interesting than changing sheets. I'm afraid again
that it's only for the summer, though."

"What's it I got to do," Midge said, "for the state?"

"I suppose I should have asked you first," Mrs. Knickerbocker said. "How do you get along with animals?"

"Animals is my favorite thing."

"Well. That's perfect, then," the lady said, and she wrote
an address on a little card. "It's the Health Services Department, just around the corner on Galisteo. Ask to see Dr.
W. Manheim."

"What's it I got to do for the state?"

Mrs. Knickerbocker seemed surprised, perhaps disturbed,
that Midge had asked the question again.

"It's working with animals," she said. "That's all they said.
I'm sure Dr. Manheim will explain. If you're not interested,
of course," she added, with only slight condescension in her
voice, "I'm sure the motels will be getting busy again soon."

"I'm very interested," Midge said, and she took the card.
"Quite very, in fact." She figured that would make Mrs.
Knickerbocker happy. It also happened to be the truth.

She left the familiar Unemployment Office and went outside. Spring trees were blooming on Alameda. Soon people
who did not want to spend money in restaurants would be
eating brown-bag lunches in the park. Eating lunch with short
green grass under your feet and tall green trees over your
head was one of Midge's favorite things, except in August
with the pesky flies around or in May when sometimes a left-
over wind came, or the rest of the winter when it was much
too cold. Come to think of it, most any time she'd rather eat
inside. Which she would treat herself to at Josie's today if
only she got the job. It was her favorite place for luncheon.
And cheap. She hadn't been there in months.

She checked the address on the card. Just around the corner turned out to be three blocks away. Turned out to be the
Belknap Building. Clifford Belknap, she knew from the papers, had been a Senator from New Mexico who was born dirt
poor and wound up richer about 16.7 times over, and after he
died they named a building after him. That was one of the
things they liked to do in New Mexico. Name buildings after
people who should have gone to jail instead.

Maybe there'd be a Jack Smith Building someday, she thought. But then again she didn't really think so.

She found Dr. W. Manheim in Room 213 of the Belknap Building. Or rather he was inside the inside of that. Inside the outside of that was one of them pretty young Spanish girls who all looked alike in a blue dress, who told Midge to have a seat and went inside and then came out in a jiffy and told her to go inside. She expected an old codger, but Dr. W. Manheim behind a desk was younger maybe than she, wearing a suit and a tie both and blowing sweet cherry smoke from a pipe.

"You're Beatrice Smith," he said, which she was surprised he knew—her reputation had preceded her, she supposed—and she sat in a straight-backed wooden chair where he nodded. "You were sent over by the Division of Employment."

"Un," she said.

"I beg your pardon?" His voice came around his pipe.

"Division of *Un*employment. If it was Employment then I wouldn't need a job."

Dr. W. Manheim chuckled, though she hadn't meant to make a joke.

Wilfred? Walter? Wallace?

"I suppose that's true," he said.

He leaned back in his chair, the kind that leaned back with him, and looked out a window. His pipe was in his hand.

"Are you aware of what the job entails?" For some reason he was asking the windowpane.

"Only that there's animals," Midge said.

"Do you like animals?" Now he was looking over his shoulder.

"Animals is my favorite thing."

He put his pipe back in his mouth and took some puffs and watched the smoke disappear toward the ceiling, as if he would find more questions in the smoke.

"You're our very first applicant," he told the windowpane.

She didn't know what she was supposed to say to that. She couldn't hardly help it if she was the first. If that was bad. Then a horrible thought crossed her mind. Perhaps because she'd be working for the state.

"Do you kill them?"

"Kill who?"

"The animals."

Dr. W. Manheim turned back to face her. *Wendell? Warren? Woodrow?* He put his pipe in an ashtray on the desk.

"Why do you ask that?" he said.

" 'Cause scientists do that sometimes."

"And you're against that?"

She hesitated only a moment. "Not for them. They do what they got to do."

"But?"

"I'm against it for me."

Dr. W. Manheim picked up his pipe and puffed it again and shuffled through some papers on his desk. He leaned back in his chair, but he didn't look away this time.

"We don't kill them," he said.

He went on to explain what they did: about the plague and the fleas and the squirrels and the prayer dogs and such. Midge listened with fascination. Dr. W. Manheim was a talking library.

"And if they ain't sick you let them go?"

"Right where we found them," he said.

Midge clasped her fingers in her lap, the way they did in school. She had worn a white blouse like a schoolgirl's that morning, a short pink skirt, and her sneakers.

"I approve," she said, firmly.

Immediately she was afraid he would chuckle. But he didn't.

"Do you want the job?" he said. "It pays one ten a week."

"I think I'll try it," she said.

"I want to emphasize the risk," he said. "Statistically it's slight. But it's there. We get a few cases of plague each summer. Sometimes none at all. But if the plague is around, the easiest way to contract it is by handling these animals. And that's what you'll be doing. We take all precautions, of course. But accidents are possible. Do you understand that?"

Midge bit the skin on her thumb. She didn't know much about the plague, except that it could strike both your houses. Your apartment and your trailer, too, she supposed.

"You got many other people doing this?"

"A few," Dr. W. Manheim said.

William? Walker? Ward?

One thing was clear in an instant. In two days she'd be thirty years old, and though she had avoided the plague so far, she hadn't exactly set the world on fire. Careerwise. Anyone with three-eighths of a brain could change a sheet. Whereas being a scientist was something else.

"It's pretty important work, huh?" Midge said.

"No queston about it," Dr. W. Manheim said.

Midge licked her lip, feeling for the scar with her tongue. She took a deep breath, expanding her chest, pressing what passed for her breasts against her blouse. Dr. W. Manheim did not seem to notice, him being a doctor and used to sights like that. She was filled nonetheless with a feeling she couldn't explain, a premonition: that the second half of her life was about to begin.

"Well," she said, casual as could be but sounding kind of nervous nonetheless, "what day do I start?"

"Ms. Leyba in the outer office will give you some forms to sign before you leave. How about starting June first?"

"At what time?"

"Let's say eight o'clock."

"I'll be there," Midge said. "With gloves on."

Dr. W. Manheim smiled appreciatively.

When she left his office she stopped at Ms. Leyba's desk and filled out forms: her name and address and Social Security and stuff. Ms. Leyba had breasts that even a doctor would notice. It seemed somehow that all them Spanish girls did.

A minute later she was out in the spring again. She felt like skipping down the street, skipping across the park, skipping the four blocks to Josie's to eat. She didn't skip because it would be unladylike. And certainly unscientistlike. She was sure Marlin Perkins didn't skip. (Also, she couldn't skip too good.) But her heart was skipping nonetheless. June first at 8:00 A.M. She would be there, all right.

As she walked she planned her celebration lunch: a half order of *chili rellenos*, green; a side order of *pozole;* and iced tea to wash it down. Then she changed her mind. The heck with iced tea, she'd wash it down with an old-fashioned chocolate malt.

She thought maybe she should call someone to come meet

her for the celebration lunch. She knew Jack would have come if he could. If he wasn't back in the pen for bad checks. She couldn't think of anyone else to call.

She opened her purse and took out her address book and turned the pages. No new names had appeared overnight. If you didn't count motels and Vanessa, no names were there at all.

"No matter," she said aloud.

She didn't mind eating alone. Not really.

Half a block from Josie's, on the familiar street, she detoured up the steps and into the library. Josie's would be crowded just now with all the downtown workers eating lunch, and she thought she might as well look it up first. She went to the reference room in the back, where they had the Encyclopedia Americana, and took down Volume 22, "Photography to Pumpkin," which she always felt was one of the best. She spread the book on a table and turned the pages until she came to "Plague." With her knees pressed together on a chair, her elbows on the table, her chin in her hands, the blue book with the gold eagle on the cover open before her, she began to read:

PLAGUE, plág, an acute infection primarily of rats and other rodents, and secondarily of man. The infective organism, *Pasturella pestis* (also called *Bacillus pestis*), is spread by rodents and is transmitted by fleas parasitic on them to man. The disease is marked by fever, chills, severe prostration and swelling of the lymph nodes in the groin, the axilla and other parts of the body. Furthermore, *P. pestis* causes hemorrhages, which are called plague spots when they occur in the skin. The black color of these spots coupled with the extremely high mortality of the disease gave it the name Black Death in the Middle Ages.

The most characteristic sign of the plague, the painful swelling of the lymph nodes in the region of the groin, is due to the relative ease with which the fleas reach and bite the legs. The swelling in the groin may attain the size of a large orange and has been called a bubo, from the Greek *boubon,* "groin." This usage gave rise to the name bubonic plague.

The article went on for three more pages. It told the whole history of the plague. How in the Middle Ages, "The dead were passed through the windows, removed from the city in carts, and buried outside the walls. When a plague patient died, the rooms were aired and fumigated, and his effects were burned." It told what they used to think caused the plague, and how they knew what caused it now. It said the plague first came to the United States in 1900, and that now it could be found all through the Rocky Mountain region as well as Kansas, Oklahoma, and Texas, on squirrels, rabbits, mice, rats, prairie dogs, and such. It said there was another form of plague also present, pneumonic plague, "death usually occurring in two to four days." It said the plague could be treated with antibiotics nowadays, but only if you found it quick enough.

Midge read the whole article through. When she was finished, she read it again. Then she closed the book.

"Beatrice Audra Smith," she thought, "what in criminy have you done?"

She sat there for a while, one leg crossed under her, not moving. Oranges, heck. Imaginary boobies the size of watermelons were growing in her groin.

She stood up and put "Photography to Pumpkin" back on the shelf where it belonged. She went to the reference desk, where Mrs. Sawyer was reading *Library Journal.* Mrs. Sawyer had white hair and had been the librarian at the reference desk for eight thousand years. Ever since Midge used to come after school to delay going home to Vanessa.

"Hello, Beatrice," Mrs. Sawyer said, looking up from her desk. Her voice seemed to quaver when she spoke.

"I'm studying about the plague," Midge said. "For work," she added.

"That's nice," Mrs. Sawyer said. Mrs. Sawyer thought everything was nice.

"You got any new stuff about the plague in New Mexico?"

Mrs. Sawyer got up, stiffly, went to a file cabinet, thumbed through manila folders. She pulled one out and handed it to Midge. There was one small clipping in it from the paper the week before, which Midge had missed. It had some of the same information as the encyclopedia, but also some other facts. In the last thirty years there had been eighty-six human cases of plague in New Mexico. Last year four cases were reported. Two of the victims had died. Soon the Health Services Department under Dr. W. Manheim would begin scanning the outlying areas to keep their annual tabs, the article said.

Wolfgang? Whizzer? Whitey?

"That's me," Midge said, handing the folder back to Mrs. Sawyer.

"That's nice," Mrs. Sawyer said.

The article made Midge feel somewhat better. Four cases out of 1.2 million people. It wasn't terrible odds. More people got hit by trucks. But when she left the library she didn't go to Josie's to eat. Instead she walked back to Unemployment, where she had parked, and she drove out to Taco Bell and ate in the car.

When she started work on June first she was assigned to Mrs. Gallegos, who would show her what to do. Mrs. Gallegos, she soon learned, had five children at home in Chimayo. This news made Midge feel good. Nobody with five kids, she figured, would run around endangering themselves to plague.

"It's a job that needs to be done," Mrs. Gallegos said. "With the proper precautions there's hardly any risk."

Mrs. Gallegos gave her blue surgeon's gloves to wear while handling the animals. "Always wear pants and thick socks on days we go in the field," she said. "It prevents getting bitten by fleas."

She showed her the Plaguemobile—really a pickup truck with a camper unit on the back that had cages in it for trapping the little animals, and cloth for trapping fleas, and test tubes and dishes and scientific equipment and stuff for the fleas and blood samples and urine Mrs. Gallegos would take from the animals they trapped. Then they would bring them back and send the dead fleas and blood and urine to laboratories in Albuquerque or Colorado Springs where they would be in-

jected into mice to see if the black death grew. If the plague
was around they would go back with dusters that looked like
long oatmeal boxes with tubes on the end and fill them with
flea killer and spray the flea killer into all the prayer dog
burrows or wherever the plague was found, which killed the
fleas but left the prayer dogs alone. Midge asked twice about
that. It left the prayer dogs alone.

All this information she ingested eagerly. And when the
next day they started going on daily field trips in the Plaguemobile to set the traps and gather up the animals—trips to
Hyde Park, or Tesuque, or Velarde—she couldn't believe her
luck. Here she was, getting paid good money to go on trips to
the country, which she loved to do, with someone nice and
smart to talk to like Mrs. Gallegos; to play with cute little
animals—squirrels and prayer dogs and mice—which she
loved to do; all of it in the service of her country: to protect
the men, women, and children of Santa Fe, of all New Mexico. To be the first line of defense against Black Death. She
was a scientist, for Chrissake, like Batman in his Batmobile,
and this knowledge seemed to redden her blood. It infused
her with a feeling that she had never known before. At first
the feeling took the form of excitement, so much excitement
that for the first time in her life she could hardly fall asleep at
night, so eager was she to wake up and go back to work in the
Plaguemobile. Plaguewoman, she could become. Or Prayer
Dog Lady at least. She had to sit in the kitchen in her pajamas
past midnight, drinking warm milk from her blue plastic glass,
till she felt drowsy enough to sleep. Later, in the second
week, the excitement calmed, enabled her to sleep again. But
this new feeling was still inside her, prowling, aware. She
couldn't give it a name. She didn't try.

At the same time an opposite feeling grew, which wasn't
good. She enjoyed her work so much that the days raced by
on the Apodaca Paint Supply calendar in the john, whether
she was out collecting traps with Mrs. Gallegos or back near
the office cleaning out the empty truck. Before she knew it it
was five o'clock and time to head on home, and it felt like she
had just arrived. But when she got home, the bad feelings
started. The trailer seemed very quiet. Very empty. She was
used to spending evenings alone. It was what you did when

your mother and father were dead and your brother Jack was in the pen and you didn't much like Vanessa. Between TV and magazines and paperbacks with frightened girls on the cover and cooking dinner and cleaning up, and an occasional chat with her rag doll, it never had occurred to her to be unhappy. But now, when she got home each evening, she was bursting with stories to tell: about what they had caught that day, and where. She was alive with gossip and chatter, but there wasn't a single soul to tell it to. After the first few days even the rag doll didn't care.

This feeling was easier to name than the other. For the first time in her life, Midge admitted to herself that she was lonely.

One night, filled with talk, she went down to the office of the trailer park and went inside. Old Man Peters came to the counter from his room in the back. She asked him some fake question about something, and then she started talking about her job. Peters grunted and made small comments, and then he came out from behind the counter with his zipper down. He started reaching toward it, and she said g'night and turned her back and hurried out the door, so as not to see him wave his thing around.

She called him an old fart psycho, to herself, as she entered the trailer and locked the door behind.

The next day she bought more paperbacks against the lonelies. *Fury's Savage Sweetness* being the best.

In Hyde Park, where people and families camped in tents and lean-tos, they caught mostly rock squirrels. In Tesuque, where a big arroyo ran between the houses, they caught mostly brown field mice. Midge liked these both fine enough. But it was the prayer dogs up near Velarde that stole her heart.

The prayer dogs lived in a town out in the desert. That's what Mrs. Gallegos called it, a town just like for people. Midge half expected to see little houses and small grocery stores and such the first day they drove up. And maybe even a post office and city hall, she joked to herself, though she wasn't sure who it was they'd write to. What the town turned out to be was a whole series of holes in the ground where the prayer dogs lived, with mounds of earth around them and escape holes farther out. Acre after acre in every direction she could see the mounds of earth that guarded the holes. They parked the Plaguemobile off the road, and looked about. Prayer dogs were everywhere in their light brown fur, looking something like squirrels only fatter. Some were taking the sun on their mounds. Others were playing and wrestling about, or kissing each other's face. Most were sitting on their back legs, sitting up tall, looking right at the truck. As if to see who was coming, friend or foe. A few had their hands clasped by their chin, and Midge decided they were praying. Mrs. Gallegos said they were eating, but Midge didn't think you could be so sure. Not just yet. Some were making a racket of yips and barks, which was why they called them dogs, she guessed, even though they weren't dogs at all. Mrs. Gallegos said she was right.

"They've got a whole assortment of barks," Mrs. Gallegos said. "Like a little language of their own. Some barks are warnings that there's something strange around, like us, so everyone should be alert. Other barks mean a coyote's near, so hurry back to your hole. Then there's one that's real loud and frantic. It means someone saw an eagle or a hawk, and everyone runs to the nearest burrow, whether it's theirs or not, and dives underground so they don't get caught. Later they'll peek out and give a different bark, which means that everything's clear."

"I wish people had a system like that," Midge said. "How do they learn all that?"

"I suppose the old teach the young," Mrs. Gallegos said. "But it could be inherited. Instinctive."

"I'll bet it's in their genies," Midge said.

They opened the doors and climbed down from the truck and walked among the mounds. They could get as close as 9.7 feet to the prayer dogs before they scampered down the holes and out of sight.

"They get used to seeing people," Mrs. Gallegos said, "with the highway so close to them."

"I wonder why they built near the road," Midge said.

Mrs. Gallegos didn't hear her joke. She had turned and started back toward the truck. Midge followed, walking in her footsteps, and took a trap that Mrs. Gallegos handed her, and together they walked back, Mrs. Gallegos carrying a small canvas bag.

"We'll put this one in the middle," Mrs. Gallegos said.

"On Main Street," Midge replied.

They put the trap in the middle of the prayer dog town, with mound holes all around. Midge set the door to stay open, the way she'd learned the day before at Hyde Park, with the squirrels, and at Tesuque, with the mice. Mrs. Gallegos opened the bag and poured a stream of rolled oats into the trap. They went back to the truck and got two more traps, and they set them at either side of the town.

"That should do it," Mrs. Gallegos said. "We'll come back tomorrow and see."

They repeated the procedure at three more villages. When they returned the next day there were prayer dogs in every trap.

"He looks so frightened," Midge said, picking the first trap up in her pale blue gloves.

"He doesn't know what's happening," Mrs. Gallegos said. "He's never been penned up like that."

"His eyes are so big, so scared."

"He doesn't know we're not going to hurt him."

Midge stuck a finger in the cage, to try to pet the animal. It squeezed against the opposite side, twisting away.

"Don't worry, Mr. Prayer Dog," she said. "We're not gonna hurt you. I swear."

"I think that one's a Ms.," Mrs. Gallegos said.

They collected all the traps and stacked them in the Plaguemobile. Some of the caught prayer dogs were men and some were ladies, some were boys and girls. All had the same frightened look.

"They don't look sick to me," Midge said.

"It's nothing you can see," Mrs. Gallegos said. "The plague, if it's there, is carried by their fleas."

"Right," Midge said. But she didn't see any fleas neither. Certainly none big enough to carry things.

Mrs. Gallegos went into the Plaguemobile and did what she had to do: taking blood from the prayer dogs with a needle, and other stuff. That part Midge didn't like to watch. Then one by one she took the prayer dogs out and let them loose again.

Back in the truck, they rode the highway south. The sinking sun lent shadows to rocks that had none of their own. It was the time of day when Plaguewoman turned into plain old Beatrice Smith again.

"Fleabags," she said as they rode.

"What?"

"Fleabags. That's what fleas carry things in."

Mrs. Gallegos looked at her, smiling, out of the corners of her eyes. Midge had her lips pressed tight together, but she couldn't hold it in. Saliva spritzed out from her lips.

Pleased with her joke, but embarrassed, she wiped the speckled dashboard with her hand.

She remembered how, when she was little, saliva used to drip through the gap.

At the office they said good night, but Midge didn't go right home. The prayer dogs were so cute with their fat bellies and bushy tails and big eyes and startled looks that she wanted to know all about them. She went to the library and looked in the catalogue—599.323, it turned out—and she found a hardback on the shelf called *The World of the Prairie Dog*. With pictures and everything. She had forgot dinner and was still reading the book when the lights of the library dimmed at five to nine.

At home in the trailer she made a peanut butter sandwich and a glass of milk. Later she tried to read a paperback, but she couldn't concentrate. When she closed her eyes she saw the prairie dogs, praying and kissing and rubbing noses and tumbling in the sun. And over and over she thought of one sentence that she had read and reread in the book: "Prairie dogs make interesting pets."

She knew she shouldn't do it. But she took him home the Friday of the third week.

She purposely called in late. She told Mrs. Gallegos she would catch up with the Plaguemobile up near Velarde. She drove out a little later in the ratty-old. And when she was letting the prayer dogs go—with Mrs. Gallegos busy in the truck—she took one and put him in a box in the trunk of her car. It was as simple as that.

She waited till it was dark before going home. She didn't want Old Man Peters to see her coming. The trailer park didn't allow pets.

She parked as close to the door as she could, turned off the lights of the car, and went inside without him. The empty orange crate she'd got from Safeway was in the corner of the bedroom, where it had been for a week. She'd never thought she'd really go through with it. She took off the top of the crate and set it on the bed. She peered out the window, making sure there was no one around. She pulled on her rubber gloves, so she wouldn't get scratched, and slipped out to the car and took him out with both hands and carried him carefully inside. She pushed the door closed behind her with her foot and hurried into the bedroom and put him in the crate, and she quickly placed the top back on the crate. She tried it to make sure it would stay, and it did. Then she slumped into a chair, exhausted, still wearing her rubber gloves.

She pulled closed the curtain on the window. She pushed a chair against it, to close it tight, so there weren't any cracks at the edge. Then she turned on the light. The prayer dog was busy, exploring his new home. It was bigger than the trap, and that, she figured, would make him happy at once.

She watched him nudge about, back and forth. She put her knees on the bed and looked closer. She sprawled on her stomach with her nose almost touching the crate.

"It's my scientific opinion," she said, sticking her finger through the crate and scratching his fur, "that you're much too cute to have the plague."

The prayer dog twisted his head to the right and nudged her finger with his nose. Midge figured that meant he agreed.

Cynomys quickly became her favorite thing.

She'd picked the name from 599.323. It had a list near the back of all kinds of prayer dogs, all of them Cynomys this or Cynomys that. She figured he was small enough that one name was enough. If he ever needed two she'd lend him hers. Cynomys Smith. She liked it because it sounded like cinnamon, which was the color he almost was, only lighter, and which she liked to eat on macaroni and cheese. Also, she just liked the sound. It was romantic, like the wind in the trees. Or like the names in a paperback. The name of the girl or of the castle, either one.

She fed him rolled oats she brought home from the truck. She fed him grass she pulled from the sides of the road. She went to an arroyo out toward the race track and filled her scrub-the-floors bucket with earth and brought it back and dumped it in his crate, to make him feel more at home. Each night she'd scoop his leavings in a spoon and drop them into the john.

At first she was afraid he would push off the top of the crate. She put a brick on it to hold it down. When she came home from work each night she would take off the top of the crate and hold him for a while, making friends. Then she would put him back.

He didn't bark or yip much in the crate. Not the way they did at Velarde. Still, she feared he might be overheard. The minute she got home she'd put on Maria Muldaur, and she'd keep the records playing till bedtime. So Old Man Peters or someone else wouldn't hear Cynomys bark.

One morning when she woke up and swung her legs off the bed, her foot brushed something soft. She looked down and there was Cynomys, curled up asleep between her sneakers. She examined his crate and saw she had forgot to put back the brick the night before. He had pushed off the top in the dark and had come on over to sleep near her bed. After that she left the brick off all the time. There were screens on all the windows, so he couldn't get out of the trailer. He'd run around, poking into this corner or that, while she dressed and ate her breakfast. When she came home after work she wouldn't see him at first. But she'd close the door behind her, and put on Maria Muldaur and call, "Hey, Cynomys, come on out!" and he'd come running from wherever he'd been, the bedroom or a closet or the john. And she'd pick him up and kiss him on the nose. Play rubby-nosey with him, like his brothers and sisters did in the village near Velarde.

One night when she was getting ready to eat she poured some rolled oats on the other end of the table, and she put

Cynomys there. He ate his oats while she ate her hamburger sandwich. Soon he nosed around near her plate, and she discovered he liked lots of things to eat besides oats and grass. He'd like most anything she had, hanging around her plate till she gave him some.

She wished she could take him outside and let him run around. But she was afraid of two things. She was afraid he'd run away and not come back, or get hit by a car or something. And she was afraid someone would see him and snitch to Old Fart Peters. So Cynomys stayed an indoor prayer dog only.

At work, no one knew he existed, or ever had. She didn't tell a soul.

With each passing day, she was bursting with the news of Cynomys. About how she had tamed him. About how much fun he was. She wanted to tell all about him, especially to Mrs. Gallegos. But she didn't dare. She was afraid she might be fired for taking him.

He didn't have the plague, that much was pretty certain. No fleabag-carrying fleas on him. Still, she dared not tell.

Instead, she talked to the only one she could, which was him. One night she told him a story while eating a TV dinner and he on the other end eating oats.

"Once upon a time," she said, reaching across the table and petting his fur, "there was a little prayer dog named Cynomys. He lived with his mother and father and brother in a prayer dog village near Velarde. He was a happy little prayer dog, running around rubbing noses with the other little prayer dogs all day, and coming home to the burrow with his mother and father at night. But one night, when he came home to the burrow, it was empty except for his brother. His brother was crying, and he told Cynomys what had happened. Their mother and father had been crossing by the road, and they had been hit by a truck. His mother and father was dead.

"Their Aunt Mable took care of them for a while, and then they went to live in a burrow by themselves, which Cynomys liked better. Till one day the hunters came, and took his brother away, and Cynomys was all alone."

Eating her frozen veal-cutlet-mashed-potatoes-peas, wiping her lips with a green paper towel, she wondered why the story she was making up was sad. As long as you're making it up, you might as well make it up happy. She gave Cynomys one of her green peas, and he began to pray as she continued the story.

"Cynomys didn't have a whole lot of friends, but he was very important because of his job. His job in the village was to be on the lookout for eagles, who could swoop down and kill his friends. Day after day, Cynomys stood out in the countryside, looking for eagles, at great danger to himself. The other prayer dogs thought he was very brave. Cynomys was happy being brave. But at night you couldn't look for eagles. Nor for hawks, neither. So at night brave Cynomys sat in his burrow alone."

Somehow the story was getting sad again. It needed a happy ending.

"So one night the prayer dog fairy rewarded Cynomys by taking him to her castle in fairy land, which was 27.8 miles from the village. And Cynomys was very happy with the prayer dog fairy. And the prayer dog fairy was happy with Cynomys, and loved him very much."

She shoveled the last of the mashed potatoes into her mouth, and she spoke without swallowing.

"You like that story, Cynny?" It was what she called him sometimes for short.

Cynomys gnawed on the green pea and didn't answer.

The next morning, a Tuesday, as she was getting into her car to go to work, Old Man Peters approached her. He was wearing his usual uniform: a blue windbreaker and gray pants. His fly was closed for a change.

"What you got in the trailer?" he said.

She felt herself grow warm under the arms and in the small of her back.

"What do you mean?"

"You know what I mean. You got a dog in there. I been hearing him bark. You better get rid of him. There's no pets allowed."

"Oh, that," Midge said. "That's just a record I got that's got barking in the background. "Maria and Her Dogs." Didn't you ever hear of it?"

Peters glared at her with bloodshot eyes, like a face with a headache.

"I ain't got a dog in there. I swear it. On my mother's Bible."

It was a heavy swear. "You better not," he said, and he turned and walked away.

She was sweating as she drove to work.

Two days passed and nothing happened. She stopped worrying about Peters. She'd put one over on him. And she hadn't really lied about not having a canine in there.

"Maria and Her Dogs!" She wondered what Maria Muldaur would think about that. She wished she could meet Maria Muldaur someday.

On Thursday Peters was waiting for her outside the trailer when she drove home from work. His right hand was picking his ear.

"You're a goddamn liar," he said. "You've got a dog in there."

"I don't," Midge protested. "I told you, it's on a record."

"A record that plays all day?"

She didn't know what to say. She looked at the ground.

Peters put his arm on her shoulder. She wanted to pull away, like Evangelina in *Fury's Savage Sweetness*. But she didn't.

"Now listen, honeybunch," Peters said, his voice almost a whisper. "I know you must like that dog, and rules is made to be broken. Maybe we can work something out."

"Work what out?" Midge said.

"Oh, you know." She could smell his breath on her face, smelling of wine and age. "I do you a favor by forgetting about the dog. You do some favors in return."

Her mind was racing. She could hear Cynomys, who'd heard her voice, scratching inside the door.

"What kind of favors?" she said.

She didn't have to ask. She could guess.

"Let's go down to my room," he said, "and see if we can think of some."

She didn't resist as he led her down to his office, his arm weighing heavy on her shoulder. He put a sign on the door that said Back Later, and led her into his room behind the office. There was an unmade bed in the corner, and a chest of drawers, an empty pint of wine on the top.

She felt herself shaking, her knees weak. She wondered if she could do it. Just once, to keep Cynomys. It wouldn't be the first time, Heaven knew. It wasn't as if she was a virgin, or something. She'd been with lots of men. Four at least. And some of them were as nasty and dirty as Peters.

"Make yourself t' home," he said. "There on the bed. Or kneel on the floor if you like."

When he turned to face her his fly was open, his thing was hanging out. It was pale and limp. All she could think of was the sign on the door: Back Later. He'd be back all right. Again and again.

Her temper exploded like it had never done before. She put her face up to his chin.

"You're a dirty old fart," she said.

Then she turned and walked—she refused to run, she walked—out of his room, out of the office, back to her own trailer. She wanted to look back to see if he was following, but she wouldn't. She didn't turn around till she was inside the trailer. Then, with hands shaking, she locked the door behind her and ran to the bedroom and thew herself on the bed.

Cynomys, who couldn't get onto the bed without her help, sat quietly at the foot of it till she was finished crying.

It was dark outside by the time she was done. A half moon was rising over KRAP RELIART TNEMTNAHCNE. She reached down and picked up Cynomys and held him in her arms on the bed. Through her wet lashes his fur seemed to sparkle. And she knew the truth of it, and she told him another story.

"Once there was a prayer dog named Cynomys," she said, while Cynomys licked her fingers. "At first he was small, like all the other baby prayer dogs. Then, when he got bigger, he got brave. He was made the lookout for eagles, and the whole village saw how brave he was. But even then they didn't know the whole story. They didn't know who Cynomys really was.

"It wasn't till the Old King died. The village went into a tizzy. They didn't know what they would do without a king.

Then brave Cynomys stepped forward, on the tallest mound in the village, and he said: 'Do not fear. It is me, Cynomys. King of the Prayer Dogs.'

"All of the other prayer dogs looked at him in wonder. And they could see it was true. They never noticed how really special he was, but now they could see. They all cheered, and became his friend. And Cynomys was their King. The best King they ever had."

She stroked his fur, as if the story were done. But she knew it wasn't. She continued speaking, alone with him on the bed in the trailer in the dark. Trying to forget Old Fart Peters.

"One day the village was visited by the Prayer Dog Fairy. She looked around at all the prayer dogs, to take one home with her to fairy land. And the one she decided on was Cynomys. Cynomys the King.

"She took him home and she was very happy. And Cynomys was, too, being fed and loved and all. But the other prayer dogs weren't happy at all. Their King was gone, and no king came forward to replace him who was as brave and good and special as Cynomys.

"Far away in fairy land the Prayer Dog Fairy knew this. Fairies know things like that. And Cynomys knew it too, being King. He knew that the prayer dogs back home needed him to return. It was only right.

"So Cynomys and the fairy shook hands and said good-bye. And Cynomys went home, and all the other prayer dogs welcomed him back with open arms. And the Prayer Dog Fairy wasn't too unhappy, neither. Because it was the right thing to do, in the end."

A cricket was buzzing somewhere outside the trailer. When she stopped talking she lay in the dark for a long time. Then she got up and changed into pajamas. She fed Cynny a large pile of seeds. Plaguewoman herself went to bed without eating.

She had loved her mother and father before they were killed and she still loved Jack who was out there in the pen. But not so's you noticed, because you took that for granted, loving your brother. Aside from them three, Midge figured, thinking back, she had never loved anything or anyone as much as she loved Cynomys. Not her dolls as a little girl or her rag doll now, or the few men who came through now and then, or her paperbacks, or even the library. Those weren't at all like this.

She was glum and morose at work the next day, not joking at all, hardly even speaking.

"Is something wrong?" Mrs. Gallegos said.

"No," Midge said, and Mrs. Gallegos looked at her, but didn't ask any more questions.

They worked in Tesuque that day, and they returned to the office early. Midge got very restless sitting around. She planned to take him back after work, and she wanted to get it over with. Horrid thoughts were growing in her head.

Finally, at 3:30, she approached Mrs. Gallegos. "I'm not feeling too good today," she said. "I think I need to go home early."

"You do look a little peaked, like you're not yourself," Mrs. Gallegos said. "Go home now. I'll take care of things."

She went to the ratty-old and started home. At first she drove slowly, as usual. Then she speeded up. An awful premonition filled her brain. Cynomys was dead!

She speeded up more, faster than the legal thirty on Cerrillos Road. But she had to stop for lights. She fidgeted impatiently on her driving pillow. There were new lights on Cerrillos Road every day.

Cynny was dead, she knew it. He was not in his crate. She'd look all over the trailer and then she'd find him in the corner. His head caved in with the brick. The bloody brick beside.

She knew who did it, too. Old Man Peters. To get even for last night. She saw herself stalking to his office, blind tears on her cheeks. He was standing behind the counter.

"You fuck!" she said. "You bastard psycho pervert!"

"What's your problem?" he said, calmly. Grinning, even.

"You killed my prayer dog!"

"Eh, what's that? I thought you didn't have a dog. Pets are against the rules. I'm sure you didn't have one, did you, sweetheart?"

She looked at him with hate. She didn't know what to say. She stalked out of the office, back to the trailer.

If only Jack were here. Jack would know what to do.

She knelt beside the poor battered body. She wrapped him in paper towels, put him in a brown paper bag. She would have liked something nicer, a pretty box or something. But she didn't have anything nice around. She drove out to the big arroyo near the race track. She dug a hole in the earthen side with her hands. She put little Cynomys in. Then she filled in the hole.

If a big rain came, she knew, it might wash his body away. Which was fine. She didn't want to know where he was.

She careened the car into the trailer park and slammed to a stop. She could not remember the last three miles, the speeding, the lights. Her mind was in the arroyo with Cynomys. The car had taken her home like a faithful horse.

She fumbled with her keys, dropped them, fumbled again, and finally opened the door. At first she didn't see him.

"Cynny?"

She kept her eyes off the floor. She was afraid to look. Then she heard the patter of his claws as he came running out of the kitchen to meet her.

"Cynny!"

She reached down and picked him up, eyes watering, and hugged him to her breast and kissed his nose. He wasn't even hurt.

Without saying a word, she said a prayer of thanks.

Then she decided she'd better not waste any time. She looked out the window. No one was there. She put Cynomys in his crate, with the top on, and carried it out and put it in the car. And, slowly this time, she drove the 27.8 miles to Velarde.

She parked at the side of the road, and she lifted him out. All across the village she could see the prayer dogs, hundreds of them, stopping what they were doing to sit up on their hind legs and see who was coming. They looked soft and small in the late afternoon sun. But they cast long shadows.

She walked to the center of the village. The nearby prayer dogs dove into holes until she passed. Farther away the others watched and waited.

When she got to the center she kissed Cynny one last time. Then she set him down on the ground.

At first nothing happened. Cynny didn't move. None of the others moved.

It must be private, Midge thought, and she started backing away.

Cynomys sniffed the ground, first in one direction, then another. The others started to twitch and bark.

She continued to back away. Cynny didn't follow. He stayed where he was, and the other prayer dogs began to run over to him from every direction. First three, then ten, then twenty. In a few seconds there must have been a hundred prayer dogs surrounding Cynomys, kissing and barking happily and wrestling in the dirt. The barking spread in circles toward the outskirts of the village, till even the farthest ones came to see.

Midge sank to her knees and watched them from afar. It didn't make any sense. They returned caught prayer dogs to the villages every week, usually three at a time, and nothing like this ever happened. A few might come to sniff and play, but that was all. Nothing like this. No . . . celebration.

There was only one explanation she could think of.

The goddamn King was home!

For twenty minutes she sat on her haunches and watched, with her hands clasped under her chin in wonderment, and the sun fading behind her. She felt herself overflowing with emotion. It was as if some dam inside her, long locked tight, had burst, and a pent-up river was pouring out, was overflowing its banks.

Finally the prayer dogs scattered in fifty-six different directions, in ones and two and threes, back toward different mounds. She roamed her eyes about, trying to spot Cynomys. To wave him one last good-bye.

She couldn't have told which one was him if her brother's life depended on it.

She walked to the car and drove back to town. It was almost dinner time. She treated herself to a giant hamburger and seventeen fries at the Guadalupe Cafe, not far from the virgin's church.

Two nights later—it was the second time around for *Fury's Savage Sweetness*—Decker knocked on the door.

CHAPTER 9

Horse Thieves

Zozobra towered over the track, sixty-two feet at least, brilliant white in the spotlights. The infield was dark except for the glow of cigarettes, hovering like fireflies, darting in dying arcs. In the grandstand at the rear, only small bulbs lit the aisles.

"Ugly bastard, ain't he?" Decker said.

Midge was on her knees, sitting on the heels of her maroon boots, bouncing slightly with anticipation. Decker and Short Bread were sitting on the ground just behind her, one on either side, the greasy paper remains of their dinner strewn around them.

"You wouldn't want them to burn something pretty," Midge said.

"Might be kicks," Decker said.

Midge gave him a look over her shoulder, past the edge of the Navajo hat that was slung on her back. "You getting drunk or something?"

"Three beers! It's Fiesta, for Chrissake. Ain't that right, Marvin?"

"Drunk or sober, Fiesta it is," Short Bread said.

Midge, her back to them both, spritzed the air with her lips. She hoped that Short Bread wasn't a wishy-washy.

But that's not fair, she decided. He wants to be both our friends. He just don't want to take sides, is all.

Sides with what? Me and Deck is together.

169

On the stage up front she could see a tuxedoed figure moving to a microphone. She began to bounce again, the creases of her boots squeaking at the ankles. She punched Decker's knee, lightly, with her right hand, Short Bread's with her left.

"It's starting," she said. "They're getting ready!"

Decker took her hand, held it in his, a rare gesture in recent weeks. On the stage the man was talking in the microphone, his Chicano-accented words resounding on all sides.

"Just one more reminder. Following the burning, everyone is invited to the Plaza downtown, to witness the crowning of the Fiesta queen, and to dance the night away. That will be at ten o'clock. In just about an hour. And now, Monsignor Joseph Brown of the Archdiocese of Santa Fe will deliver the invocation. Let the Fiesta begin!"

The crowd broke into applause that rolled across the infield. The man left the microphone, disappeared into the darkness. He was replaced by the fall figure of the Monsignor. Not as tall, however, as Midge remembered.

"Do you think he's nervous?" Midge said.

"Nah," Decker said. "They give vocations all the time."

"I mean tomorrow. About the race."

Nobody answered as the Monsignor's voice boomed out over the grounds, hovered over the infield, bounced back off the grandstand, rose up toward the moonlit clouds overhead, asking for love, for joy, for peace, for nobody getting shot.

The usual.

So Midge assumed, because she wasn't paying attention to the words. She was watching the giant arms of Zozobra beginning to move, ever so slowly, high above the Monsignor's head. Then the Monsignor was gone and all eyes were on the puppet's arms as they raised up high in the air, first in a wave, then in an aimless thrashing. From the loudspeakers on poles all around, replacing the Monsignor's voice, there was a low moaning, a groaning, that began to grow louder as the puppet's arms waved about.

"Why's he groaning like that?" Decker said.

"He's moaning 'cause he's Old Man Gloom," Midge said loudly, not taking her eyes from the puppet. "That's why they got to burn him. To start off Fiesta right. To get rid of all the sadness in the world."

"My dime to your nickel it don't work," Decker said.

"He's a stands-for," Midge said. "He stands for all the moaners and groaners that live among us. Certain of which shall be nameless, even if they share a trailer with me."

She took his beer from his hand, leaned her head back, drank a long, glugging drink. Three entire swallows. As she handed the can back, as he took it from her, he said, "A regular drunk. I'll make you a drunkie yet!"

Midge smiled vaguely. "Might take you thirty-one or forty-one years." She belched with the taste of beer and red chili. "You planning to stick around that long?"

This last she said real low. Mumbled, actually, so neither Decker nor Short Bread could hear it.

"What?" Decker said.

"Nothing. Look at that! She pointed toward the puppet's face. His eyes were glowing orange, like hot coals. His arms were thrashing harder. His mouth was opening and closing as if in pain as the moans from the speakers grew louder.

Stop being a twerp, she told herself. It's Fiesta, for Chrissake. You be a twerp, you'll ruin everything.

She wasn't sure why she was doing it now. Decker was being wonderful. So friendly with Short Bread and all.

Maybe that was why. It wasn't natural.

Is that what love is all about? she asked herself. Being suspicious when your man is happy?

That was only love among the twerps.

She lifted his hand, lowered her face, pressed her lips to his knuckles in the dark. The bad feelings melted away, even before the burning. She could feel the 6 percent alcohol in her brain.

She pressed his hand to her cheek. Decker didn't wear any rings. She wondered if he would wear a wedding band. Probably not. Rings is for queers, he'd say. But who cared? Even lots of ladies didn't wear wedding rings nowadays.

She was pretty sure that she would wear one, though.

At least in the beginning.

If Blue Lady won, that is.

Which she would. Midge was sure of that.

Suddenly the spotlight went out. The track was in almost total darkness. Then, at once, eight bonfires blazed into being, ranged in a line across the front of the puppet. From the eerie glow a single figure emerged, slim, clad only in pink tights, and began to dance behind the flames, his shadow, bigger than life, visible on the puppet's broad skirt.

"Who's that?" Decker said.

"The fire dancer. He'll dance around for a while. Then he'll set fire to Zozobra."

"They sure know how to torture a guy," Decker said. "They did that to some guy in prison. Only there wasn't any music. They just tied him to his bed and set the mattress on fire. They didn't bother with dancing."

Midge pretended not to hear. Short Bread shook his head. From the loudspeakers on all sides, Zozobra's moans grew louder.

"There he goes!" Midge said.

The dancer had taken a torch from the nearest fire, was holding it over his head as he danced back toward the puppet. Still dancing, he touched the torch to the edge of Zozobra's skirt. At that moment eight other figures, clad in white, their faces hooded like ghosts, ran at Zozobra from all sides and touched their torches to the skirt, like the Romans slaying Caesar. At once the skirt was in flames, and then, as if in some interior shaft, the flames raced skyward, up his spinal column, to his head. His eyes bulged and glowed, his huge lips twisted in pain as his head went up in flames, his arms still thrashing like the halves of a severed snake.

As the giant flames leaped into the night they were capped in the darkness by blossoms of fireworks that began to explode overhead, reports echoing off the grandstand like cannons, fireworks trailers falling like shooting stars as children screamed in delight and adults watched awestruck. Zozobra continued to moan, little left of him now but his voice, his lips, one arm that had not fully caught fire hanging from its wire tower like a disembodied warning. Till at last, while the fireworks continued to erupt overhead, that arm too caught fire, amid a great roar from the crowd. In another moment there was nothing left at all.

The moaning from the speakers stopped. The mariachi band began to blast its trumpets as the fireworks continued above, vaulting, leaping, exploding electric flowers. A jubilation.

"It's the fuckin' Fourth of July," Decker shouted over the noise of the crowd.

"It's a pagan ritual," Short Bread said. "It's a genuine pagan ritual. You can't hardly find them no more."

"I guess you liked it, huh."

"A pretty good show," Decker said. "They put on a pretty good show."

Midge basked in their praise as in the glow of the fireworks, as if they were her fireworks, her Zozobra, her Fiesta. It was important somehow that Decker from New Jersey, Short Bread from Albuquerque, admire everything there was about Santa Fe. It was as if her home town was a reflection on her.

"It burned pretty good," she said. "Sometimes it goes up too fast. This year was just about right."

"What happens now?" Decker said.

As he said it the lights went on on all the speaker poles and in the grandstand. People were standing, shaking out blankets they had been sitting on, folding up folding lawn chairs, milling about, moving in slow clusters toward the exits and the parking lots.

"People go back to the food booths to eat some more," Midge said. "Or downtown to the Plaza where they can buy all kinds of desserts and watch the crowning of the Fiesta queen like they said, and drink beer and walk around the Plaza just saying hi to each other and having fun. Or else they go to the Jockey Club and places like that, to dance."

"Drinking beer sounds good to me," Decker said.

"So does dessert," Short Bread said. "I'm buying."

Dancing sounded good to Midge, but so did the others, actually. Decker was being so good she thought maybe she should let him off the hook about dancing. There'd be plenty of other times to dance.

"Well, let's go then," she said.

They began to inch forward, following the crowds moving slow as a glacier across the ramps over the track and toward the parking lots. If she closed her eyes Zozobra was still burning bright. Her mind was a jumble of thoughts and images: how sociable Decker could be when he wanted to, like with Short Bread just now, the two of them gabbing again. Of Cynomys, who she'd been thinking about before while they talked, and how she knew it had been the right thing to do to return him to his friends in Velarde. About the race tomorrow, the baby inside her, Blue Lady, Terry Blodgett and Kathee Praline and Fool, the horses in the van being sent away to be killed.

Her thoughts snagged there, on the doomed horses, like a coat caught on a nail. They pranced in her mind, like unicorns about to lose their horns. Fireworks seemed to light the furthest parts of her brain. Such poetry as was in her, seduced by the Fiesta spirit, merged with her natural well of mischief, gave birth to a ready-made plan. She did not so much turn it over in her mind as leap around it, like the fire dancer, studying it in an instant from all sides, perceiving the rightness of it. Till her small body could barely contain the idea.

She kept silent until they reached the parking lot.

"We're over there," Decker said.

"I'm two rows back," Short Bread said. "Should we meet down at the Plaza?"

"Right on," Decker said.

Midge stepped between them, pushing their stomachs, like a referee separating fighters.

"Hold your right-ons," she said. "First of all, there's gonna be eight zillion people in the Plaza, so we won't find each other like that. We got to go all in one car." Her face was flushed with excitement as she spoke. "Second of all, me and Deck was supposed to go dancin' at the Jockey Club." Decker opened his mouth, started to protest, weakly. She reached up and put her hand on his mouth. "Third of all, I don't want to go dancing no more. I got a better idea."

She waited for them to react, her mind tumbling ahead of itself so that for a moment she thought they already knew the plan.

"Well?" Decker said.

"Well what?"

"What's your idea?" As long as it wasn't dancing, he figured, it couldn't be bad.

Midge looked about, at the people moving toward their cars on all sides, mothers trying to keep their children together, teen-aged boys yelling beer-soaked remarks, headlights of a solid line of cars moving slowly among the masses of people toward the exit.

"I can't tell you here," she said. "Let's go to the car."

They worked their way through the lanes to the ratty-old. Decker unwrapped the wire and climbed in and slid across the seat to the driver's side. Midge climbed in next to him. Short Bread got into the back and closed the door. People were passing on all sides of the car. Midge twisted in her seat so as to face them both, and so's not to crush the Navajo hat on her back.

"What this Fiesta needs," she said, her nervousness making her sound like an after-dinner speaker, "is a little more excitement. What I think we need to do is to free them doomed horses."

Decker squinted at her in the darkness of the car.

"How's that again?" Short Bread said.

"We saw them this afternoon," Midge explained. "Horses from the race track being sent off to be killed. Only that was about six o'clock, and this being Friday, and Fiesta night also, I'll bet anything they didn't kill them yet. They must be up in that corral by Mountain Packing, waiting for tomorrow. And tomorrow being Saturday and still Fiesta, and then comes Sunday and Labor Day, they might not come to kill them till Tuesday. By then them horses could be very far away. To Espanola, even."

"They'll only go round them up and kill them anyway," Decker said.

"Maybe," Midge said. "In which case there's nothing lost. And maybe some of them will get away. In which case we done a good deed, and saved some horses that tried their very best, even though they didn't win."

Decker's eyes were shining in the dark. The old getaway juices were beginning to stir.

"There might be a night watchman," Short Bread said.

"We'll trick him," Midge said. "All we got to do is open them gates, and the horses'll run away."

"You realize it's against the law," Short Bread said. "Those horses are private property."

"Of someone who wants to take beautiful horses," Midge said, hotly, "and squeeze them into dog food cans. Horses are a part of nature. They got no right."

Decker, twisted in the seat now, was leaning toward both of them. "Making book is against the law, too," he said to Short Bread, "except if you don't get caught."

Midge squeezed Decker's hand on the seat.

"I'm for it," Decker said.

"Me, too," Midge said.

Short Bread smiled, his teeth glowing like snowflakes in his dark face. "It's your show," he said. "Why the hell not? The ponies have been good to me. One good turn deserves another."

"Right on," Midge said. "Now there's your right on!"

They looked from face to face. Decker was grinning eerily, as if the deed already were done.

"We got to hurry," Midge said, "so we can still see the Fiesta queen. The first thing we got to do is get outta here. And two cars is too many. We'll get lost. Why don't you get your rental," she said to Short Bread, "and drive it to the 'Chantment Trailer Park, right down the highway. We'll pick up a pack of beer and meet you there. Then we can drive into town in one car."

"Whatever you say," Short Bread said.

He opened the rear door and eased his bulk out. "I'll see you down the road," he said, and he closed the door and gave a little wave. He was surprisingly graceful, considering the roundness of his shape.

Midge and Decker both turned back in their seats. Their glances met. Decker reached his arm around her neck and pulled her to him. Their lips came together, and they kissed. Long and firm and wet.

Midge touched his cheek with her hand. They pulled apart and straightened in the seat. Decker found his keys in his pocket, inserted one in the ignition. Midge reached behind her and lifted the Navajo hat onto her head. A cowgirl. She couldn't imagine why it used to make her feel squashed and dumb.

"Let's go, Clyde!" she said, and she began to bounce lightly in her seat, with her arms out in front of her, as if she were riding a horse, holding the reins loose. The only real horse she'd ever ridden was the electric one outside Woolworth's on the Plaza, 10 cents a ride when she was a kid, 50 cents now, she imagined.

Decker started the ignition, turned on the headlights, felt flooded once again with power, with a stirring in his loins.

"How come you called me Clyde?" he said.

Midge, still riding, peered through the broken windshield at the West of long ago.

"I'm Dale Evans," she said, whipping the seat with her hand. "So you must be Bonnie and Clyde."

Just inside the entrance to the trailer park, across from the office to the left, gravel and log dividers marked off six parking places, for visitors. Short Bread's white rented Futura was parked in one of them, Short Bread leaning against it, when Midge and Decker swung off the road and pulled in alongside him in the ratty-old. They climbed out and approached him in the dim light, Midge carrying a cold six-pack of Schlitz.

"All set?" Short Bread asked.

Midge placed the six-pack on the fender of the Futura.

"Decker thinks we should use your car," she said, "since being rented it will be less noticeable if we get noticed."

"Also," Decker said, "it'll do ninety or more easy, professionally speaking. The ratty-old can't do sixty. It'd be useless in a high-speed chase."

"Now hold on," Short Bread said, hoisting his belly with his hands. "Who said anything about a high-speed chase? We're supposed to just open up some gate, correct?"

"Correct," Midge said. "That's what I been telling him. And if there's a watchman, I can trick him with the ratty-old. I could tell him my car broke down, could he please help a dancer in distress. He ain't gonna believe me with a new white Futura."

"And what happens if they come after us?" Decker said. "You wanna get shot down like dogs, without a chase?"

"Who said anything about shooting?" Short Bread said.

"That's what they do to horse thieves around here," Decker said. "They shoot first and ask questions later."

"We ain't horse thieves," Midge said.

"What would you call it, then?"

"Horse rescuing. That's all we're doing is some sincere horse rescuing. All we got to do is open the corral and shoo them four horses out, and slip away in the dark."

"That was the extent of the plan," Short Bread agreed.

Decker pawed at the gravel with his worn shoe. "Okay," he said. "It's a democracy, I guess. If you wanna be amateurs all your life, we'll do it your way. But don't say I didn't warn you."

"We won't say you didn't warn us," Midge said.

She led the way around to the ratty-old. All three squeezed into the front seat, Decker behind the wheel, Midge making herself slim between the men. She pulled the tabs off two beers and handed them each one, taking a swig from Decker's before she did. Decker started the ignition, switched on the lights. All three saw a figure in the office window quickly pull out of sight.

"Who was that?" Short Bread said.

"Old Man Peters."

"You think he heard us?"

"Couldn't be," Midge said. "He couldn't have, I don't think."

The car lurched backward on the gravel as Decker threw it into reverse. Gravel sprayed and the tires whined as he spun the wheel and sped onto the macadam, out toward Cerrillos Road.

"Let's burn rubber," Decker said.

"KRAP RELIART TNEMTNAHCNE," Midge said.

"The Lord is my shepherd," Marvin Kimberly said, and he held tight to the wired door.

The Mountain Packing Company Inc. was a network of corrals, squat buildings, and loading bins situated on the Old Taos Highway, at the top of a steady grade, six blocks north of the Santa Fe Post Office, eight blocks north of the Plaza. To the south of the slaughterhouse—for that's what it was, by any other name—the highway dipped sharply into town. To the north it leveled across a piñon-and-juniper-studded plateau before dipping again near Tesuque. To the east and west were rolling hills dotted with twisted trees and shrubs, expensive new adobe homes nestled among them. The company was building a new plant out on the Albuquerque Highway, and planned to tear down the outmoded old one and sell the expensive land underneath to developers. But that move was a year away.

The ugly commercial buildings were considered an eyesore, and the company had earned the scorn of the community by resisting for years a growing pressure to relocate. When people read about the freed horses in the paper the next day, Midge figured, they would have a real good laugh on Mountain Packing.

This went through Midge's mind as they rode into town, Decker unable to speed because of the traffic. She told him to turn right on Paseo de Peralta, which looped the downtown area in a half circle. Even from there, several blocks away, they could hear mariachi music from the Plaza. A halo of light and noise seemed to hang over the whole downtown area as they skirted the edge of the Fiesta revelries.

Beyond the post office they turned right again, onto the highway. There was less traffic here, and none at all as they climbed the hill toward Mountain Packing.

"Drive past it," Midge said. "We'll see if there's a guard."

They drove past the low, dark building. A watchman, looking bored, was sitting on a wooden chair under a light near the front. As they passed he stood up and started walking around to the back.

"He must check around every few minutes," Decker said "He must be the only one."

"They wouldn't have more than one," Midge said. "Nobody wants to work Fiesta night."

Decker pulled off the road around a bend, and doused the lights. They were all slightly nervous. None wanted to be first to chicken out.

"Here's the best plan," Midge said. "When the guard comes out front again, you guys sneak around to the back. I'll drive up to the front and stop there, to ask him some directions or something. That'll keep him busy while you let out the horses. Then run down the hill and I'll pick you up at the bottom. Whattaya think?"

"Sounds good to me," Decker said.

"Don't be too far down the hill," Short Bread said. "I'm not in shape for running."

"When we get back to the car," Decker said, "slide over and let me drive. In case there's a high-speed chase."

Midge and Marvin groaned.

"Look, there he is," Midge said. "He just made a quick check. Get going."

Decker and Short Bread slipped out of the car and in among the sparse vegetation at the side of the road. The clouds that had been threatening a storm all evening covered the moon. From twenty-three feet away they couldn't be seen. Midge made a U-turn on the side road without turning on any lights. Then she switched them on and drove down the road, slowly, like a person who was lost, and rolled to a stop in front of the packing plant.

"Hey," she called to the night watchman, who was sitting on his chair near the front door, about eighty-one feet from the road. The watchman got up and ambled on over to the car. He was pretty young, twenty-five and a quarter, with blond hair and a flashlight in his hand and a gun attached to his belt.

"Which way is Santa Fe?" Midge said.

"Santa Fe? That's Santa Fe right down there." He pointed to the bottom of the hill, where the lights of the city spread out for miles in every direction. Midge always marveled at how the city looked so big at night. Much bigger than it looked in the day.

"I just was down there," Midge said. "They told me Santa Fe's up here."

"Who told you that?"

"Some young guys drinking beer."

"They was putting you on," the watchman said. "It's Fiesta, everybody's having a good time. They was joking with you."

"Oh. It's no joke when you come down from Denver to

visit your sister who just had a baby, and you're late, and don't know your way around, not knowing these parts at all." She strained to hear the sounds of horses running away. All she could hear was the faint violins from the mariachis on the Plaza, all the way up here. "What is this Fiesta, anyhow?"

"A big celebration," the watchman said. "The whole town joins in."

"Why not you?"

"Someone's got to work," the guard said.

"What they celebratin', anyway?"

"I don't know. Capturing Santa Fe from the Indians. Something like that."

"The Indians took over Santa Fe?" Midge said. "I didn't know. I ain't seen the papers for a few days."

She thought maybe she had gone too far. But the watchman didn't catch on.

"This was a long time ago," he said.

"Oh."

She thought of a few more jokes—such as why are they first getting around to celebrating it now?—but she didn't say them. She still didn't hear the horses, but she figured four horses could tiptoe pretty quiet if they wanted. Decker and Short Bread sure had enough time by now.

"Well, thanks for the directions," she said to the watchman. She hoped he wouldn't get in trouble over the missing horses. "Hey, I got this beer here," she said, and she held up the remaining four-pack. "Why don't you take it? Since you're working on Fiesta and all."

"I better not," the guard said.

"Not even one?"

The guard looked around in the dark. "I guess one couldn't hurt," he said. Midge twisted out a beer and handed it through the window.

"Nice talking to you," she said, and started up the car. "Viva la Fiesta," she said as she drove off.

And bit her lip. How dumb could she get? Here she set up this perfect alibi about being from Denver, and then she goes and says "Viva la Fiesta" like a native.

"Not too bright," she said aloud.

Halfway down the hill she turned off the lights and pulled to the side of the road. There was nobody there. She blinked the lights so they would see her. Nobody came.

She waited another minute. Then she decided to go see. She crept out of the car, invisible in her black dress, black hat, maroon boots, and ran low to the ground around toward the back and up the hill toward the corral. When she got close she hid behind a bush. She could just make out the shapes of Decker and Short Bread fussing near the gate. Decker's white shirt especially.

Quietly she ran over. Decker and Short Bread froze with fear as they heard her coming. Then they saw it was her.

"What's goin' on?" she whispered.

"Fuckin' lock won't open," Decker said. He was picking at a padlock on the gate with a knife. "I thought you was taking care of the guard."

"I thought you was done," Midge said. "Anyways, I give him a beer."

"That should knock him out," Decker said.

"Yeah. Where'd you get the knife?"

"It's mine," Short Bread whispered nervously. "Swiss Army. A blade for cutting short bread. Toothpick, tweezers, nail file, scissors, corkscrew. It comes in handy."

"Nothing for picking locks," Decker said, yanking at the lock again in frustration.

"I didn't know you was Swiss," Midge said.

Nobody answered. Decker still was working. The moon peeked momentarily between the blowing clouds overhead, brightening the scene for a moment like a dark curtain parting.

"Holy cow!" Midge said.

"What?" Decker said, looking around nervously.

"Them horses! Look at all them horses!"

"There must be twenty," Short Bread whispered.

"Nineteen at least! I thought there was only four."

The corral in front of them was two-thirds filled with horses, most of them asleep standing up, the moon glinting off their coats.

"They're mostly Thoroughbreds, too," Short Bread said. "Most of the trainers must have sold off their pigs this week, instead of paying to transport them to Sunland or Phoenix for the winter."

"They must've done the same with their horses," Midge said. "Holy cow!"

"Quit gabbing," Decker said, twisting the lock in his hand. "It's done." He pulled off the lock and tossed it away in the bushes. None of them moved. "Well," Decker said. "If you're gonna do it, do it. Before that guard comes around."

"You open the gate," Midge said to Short Bread.

"It's your show, Little Lady," Short Bread said.

It was the first time he had called her that in front of Decker. It felt good. She looked from one to the other, grinning, and pulled open the gate.

All three moved off to the side, to make way for the horses. Nothing happened.

"They're mostly asleep," Short Bread whispered. "They don't know what's going on."

"What should I do?"

"Go on in and wake 'em."

Hesitantly, she stepped through the gate, into the corral. She approached the nearest horse and petted its face, the way she'd done with the three Blue Ladies. The horse didn't move.

"It's me, Midge," she said. "Let's go."

The horses didn't move.

She gathered up her courage and reached up and tugged its ear. "It's me, Dale Evans," she said in her deepest voice. "Let's move it."

The horse blinked, responding to her tug. She tugged again. The horse began moving beside her toward the gate. Others came awake, began to mill about.

"This way!" Midge shouted, backing toward the gate. "It's Dale Evans. Let's go!"

The first horse reached the open gate and walked through.

"What'd you yell for?" Decker said. "The guard coulda heard!"

"I forgot," Midge said. "They wouldn't move."

"We better scram," Short Bread said.

The first horse, outside the gate, began to prance about in his unexpected freedom. He let out a long, low whinny. In an instant the other horses were awake, were making their way toward him through the open gate.

"They're coming!" Midge said.

"They can smell the death inside," Short Bread said. "They want to get away from it."

Suddenly the small bright beam of a flashlight appeared at the side of the building.

"The guard!" Decker said. "Let's go."

Ducking their heads like turtles, they ran down the hill in the dark. Halfway down they stopped, sliding on the sandy surface, and looked back. The watchman's flashlight still was by the corral.

"What's that noise?" Midge said.

They could hear a deep rumbling not far away. The ground beneath them was shaking.

"It's the horses," Short Bread said. "They're stampeding down the hill."

"They're supposed to go the other way," Midge whispered. "Out toward Tesuque."

"I guess you forgot to tell them," Decker said.

"This way they'll end up in town!" Midge said. "By the post office. By the Plaza!"

The tension inside Decker broke. "Whoopee!" he screamed at the moon, at the top of his voice. "Viva la fuckin' Fiesta!"

On the top of the hill the flashlight beam swung toward them. It didn't reach anywhere near. Behind it the voice of the young watchman drifted down in the night: "Big fuckin' joke! Big goddamn fuckin' joke!"

"I think it's time to scram," Short Bread said.

They ran across the hill toward the road, Midge in the lead, and scrambled into the car, Midge in the middle, Decker behind the wheel in case of a high-speed chase. There was no time to wrap the wire. Short Bread held the door closed with his hand as Decker fumbled for his keys. For a getaway, Short Bread thought, he fumbled a lot with his keys.

"I feel bad," Midge said. "You think they're gonna blame the watchman?"

"I doubt they'll give him a raise," Short Bread said.

Decker started the ignition, but didn't turn on the lights.

"They was gonna kill them horses," he said, slowly. "They was gonna march them into the building tomorrow, or whenever, one at a time, and they was gonna chop their heads off. Then they was gonna saw them into little pieces with electric saws, and the bad parts they was gonna grind up like chopped meat and put into little cans for stupid dogs to eat horseburgers, and the good parts they was gonna put on a fancy boat and send to Paris, France, for the Frenchies to eat like snails between screwing their sister. Now," he said, pausing, "you wanna go round up them horses and bring them back, or what?"

Midge looked at the side of his face. Her eyes were glistening. She squeezed his thigh, tight. Then she turned in the seat as best she could between them, and looked toward the rear window.

"Viva la Fiesta!" she shouted.

Decker released the brake with his hand and burned rubber.

A second later he switched on the lights and jammed the brake with his foot. The car skidded to a stop on the shoulder of the road, and stalled. The headlights were filled with the rumps of galloping horses.

"Look," Midge said, "they're going right down the highway. It's lucky there ain't no cars coming up."

The rumps disappeared beyond the arc of light, the hooves rumbling on the asphalt like the storm that never came. Decker cursed till the engine started again.

He lurched the car back onto the highway, following the horses down. The road dead-ended at the post office, dividing and circling the building on both sides. The galloping horses, sensing the three-story stone building looming in front of them, had veered to the right, around the building, into Lincoln Avenue. The building had blocked off the lights of Fiesta, the smells of the food, the noise of thousands of people crowding into the Plaza a block ahead. By the time the horses saw and smelled and sensed what was just ahead they couldn't turn back. The avenue was like a shoot leading straight to the corral of the Plaza, a corral alive with people, music, flags.

"Better park here," Short Bread said. "We can't get any closer."

Decker pulled into a no-parking zone. The three of them got out and ran down the avenue, chasing after the horses.

"It's a fuckin' stampede!" Decker said.

"What if someone gets hurt?" Midge shouted.

They caught up with them at the edge of the Plaza where some of the horses, seeing, smelling, hearing the large crowd, had come to an abrupt stop and begun to mill about. Other horses had veered across the sidewalk into Palace Avenue, the north side of the Plaza. People crossing the street to the center of the Plaza shouted, screamed, backed away from the frightened horses, giving them plenty of room.

At the center of the Plaza a temporary stage had been erected, facing north, and on it now, illuminated by floodlights and the extra lights of two Albuquerque television stations, were a mariachi band in turquoise uniforms and fringed hats, the Fiesta queen and her court, master of ceremonies Toby Trujillo, and the slim, dark form of the Monsignor. The Monsignor was at a microphone, addressing the huge crowd.

"The Fiesta queen is normally crowned by Archbishop Flores himself," the Monsignor was saying. "As you all know, the Archbishop had to leave this morning for a solemn conclave of the College of Cardinals in Rome. Therefore it will be my privilege and pleasure . . ."

The people crowded at the front near the stage were listening intently to the Monsignor. Those in the back were turning away as the band of horses suddenly materialized behind them, milling and rearing in confusion. Children screamed in fright and squealed in delight as they saw the towering horses. People moved away, giving the frightened horses room to rear and turn. At the edge of the crowd people were petting some of the calmer horses who were standing docilely, accustomed to the noise of the track.

"Where these fuckin' horses coming from?" a policeman shouted to another as they ran to move back the crowds.

"From Mountain Packing!" Midge shouted to him as she and Decker and Short Bread ran by. "The doomed horses has been freed!"

Decker yanked her away from the cops and into the middle of the crowd. The whole Plaza was in an uproar now over the horses, people pressing closer to see while a line of policemen tried to keep them away. The two TV cameramen had swung their lights away from the stage and were filming the horses, the commotion, the crowd, artificial lights illuminating a dream run wild.

"Therefore it will be my privilege and pleasure . . . ," the Monsignor said again, not certain what was happening. But he had to stop as the hubbub of the crowd covered his words. Toby Trujillo, wearing a black tuxedo, peered from the edge of the stage to see what was going on. The walkie-talkies of the police on all sides of the Plaza were crackling with consternation about what to do with the goddamn fucking horses.

"Take down those barricades!" an officer shouted, pointing to wooden police horses blocking traffic in the northeast corner of the Plaza. Rookie cops swung the wooden barricades away, and the line of uniformed officers that had been holding back the crowd moved toward the milling horses, shooing them up the street. When the horses saw the opening they broke into a trot up Palace, out of the congested Plaza. Several swung left into Washington Avenue. Others went straight and then veered right into Cathedral Place. When most of the horses were gone the barricades were put back in place so they couldn't return. Only three horses remained in the Plaza, standing quietly, being petted by men, women, and children no longer afraid.

Midge felt relieved that no little girls had been trampled.

"Look, there's the queen," she said, pointing toward the stage, her chest throbbing with excitement. "Let's go see the queen."

She took Decker's hand and pulled him through the crowds to the edge of the platform, Short Bread following behind. One of the docile horses had been led toward the stage by a bunch of teen-aged boys and was within seven feet of it now. The crowd was buzzing with talk, laughing, joking, reveling in the unexpected diversion now that the danger was gone.

"They're from Mountain Packing. . . . They were due to be slaughtered. . . . Someone opened the gate. . . . Serves the bastards right. . . . Viva la horses! . . . Viva la Fiesta! . . ."

The horses were being petted and rubbed by the people closest to them. Those farther back were cheering. The stage, the Monsignor, the queen were forgotten.

"I wonder who the hell did it," they heard one of the cameramen say.

"She did!" Decker yelled up to the cameraman on his platform.

"Who did?" the man yelled down.

"This lady right here!" Decker said.

"Stop it!" Midge said, and made herself small behind him. But Decker took her shoulders, moved her in front of him.

The cameraman was kneeling down on his platform. "Is that the truth?" he yelled.

"I didn't mean no harm," Midge said, tears beginning to well. Why had Decker ratted on her like that?

"Harm, hell," the cameraman said. "You're the hero of the night. Can't you see?"

Midge looked around but all she could see was people taller than her screaming and cheering and joking, and horses among them. And the queen and her court and the Monsignor sitting quietly on the stage.

"Hey," the cameraman said. "Why don't you get up on a horse?"

Midge shook her head. "I can't ride no horse. I never did."

The cameraman was looking at Decker, at Short Bread, at the people pressed around them. "Put the lady on a horse," he yelled. "That's the girl who saved the horses! Put her up on one."

Before she could protest further the crowd was around her, lifting her, hoisting her onto the horse nearest the stage.

"Deck!" she screamed. "Help me!"

Decker shook his fist in encouragement. "It's just like the electric at Woolworth's. Just hang on!"

"Hang onto what?" she shouted. She was sitting on the horse now, or rather leaning over its neck, hanging onto its mane for dear life, even though the horse was standing still. Short Bread shoved his bulk through the crowd till he was beside the horse's head. He unbuckled his enormous belt and pulled it off, and he looped it over the horse's head.

"Hold onto that," he shouted, giving Midge the end of the loop, like reins.

The television floodlights both swung to Midge now, sitting on the horse in front of the stage. The people nearby cheered. She could be seen throughout the Plaza. People asked who she was, and the word spread back in waves: "That's the girl who freed the doomed horses!" Cheer followed cheer as more people heard and understood.

"Walk her around!" someone nearby yelled. Others surged around to tug at the horse's head. Short Bread shoved them away. He took hold of the belt himself.

"How you doing?" he yelled up at Midge.

"Okay," Midge yelled back. Her face was flushed as she looked out at the crowd in three directions. On impulse, she let go of the belt with one hand and waved to the crowd. A new cheer rose, louder than all the others.

"Hang on," Short Bread called. "We're gonna take a little walk."

"Okay," Midge said. She couldn't believe what was happening. She figured she would wake up in bed any second.

Short Bread motioned with his fat right arm for room. The crowd moved back slightly. With his hand on the belt under the horse's neck he led it slowly across in front of the stage, then around to the side. The TV lights followed, the cameras rolled, wave after wave of cheers bounced off the buildings that squared the Plaza and up toward the passing clouds as Midge, circling the stage on horseback, waved and waved.

"Way to go!" she heard a beery voice yell that might or might not have been Decker's.

"Viva la Fiesta!" shouted another voice.

"Viva la Fiesta Queen!"

"Viva la Fiesta Princess!"

Round the perimeter the horse moved, Short Bread leading it, Midge waving to all the cheering faces, men, women, children, some in every day clothing, many in costume like herself. She had no idea how many people were cheering her, she couldn't even guess. Thousands. Thousands. For the first time in her life she couldn't even think of a number. Just thousands. Thousands of ordinary people.

They came around to the front of the stage again. Suddenly she got all shy. "Let me down," she said.

Short Bread stopped the horse and caught her as she slid off. Her face was wet with perspiration, her skin seemed to glow. On the stage the Monsignor had returned to the microphone, was beginning to talk again. But every time he spoke, boos drowned him out.

"We want Joan of Arc!" someone yelled.

The TV lights lit up the stage again. Still they wouldn't let the Monsignor talk. He turned and left the microphone, to confer with the master of ceremonies. The emcee nodded vigorously. He came to the edge of the stage and knelt over it near Midge.

"Hey, miss," he called.

Midge didn't hear him. She had her back turned, she was looking for Decker. People turned her around, pushed her toward the platform.

"Come up on the stage," the emcee said.

Midge shook her head no, shyly.

"A favor for the Monsignor," he said. "The Monsignor would like you on the stage."

Midge shrugged, not knowing what to do. Her shrug was taken as acquiescence. Willing hands lifted her onto the stage. The emcee led her to the Monsignor, and another roar rose from the crowd as she stepped into the lights and the people saw her on the stage. All she could think was how glad she was she'd gotten dressed up, in her maroon boots and black cowgirl dress and Navajo hat. Unlike Decker and Marvin, wearing civvies. And how glad she was that she had washed her hair today.

The crowd continued cheering, having fun with it, as she stood beside the Monsignor, who had something in his hand on the other side of her. She couldn't see what it was. The people finally quieted after the Monsignor held up his hand for silence.

"As most of you know," the Monsignor said into the microphone, "this lady beside me is the lady who freed all these beautiful horses that have joined our Fiesta celebration." The crowd laughed, then cheered. "Before I ask her her name, I want to remind any officials of the Mountain Packing Company who may be in the crowd"—boos split the Plaza for a moment—"and also the police that nobody in this Plaza to-night was an eyewitness to the deed. So nobody can testify in court." More laughter from the crowd. "Also, anything she tells a priest is privileged information." More laughter, then cheers for the Monsignor. He had a reputation as all business. They had never heard him like this. "If she says that she just happened to be passing the corral on the way to Fiesta, and the horses one after another leaped the fence and followed her, no one here can say that that isn't the way it happened!"

More cheers, more laughter. Midge was laughing along with them, while tears ran down her cheeks.

A shadow crossed her face. The Monsignor was leaning down, talking just to her.

"What's your name?" he was saying.

"Beatrice. Beatrice Smith."

"Her name," the Monsignor said into the microphone, "is Beatrice Smith."

Vigorously, Midge tugged at his sleeve. He turned to her. She stretched as tall as she could and talked into his ear.

"Correction," the Monsignor said into the mike. "Her name is Midge. Midge B. A. Smith."

Her eyes scanned the crowd in front of the stage, to find Decker's face. To see if he was pleased with the correction. She couldn't find his face in the crowd.

"And now," the Monsignor said into the microphone, "before we conclude our activities here with the crowning of the official Fiesta queen, I think it is only fitting, in the light of the evening's events, that we first have another coronation. Midge B. A. Smith," he said solemnly, turning to face her, holding a silver crown in both hands, "by the authority vested in me, I hereby crown you the unofficial Fiesta princess!"

The crown glittered and sparkled in the lights. Her tears were flowing faster, she was fighting back sobs. But she held perfectly still, her hands straight at her sides, as the Mon-signor set the crown on her head, then leaned over and kissed her cheek while flashbulbs flared and the crowd cheered louder than ever. The cheering continued as, prodded by the emcee, one by one the Fiesta queen and the girls of her court —one of them missing her crown—walked up in their beautiful evening gowns and kissed her on the cheek. Midge stood still, accepting all the kisses quietly, brimming liquid eyes looking out at the television lights, bright white lights that blotted out the crowd, the Plaza, the sky. The lights became colored halos, red, blue, yellow. The halos became round picture frames, antiques. The frames filled with ancient photos: of her mother in the kitchen making supper; her father in his mailman's hat; Jack in his black baseball cap; Aunt Vanilla on her bed all naked entertaining men without no piano, which she had seen once when they went to live with her; Eddie Garcia who stole a basketball with them before he went and got killed in Vietnam; a doctor in a white coat, doctor what's-his-name, who tried his very best to make her pretty. The pictures began to bob, to dance, as music blasted from the mariachi band behind her, the band striking up, she realized, for her, the invisible people cheering, she realized, for her. And she wasn't nervous at all. The people were glad the horses had been stole, and it was her who had stole them— she couldn't have done it without Decker and Short Bread, of course, but still it was her idea—and there they were, all her friends and neighbors, applauding and cheering for her, and it was right! Without moving a muscle she saw herself climbing back onto the horse, looking as pretty doing it—looking almost as pretty doing it—as Kathee Praline; the horse walking slowly with her on its back, out of the cold and lonely world of the twerps; walking toward some bright land of the future. The land of all her fairies, it must be. Or was it, instead, the land of ordinary people? All these pictured thoughts tumbled through her head in a moment. It was only a moment, she knew, and this caused another thought: that anyone who could think so many thoughts in one moment just wasn't as daffy-dumb as she liked to think. And this thought led to another: that of course she had known this all along.

A wave of apprehension made her shudder, momentarily, in the cold sweat of the night. In the circles of the light she saw the oil painting at home on the wall of the trailer: of her without her lip. It was gone; she knew, suddenly, that it was gone. Some misguided fairy had crept onto the stage, here in front of the cameras, in front of the people, and stolen her lip away. Frightened, she reached up with her tongue, she licked her lip. For three-eighths of an instant it was true. Her lip was smooth as ice. Smooth as a baby. Then she found it with her tongue: the ridge, the roughness, the scar. The imperfection. She drew a deep breath, her first real breath in nineteen seconds. The apprehension passed off into the night.

It had only been a moment. A jiffy-and-a-half at most. She waved to the crowd, to the lights, acknowledging the cheers. Then she ran across the stage after the last maid-in-waiting, the one who didn't have a crown. She took the girl's hand, a dark-haired Spanish girl like all the rest.

"It's yours," Midge said.

She lifted the silver crown off her head with both hands and handed it to the girl. At first the girl looked toward the Monsignor and said no. Then she took the crown.

"Thanks," Midge said.

She stood on her toes and kissed the girl on the cheek. The lights still were on them, though Midge had forgotten them. The cheers erupted again.

In an instant the stage seemed darker as the TV lights went out. The emcee was at the microphone, trying to get order so the show could continue. The Monsignor walked over to Midge near the side of the stage and reached out his hand to shake. Midge took his hand, as if he were a man. She stood on her toes and shouted into his ear over the noise.

"That's the second time in my life I stole something, if you don't count the basketball or Cynomys. And both times you kissed my cheek!"

The Monsignor had little white hairs growing out of his ears, she noticed.

"I'm not sure I understand," he said.

"The Virgin Mary," Midge said. "From the church."

The Monsignor cocked his head and looked at her. "The virgin of Santa Anna," he said. "I thought you looked familiar! That was a long time ago."

"A long time," Midge agreed.

They stood in silence for a moment. On all sides the crowd was quiet now, listening to the emcee.

"At least they fixed the table," Midge said.

The priest looked puzzled, looked in pain, almost, but he didn't say anything.

"I think I'll go now," Midge said. "Thanks for everything."

When the Monsignor didn't respond she turned and stepped to the far edge of the stage, looking for Decker. She didn't see him, but she saw Short Bread pressed in the front row.

"Help me down," she shouted.

"Jump," Short Bread said.

Without hesitating, she jumped. Short Bread caught her against his bulky chest, and she slid down his body to the ground. He was sweating as much as she was. She squeezed his stubby hand, kissed him on the cheek.

"You was something else, Little Lady," he said. "You was something else."

She knew she should let go of his hand, but she couldn't. She had to hold onto somebody.

"I was Miss America," she said, wiping her eyes with her sleeve, licking the sweat off her lip. "For a few seconds up there I was Miss America!"

"You was the head queen," Short Bread said.

On the stage the emcee was still talking. The TV lights were on again, Fiesta Queen Abigail Ruiz was moving toward the mike. Midge was invisible again below the front of the stage.

"I got to go now," she said to Short Bread.

"Don't you want to see the other queen?"

"I want to, but I can't. Please come away with me."

"Whatever you say. Is something wrong?"

She didn't answer, but, still holding his hand, began to squeeze through the crowd, pulling him behind her. It was slow going near the stage. It loosened as they got further away. Finally there was room to breathe, where fewer people were milling in the street. She led Short Bread around the corner, into the relative calm of San Francisco Street. Then she turned and pressed her face into his mushy chest.

Short Bread was hesitant to touch her. When he felt her sobs he put his arm around her, gently stroked her hair. For several minutes they remained that way, till Midge pulled away and wiped her face with her sleeve. Short Bread pulled out his dark blue handkerchief and gave it to her. She used that, too, and stuck it in her sleeve as if it were lace.

"Tears of joy," Short Bread said, smiling, with snowflakes.

Midge shook her head, sniffling behind her hand.

"He's gone," she said. "Decker's gone and left me."

Short Bread put his hands on her shoulders. Searchingly he looked at her face.

"How do you know that?"

"He ain't here, is he? If you're here, why ain't he?"

Short Bread looked around, taking a deep breath. He didn't answer.

In the Plaza behind them, the noisy crowd was cheering the Fiesta queen.

CHAPTER 10

A Shortage of Genies

"He's like them pigeons up there," Midge said.

"What pigeons?" Short Bread said. He looked into the night sky and saw nothing.

"There's ninety-seven pigeons that live in the Plaza. I counted 'em one time. Ninety-seven. They walk about on the sidewalk among the people's feet, eating bread crumbs from lunches and things. If there's a big noise they take off and fly, once around the Plaza, and land on that building up there. Then when it quiets down they come on down again, to eat some more. But at night they're never here. At night they just disappear. No one knows where they go. To a pigeon night-club, I made up once. Or a pigeon hotel. They're just gone. Poof. Like Decker."

"But the pigeons always come back the next day," Short Bread said. "Don't they?"

"Yeah. Only Decker ain't no pigeon."

She was vaguely aware that her logic wasn't too good. Short Bread didn't seem to mind. Who could be scientific on Fiesta night in the middle of San Francisco Street with the mariachis blasting the only song they knew and the people laughing and drinking beer and three rescued horses still among them under the full-moon globes of street lights and not a single soul missing from the jam-packed Plaza except Decker? Not even Marlin Perkins would be scientific if Decker had gone and left.

199

"Maybe he just went for dessert," Short Bread said.

"With me up there being Miss America? He don't even like dessert. You're the one who likes dessert."

Short Bread strained his eyes, peering into the throngs, in patches of light and dark. In vain.

"There's a book about that," he said.

"About what?"

"In New York City, in Central Park, there's a pond with ducks in it. The ducks are there in the spring and summer and fall. But in the winter the ducks are gone. This boy Holden has a kid sister named Phoebe who's always asking him where the ducks go in the winter."

"Where do they go?" Midge said.

"Holden doesn't know. He doesn't know what to tell her."

"What about the guy who wrote the book?"

"He doesn't know, either."

"That's the modern world for ya," Midge said. "People writing books about stuff they don't even know. I betcha I could even write books like that." She wiped her nose with the handkerchief. "I bet old Willie Cather woulda knowed. Did he know the name of the castle, at least?"

"What castle?"

"The castle in the book."

"This book doesn't have a castle," Short Bread said.

Midge peered into his face, to see if he were teasing. He didn't seem to be.

"Every book I got has got a castle. Yours ain't one of them school books, is it? I never had much fun with them."

"This one is fun," Short Bread said. "I'll get you one. I think you'll like it."

"Yeah," Midge said. "I guess I'll be having lots of time to read again. Now that Decker's gone."

She stuffed the blue handkerchief back into her sleeve. For the second time she pushed her face into Short Bread's ample chest. He let her pillow it there, his arm resting lightly around her bony shoulders.

Like Clarissa.

Precisely like Clarissa.

He had been struck by the resemblance the first time he saw her at the track, months ago. He had been too shy—too afraid of the pain, perhaps—to speak to her, until tonight. It was not a physical resemblance, it was no one thing he could name. Not her mannerisms, either, so much as her . . . innocence? That was not precisely it, but it was the closest he'd been able to come to giving it a name, in all the many times that he had watched her, bending down to pick up tickets among the taller people's feet.

"Why don't we look around in the crowd?" Short Bread said. "Maybe he's just lost in the crowd."

"It won't do no good," Midge said.

"It can't do any harm."

She shrugged and walked beside him, back into the Plaza. She reached out and took his hand. Her shyness was secondary now. Her overpowering need was to hold someone's hand.

In the center of the Plaza, behind the stage, vacant now except for the musicians, people were lined up at makeshift booths to buy desserts: candy apples, cotton candy, squares of ice cream on sticks capped with hard chocolate and peanuts. They walked up and down the lines, peering at the people. No Decker. In front of the stage, where only a few minutes before Midge had been hoisted onto the horse, people in Fiesta costumes were dancing while others crowded around to watch. They worked their way over to look.

"I don't think he'll be dancing," Midge said.

He wasn't among the watchers, either.

On the four sides of the Plaza, people were strolling in a big square circle, counterclockwise, laughing, joking, drinking beer, calling out to people they knew. Some of them wore masks. They stood for ten minutes in front of the Palace of the Governors, watching the strollers go by. No Decker.

"It's no use," Midge said. "He's gone."

She led Short Bread out of the Plaza, into Washington Avenue. A lone horse was looking into the window of the Washington Avenue Deli. As if it wanted a frank with sauerkraut.

"Blue Lady likes green chili," she said.

"How do you know that?"

"Terry Blodgett told me."

"You know Blodgett?"

"We was introduced this afternoon. I went down to meet Blue Lady."

"He's a good man," Short Bread said.

"Yeah. I wonder what happened to them other horses. Hey, Cop! I mean, Officer. What happened to all them horses?"

The policeman was standing near the wooden barricade. "They scattered up that way," he said. "There's some of them grazing by the Cathedral. I understand the company's going to round them up at dawn. When the people are gone and they can see what they're doing."

"A good plan," Midge said. Disheartened.

She led Short Bread up the block to the Cathedral. The clouds were gone now and the church with its truncated spires was gleaming in the moonlight. In the enclosed park that belonged to the church the wrought-iron gate was open, and half a dozen horses—seven to be exact—were chomping on the church's flowers.

As they watched, three boys led one of the horses out of the gate.

"Where you taking him?" Midge said.

"We're gonna hide him," the smallest boy said. "So they won't take him away and kill him."

"Stop blabbing," one of the others said. "Maybe she's a cop."

"That's the lady, dummy," the first boy said. "That's the lady who freed them loose. Ain't you!"

Midge smiled, but didn't answer. "She's the one," Short Bread said. One of the boys made a fist in salute, and the three boys led the horse up Palace Avenue and left into Ortega.

Midge and Short Bread continued to watch the horses eat, holding the wrought-iron bars as if peering into a cage. Or out of one.

"The last rites of the church," Short Bread said.

He wanted to keep her mind off Decker. He was amazed at how well she was taking it.

At the far side of the church they became aware of a red light spinning. They saw it pull away, moving slowly this close to the Plaza. It disappeared around a curve, and then they heard the siren.

"I hope no one got shot," Midge said.

They continued watching the horses in the garden, till Short Bread became aware that Midge was shaking.

"You cold?" he said.

"I think I better go home now," Midge said.

This time it was Short Bread who took her hand. They walked in silence the three blocks to Federal Place, and around to the post office. The car was where they had left it. Three empty beer cans had been abandoned on the roof. Short Bread pitched them, one at a time, onto the federal lawn.

"Would you like me to drive?" he said.

Midge nodded, and, taking a deep breath, found the keys in her purse and gave them to him. She slid in from the driver's side, across to the other. Her hands had started to shake. Short Bread squeezed himself behind the wheel.

"You didn't get your dessert," Midge said.

"I'll survive."

He started the ratty-old, and before she could count to 267 by threes—which she was trying to do so as not to cry—they pulled into the trailer park. They hadn't said a word during the ride.

"That one," Midge said, pointing to the cream-colored trailer, and Short Bread pulled up alongside it. She noticed —the information taking a long time to penetrate her brain— that a light was burning inside.

"A light's on," she said, matter-of-factly. "I didn't leave no lights on."

Then she jumped up in the seat, hitting her head on the roof of the car. "He's home!" she said, ignoring the head clunk. "Deck's home!" She unwrapped the wire quickly and scooted out of the car and up to the door, knocking with her fist.

"Gimme the keys!" she said to Short Bread, who was having trouble easing himself from behind the wheel, and she pounded on the door again. When Short Bread got out he handed her the keys. She found the right one and slipped it into the lock and opened the door.

"Deck?" she called. "You home? It's me. Midge!"

She ran into the bedroom, where the light was on, but nobody was there. She ran into the kitchen, where the light also was on. It, too, was empty. She ran back to the living room. Short Bread had followed her inside. He was standing beside the coffee table where the first night Decker had knocked on the door he had spilled his beer. Short Bread was pointing down at the table.

"It looks like a note," he said.

She reached down and picked up the paper, a torn piece of paper with words on it in a ball-point pen that didn't write too good. The words were printed unevenly. They said:

> Dear Midge B. A. Smith—
>   You looked kind of pretty up their tonite. But I got to split anyway. Because it is time. I ain't the marrying type.
>   Take care of yourself, Midget.
>   Your friend always,
>   H. Decker.

The paper rustled slightly in her hand as she read the note.

"Midget," she said, with resignation. "He always wanted to call me Midget. I guess he didn't mean no harm."

She plopped down onto the sofa, her booted legs splayed wide in front of her, her fists pressing her skirt between her knees.

"He's gone," she said. "I knew it."

She held out the note. Short Bread hesitated, then took it from her and read it. Gently he laid it down on the table. He expected her to cry—he felt a bit choked himself—but she didn't.

"I think I could use a drink," he said. "I bet you could too. Is there anything here?"

"There's prob'ly beer in the fridge," Midge said. "Wait," she added, pushing herself up from the sofa. "There's some real stuff, too. For toothaches and stuff." She went into the kitchen, Short Bread following as far as the doorway, and reached around in a low cabinet of pots and pans and pulled out a dusty, unopened bottle of Early Times. "I got good teeth," she explained, wiping off the dust with her hands, wiping her hands on her Fiesta skirt. "But I guess this is toothache enough. Toothache of the belly."

She twisted the top of the bottle, but it didn't open.

"You want me to fix some drinks?" Short Bread said.

"Sit," Midge said, nodding toward the two green wooden chairs at the kitchen table. "I can do it."

"You forget I'm a bartender."

"It's my *casa*," Midge said.

Short Bread obeyed, sat near the table. Midge twisted the top of the bottle again, gritting her teeth, her face growing red, till at last the cap twisted loose. She took down two water glasses from a metal cabinet, opened the refrigerator, pulled out an ice tray, strained again to free the imprisoned cubes, filled the glasses high with ice. Then she poured in the bourbon, almost to the top. She set one glass in front of Short Bread, the other across the table from him, and she sat there, her posture erect, her hands clasped on the table.

"You ever drink bourbon before?"

Midge shook her head no. She'd forgotten it was there till now. Left over from Jack.

"You better go easy," he said. "It's got quite a kick."

"Like Decker," Midge said.

Short Bread sipped the bourbon, absorbed the burning in his gut. Midge stuck her tongue into her glass, rolled it around in her mouth. "It tastes like medicine," she said.

"Sometimes medicine is the only medicine," Short Bread said.

"Yeah," Midge said. "I guess."

For twelve seconds they looked into their glasses, saying nothing. The ice in Midge's glass was breaking up. Was cracking apart.

Short Bread spoke first.

"Does it hurt?"

"Yeah," Midge said. "It hurts bad."

Short Bread took another drink of bourbon. His fat arms below the short sleeves of his dark blue shirt seemed to stick slightly to the table. The table hadn't been washed too well.

"Why do you think he left?" he said. "Did you have a fight?"

Midge shook her head no. "We didn't have no fight. I mean, we always fight. But it don't mean nothing. It's sort of like a game." She sipped her bourbon, closed her eyes, gritted her teeth, forced herself to swallow it. It burned like green chili. "He was upset about the baby, I think."

"What baby is that?" Short Bread said.

He was looking intently at her face. His eyes seemed to focus, unconsciously, on the small scar on her lip. Habitually she flicked her tongue up to lick it. She took a deep breath before answering.

"I got a baby in me," she said.

"Decker's?"

"Yeah."

Short Bread's glass was sweating, the outside was cold and wet.

"He didn't want it?"

"Nope. He wanted me to get a 'bortion."

"What did you want?"

Midge closed her eyes, made a fist, blew into it with her lips. "You want some peanuts?" she said. "I got some peanuts somewhere."

"I don't want peanuts," Short Bread said. "What about the baby?"

Midge looked at the ceiling. She reached behind her and pulled the Navajo hat onto her head. No longer a cowgirl, she once more felt squashed and dumb. She took another drink of drink.

"I don't know," she said. With her index finger she wrote numbers in the wetness of the table from the glass. 1. 2. 7. "I don't know what I want. I mean, I don't want to raise up no child. Like it would be bigger than me. But I don't want to kill it, neither. A cuddly little baby would be cute, ya know? Sort of like a puppy. Especially if I made it myself. Only I don't think I could make one myself." She still was looking down at the table. "Only I'd sort of like to find out." She traced more numbers. 3. 5. 8. Then she looked across at Short Bread. "Only that ain't no good reason to have a kid. Is it?"

Short Bread studied the ice in his glass. Now it, too, was cracking.

"I'm not sure what's a good reason," he said. "It might be as good as any."

He threw his thick neck back and swallowed a long drink.

"I don't like this stuff," Midge said. She got up from the table and went to the refrigerator and got out a DDP. Sitting back in her seat she pulled off the tab. The soda-pop fairy didn't come. Hardly any fairies had been around lately.

"So what did you decide?" Short Bread said. "That doesn't explain why Decker left tonight."

"I guess because of the bet," Midge said.

"The bet?"

"The bet I told you about."

"You never told me what it was."

"Yeah." She rubbed her face with her hands. She pulled the chin cord from under her neck and removed the Navajo hat. She set it on the table between them, like a small black mountain. "I guess I can tell it now. Ain't no more Decker to get mad."

"The bet had to do with the baby?"

"I was supposed to have it killed. Then I got this idea. Blue Lady's my favorite horse. Decker said she was gonna lose tomorrow. I figured out scientific that she would win. So I made Decker a bet. If Blue Lady lost tomorrow, I'd get it done. But if Blue Lady won, then I could keep the baby, and me and Deck would get married."

Short Bread whistled softly. "That's some bet," he said.

"Yeah." She drank some DDP. "I guess it come to Decker that he would lose. So he ran and left me."

"He could have waited till tomorrow. Till after the race. Blue Lady still could lose."

"I guess he got afraid," Midge said.

Short Bread pushed himself away from the table. He stood and paced about in the small kitchen. Two cereal bowls were in the sink, unwashed. He looked out a small window behind Midge, his back to her, out into the night. The window had curtains on the sides, with tiny, faded blue flowers.

"Do you love him?" he said.

In the night he could make out several more trailers. There was no response. He paced back and sat on the chair again.

"He's a creep," Midge said.

"That may be," Short Bread said. "If you say so. But that wasn't the question."

"What's it matter now? He's gone. The closet in the bedroom's open. He even took his shirts and stuff."

"Just for the record," Short Bread said.

Midge looked down at the table. She spritzed with her lips, noise only, no saliva.

"How should I know?" she said. "I ain't never loved no one before."

"Then you do?"

"Well, of course I do," she said, looking into his face. "Wouldn't you? I mean . . ." She looked at the table again. "Yeah . . . Don't ask me why."

Short Bread reached into his pocket for his handkerchief, but it wasn't there. It was sticking out of Midge's sleeve. He saw an almost empty roll of green paper towels on a counter. He got up and tore off a sheet. Still standing, he mopped his face.

"Why is he a creep?" he said.

" 'Cause he went and left me. Why do you think?"

"I don't mean that. Before that. Why was he a creep before that?"

Midge felt her face grow hot. She squinted up at Marvin Kimberly. She wondered for a second what he was doing there at all. Her voice was hostile when she spoke.

"Why you asking all these questions?"

Short Bread crumpled the paper towel. He sat on the chair again. "I'm sorry," he said, softly. "I didn't mean to intrude."

"Yeah," Midge said.

"I just thought you'd feel better if you talked."

"Yeah," Midge said.

She reached her hand halfway across the table, spread her fingers down beside the hat. Short Bread, after a moment, reached out and squeezed her hand.

"I'm sorry too," Midge said.

For nine seconds they didn't speak. Short Bread slowly took his hand away. Midge left hers there, playing one-handed piano on the table. The way she used to think Vanessa entertained men. Before she saw.

"He ain't really a creep," she said. "I only said that now 'cause I was mad. He's just real unhappy, is all."

"What's he so unhappy about? Aside from the baby, I mean."

"It ain't the baby," Midge said. "I mean, that's just now. It's a shortage of genies, is what it is."

208

"I beg your pardon?" Short Bread said.

"Well, look for yourself," Midge said. "What's he got to be unhappy about? He's out of the clinker, right? And he's going straight, so he won't go back there no more. And he's got all of his health, no aches or pains or nothing. And we got this nice trailer to live in, rent free. And with me working we got plenty of money for food and beer, and even with the Welfare there'll be enough, whether Decker wants to work or not. And he's got this person who loves him very much, and even if she ain't too pretty she's pretty good in the . . ."

She stopped short, caught herself up, felt her face go red as an apple. Short Bread smiled snowflakes.

"Don't you laugh at me!" she warned.

"I ain't laughing," Short Bread said, laughing. "Midge B. A. Smith is one sweet peach!"

"Well, you might not think so," Midge said. "But certain gentlemen knows. Not the least among them Horace Decker."

"I'll bet he does."

"You bet your bejesus he does!"

"So what's the problem then? Why's he so unhappy?"

"That's exactly the problem," Midge said. "He ain't got no reason to be unhappy. But he's unhappy all the time. So it must be a shortage of genies."

Short Bread held his glass up to the light, his drink half finished, and peered through it. "Maybe it's this bourbon," he said. "I'm still not sure I follow."

"It's simple," Midge said. "You know what a genie is?"

"I think so," Short Bread said.

"It's scientific," Midge said. "We all got these genies inside us. Lots of genies that live inside our cellblocks. They got these special powers, sort of like magic. Each genie controls certain things. Some genies decide what color hair we got. Some genies decide what color eyes. The mother has genies and the father has genies, and they get together in the baby and decide. Like with me. My genies decided I should have light brown hair. And light blue eyes. And I should be four feet eleven. Genies do all that stuff. You understand so far?"

"I gotcha," Short Bread said.

"Well, the problem is that sometimes the genies ain't perfect. Like with my lip. I didn't have enough lip genies to go all the way across. So I was born with this hole in my lip. So the doctors had to fix it up when I was a kid. There's still this little scar here," she said, pointing, "which you might have noticed."

"Oh, yeah," Short Bread said. "Now that you mention it."

"It's tiny," Midge said. "I don't think Decker even noticed. But it don't matter, I kind of like it. Because if that's what the genies decided I should have, then I guess it's what I should have."

"I suppose you could look at it that way," Short Bread said.

"It's the only way to look at it. 'Cause what choice do you have? The genies always know best."

"And Decker?" Short Bread prompted.

"Yeah," Midge said. "Decker is a little more complicated. He's got his dark-hair genies and his brown-eye genies and his five-foot-seven-and-a-quarter genies. But Decker's got a shortage of happiness genies."

"I haven't heard of those," Short Bread said. He took a long drink of his now-watery bourbon, almost draining the glass. A powerful sadness overcame him.

"There's genies for everything," Midge said. "Happiness and sadness, too. I bet you can think of plenty of people who have lots of sadness in their lives. Lots of bad things happen, sickness and dying and stuff. But still they're pretty happy most of the time. Not right away, of course, when something bad happens. But after a while it's over, and then they get happy again. You know any people like that?"

Short Bread nodded his head.

"Well, those people got a lot of happiness genies. They got the right amount, at least. Like me. But Decker don't. Decker's got a shortage. So no matter how good things get, he's never really happy. Not for much at a time. His sadness genies always comes out the strongest."

She wound down suddenly, like a record reaching the end. Short Bread was looking past her, as if lost in thoughts of his own. But he'd heard. He looked across the table into her eyes, something in his voice still far away.

"Why do you love him, then? If you can't make him happy?"

"Love got nothing to do with it," Midge said. "You love someone or you don't, right? That's what I figure, at least. The genies can't make you love, you do that yourself. You love someone or you don't, a shortage of lip or no. You love some- one or you don't, a shortage of happy or no. You do the best you can to make them happy. That's all you can do. Don't you think?"

Short Bread didn't answer right away. He lifted his empty water glass. "You mind if I have another?" he said.

"Help yourself," she said. "My *casa* is your *casa*."

She remembered when she'd said that first. Her underwear was soaked, her Fiesta dress was soaked, from all this bour- bon, from all this babbling. She noticed as Short Bread fixed his drink that under his arms he was sweating too.

"My feet is killing me from these boots," she said. She crossed her legs at the knee and pulled off first one boot, then the other, and wiggled her small toes. One of her nails had pushed a hole in her sock.

Short Bread eased himself onto the chair again. She thought of suggesting they go in the living room, but she liked sitting here like this. Short Bread had been right, too. Talking made things feel better. She wished she could prove that to Decker. And remembered again that he was gone.

"I'm just gonna drink this drink," Short Bread said. "Then I'm gonna go find Decker."

"What do you mean?" she said. She was afraid he was get- ting drunk.

"I mean just what I said, Little Lady."

"Decker's gone," she said. "He must've got a hitch. He could be anywheres by now."

"Maybe," Short Bread said. "And maybe there's no one leaving town this late at night. Maybe he's drinking him- self silly in some bar, and he's gonna split by bus in the morn- ing."

"And what if he is?" Midge said. "What if you found him somewheres? You gonna tie him up and bring him back in a cage? I don't want him like that. He's got to come back by hisself or not at all. An' I don't think he will. I think he's long gone."

"I wouldn't bring him back if I could," Short Bread said.

"I just thought maybe he could use someone to talk to. Like you."

"Like me? I don't need no one to talk to."

"Well, you're special," Short Bread said.

Midge smiled, then couldn't stop herself from laughing. She squeezed her lips shut with her fingers. "I guess I been talking your ear off," she said.

Short Bread smiled back. "I got two of them," he said.

Midge got up from her chair and walked about in her stocking feet, placing the heel of one foot against the toe of the other, as if she were measuring the floor. She refused to allow herself to think that Decker might come back. She walked that way—heel, toe, heel, toe—right up to Short Bread, and stood beside his chair.

"Can I call you Marvin?" she said.

"Whatever you like," he said.

"Tell me something, then. Why you being so nice to me?"

"Who's being nice? I'm drinking your bourbon, that's all."

"Okay, you're a meanie. Why you being so mean to me?"

Short Bread's right hand tensed into a fist, involuntarily. He lifted his glass with his left hand, drank half the drink, let his hand relax. He found that his breathing was rapid, his chest was heaving. He waited till it calmed.

"I guess I like you," he said.

"I know," Midge said. "But why?"

He didn't answer. Instead he rolled the edges of his short sleeves a little higher around his thick biceps.

"Can I do something?" Midge said.

"What?"

"Can I touch your hair?"

"My hair? Why do you want to do that?"

"Just a quick touch. For science. I ain't never touched a colored person's hair. A black person, I mean."

"Be my guest," he said, and, though seated, he lowered his head further. Tentatively she touched his hair. Like the first time she'd touched Cynomys. She took her hand away.

"It's woolly," she said. "It feels nice."

"Colored genies," Short Bread said.

Midge smiled and walked back to her chair, walking normal this time in her socks

"You want to sit in the living room?" she said. "It's softer."

"I told you," Short Bread said, "I'm going to find Decker."

"When you finish your drink. You ain't finished yet."

"Right," Short Bread said. "When I finish my drink."

He stood and followed her into the living room and eased down into the sofa with a grunt. Midge sat cross-legged on the floor beside the coffee table, where she'd sat the first night of Decker.

"I could put on a record," she said.

Short Bread shook his head. "I owe you some talk," he said. "You talked to me. I ought to talk to you."

"Shoot," Midge said, cheerily. "What do you want to discuss?"

Short Bread wiped the sweat from his chin with his shoulder. He set his glass down on the coffee table.

"You know that person you mentioned before," he said, "who even if she ain't too pretty she's pretty good in the sack?"

"Yeah."

"I think she's very pretty."

Midge snorted and smiled at the same time, and turned it into a spritz. "Don't start shitting me," she said.

"I'm not," he said, quietly. "You remind me of the most beautiful person I know in the whole world."

"Marilyn Monroe?"

Short Bread smiled. He was speaking softer, slower now than he had done all evening. "Her name is Clarissa," he said.

Midge clasped her hands in her lap. She felt of a sudden like the Monsignor must feel when he's about to hear a confession.

"Is she your girl friend? A girl friend that . . . left?"

Decker kept burning in her stomach. Whenever she thought of him. It was better when she didn't think of him.

"No," Short Bread said. "She's my daughter."

"But I thought . . . I mean . . . I didn't know you was married."

"I'm not. I used to be."

He reached forward and picked up his glass and drank a drink, holding onto the glass this time in his fat fist, looking through the side, as if what he wanted to say was written in the glass. Then he came back from his moment's dream and looked at her.

"I was married when I was twenty-three," he said. "That was fifteen years ago." He was still talking slowly. "I was very different then. A lot slimmer, for one thing. I worked in a bank. I was the first black assistant teller in the Albuquerque Federal Savings and Loan. I grew up watching this little girl grow up across the street from us. Her name was Yolanda. Yolanda James. She was a lot younger than me but she grew up pretty quick. Filled out, if you know what I mean. She was this soft cocoa color, with flashing eyes. All of a sudden she was in high school and she didn't seem so much younger anymore. She was seventeen, and I was twenty-three. I used to go to the high school basketball games, to watch her leading cheers in her green-and-yellow outfit. We got married right after she graduated. Her folks was mighty happy, her marrying this up-and-coming young banker. I guess I was the happiest, horniest young man in the world."

Midge sat enthralled by every word. Nobody had ever told her a story like this before. And a true one, at that! It was as if all her years of telling stories to her rag doll, and then to Cynomys, were being paid back now. Here in her living room.

"We were happy for a year," Short Bread continued. "Yolanda liked to get all dolled up and go out. I loved to show her off, everywhere. Then the baby came. The most beautiful little girl you'd ever want to see. We named her Clarissa. Clarissa Kimberly."

"That's nice," Midge said.

She felt herself growing all teary, without knowing why. As if she knew something bad was coming, without knowing why. Because something bad always happened in these kind of stories, before the happy ending. Then she remembered it wasn't a story at all.

She tried to picture Short Bread as a skinny young banker. It was hard to imagine.

"Clarissa was a doll," Short Bread continued. "At first Yolanda had fun with her, playing with her all day while I was away at the bank. I was a full teller by then, doing real good. I'd be a branch manager someday, the cock—— . . . the gen-

214

eral manager used to tell me. Then we found out about Clarissa."

"Found out what?" Midge said.

"She was a year old when the doctor noticed. Something was wrong with her. She wasn't doing things exactly how a baby should. At first he said not to worry. Maybe it would pass. But it didn't. We didn't even see anything wrong, at first. But when she was two years old, anyone could tell. There was something wrong. She had brain damage, the doctor said. She was born that way, there was nothing anyone could do. She'd grow up physically okay, the doctor said. But not mentally. She'd get to be about as smart as a five-year-old. But that was all. No matter how big she got after that, she'd still be a five-year-old in her head."

Midge looked down into her lap, her legs crossed under her on the floor, her knees pale bumps at the edge of her Fiesta skirt. She pressed her lips together.

"A shortage of genies," she said, quietly.

Short Bread drained his drink into his mouth. He placed the empty glass delicately on the table.

"Yolanda couldn't cope with that," he said. "I think she was getting bored anyway, stuck in the house all day with the baby. When she heard that Clarissa would never grow up— would never be able to take care of herself—that was too much. She started leaving the baby home alone, going out, running around. I didn't blame her a whole lot. I was pretty shook myself. But it couldn't go on like that. Finally I told her if she was so miserable, she should go away for a while. Have a good time. Do whatever would make her happy. It would be better than taking it out on me and the baby. She thought it over for two days. She said it was a good idea. She said she'd go visit with her cousin in California. Just for a few weeks. I took her to the train station the next day. We said good-bye. We pretended she was coming back. We both knew she wouldn't come back."

"And she didn't?"

"It's the last I saw of her."

Short Bread reached for the glass, took another drink, though the glass was empty.

"You want more Early Times?" Midge said.

He shook his head no and studied the glass. The glass had a yellow flower pattern. He couldn't tell if it was glass or plastic.

"What happened then?" Midge said. "With Clarissa."

"Yolanda's mama would come stay with her during the day, while I was at work. But then she had to go back to work herself. I didn't know what to do. I hired people to stay with her in the day. But when she got bigger it didn't work out. When she was six years old she was still like three. Finally I had to do what I hated. I had to put her in a home."

"A home?"

"For retarded children. She's been there eight years. She's fourteen now. She's beautiful, with soft cocoa skin, perfect teeth, big eyes—only they don't quite flash, like her mother's. I go to see her every other Sunday. We play checkers, do cutouts. She shows me her coloring book from the week before." He hesitated. "She doesn't stay in the lines too good."

"Who wins?" Midge said.

"Who wins?"

"At checkers."

"She does," Short Bread said. He looked from the sofa to Midge's face where she sat on the floor. He couldn't make out her expression. "She wins every time."

Midge was playing with the hem of her dress. "I figured she did," she said.

Short Bread seemed to relax further into the sofa. As if some tense energy were spent. He crossed one fat leg over the other.

"I quit the bank soon after," he said. "I figured if life was gonna be like that, I'd live the way I wanted. I loved to eat, so I started to eat whenever I felt like it, and didn't worry about keeping in shape. I loved to play the horses, so I started playing the horses every day. I liked to talk to people, I liked to drink in bars—not hush-hush like in a bank—so I'd get jobs tending bar at night. You get to talk to people, to listen to their troubles. I like that. It's human."

"Like tonight," Midge said.

Short Bread ran his finger along the rim of his shoe. His speech became slower again.

"Tonight was different," he said. "You know why I talked to you on that food line? Because I felt like talking to you all summer at the track, only I didn't have the nerve. Because you remind me of Clarissa."

"Because I'm dumb," Midge said.

"Now who's shitting who? You're smart as a whip, and you know it."

Midge, looking at her lap, tried not to smile at what he said.

"It's because . . . I don't know exactly why. You just remind me of her, that's all. Clarissa is so trusting, so innocent. She wouldn't hurt a fly. I think you're sort of like that."

"Oh, yeah? You just ask Decker. I hurt him with my twerpy tongue. I hurt him plenty of times."

There was that burning again, in her stomach.

"On purpose?"

"No." She bit at the base of her thumb. "Sometimes."

"I almost forgot about Decker," Short Bread said. He uncrossed his legs and worked his way up from the sofa. "I'm supposed to be out finding him."

"Decker's in California by now," Midge said, looking at the floor. "With Yolanda."

"My guess is he's drinking himself silly, right here in town."

He started toward the door. Midge scrambled up and ran to him.

"Marvin?"

"What?"

"Thanks."

"Thanks for nothing," he said. "I'm going after Decker. You gonna come to the track tomorrow?"

"I got to," Midge said. "For Blue Lady."

"Good. I'll see you there."

"Marvin?"

"What?"

"You ain't gonna find Decker."

"Maybe yes, maybe no," he said.

He found the handle and pulled open the door. She reached with her thin hand and touched his chest.

"If you find him . . ."

He waited.

"Don't say I want him back."

Short Bread put his hands on her shoulders. He looked into her eyes. Deep into her pale blue eyes, where he could tell that no one had ever looked before. He didn't want to speak, or to leave. He wanted to stand there, hands on her shoulders, feeling whatever it was that he was feeling. But he spoke right away.

"Why not?"

"Because. If he wants to come back . . . by himself . . . he knows where to find me."

Short Bread turned away from her, blinked, ducked his head twice, nodding. He stumbled for a moment on the steps. Then he was gone.

CHAPTER 11

The Mermaid

She stood in the doorway and watched him disappear across the dark of the trailer park toward where his car was lighted out front. It was a romantic pose, it occurred to her, right out of one of her paperbacks: standing in the doorway of your house at almost midnight, watching a man go away. Even if he wasn't your lover and there was a hole in one of your socks.

It occurred to her that she never got to stand in the doorway watching Decker leave. Decker never left by himself, especially not at night. He would stretch out on the bed after dinner with a beer in his hand and watch whatever was on the TV. If she was feeling romantic she would curl up on the bed and watch with him. But if he was all engrossed and the program was too especially dumb she would get up and go into the kitchen and read a paperback.

There was some significance, it occurred to her, that she never got to watch Decker leave. Even tonight, when he had left for good, it was not Decker she got to see leave, but Short Bread. She did not know what this significance was.

She closed the door of the trailer and locked it—in case Old Man Peters was feeling some Fiesta-night jollies—and picked up Short Bread's empty glass from the table and put it in the kitchen sink. She pulled on her pale blue dishwashing gloves and washed the glass and the two spoons and the two cereal bowls that were sitting there from breakfast. The last dishes she'd ever wash for Decker, it occurred to her.

As she pulled off the gloves and washed her hands to get rid of the rubber-glove smell, it occurred to her that she was doing a whole lot of occurring. All day long, this had been occurring to her and that had been occurring to her. This was very unusual, she realized. (There it was again!) She was not the occurring type.

She dried her hands on a paper towel, carefully, and then she didn't know what to do. She had not been alone in the trailer at night since Decker had knocked on the door, eighty-seven nights ago. She sat at the kitchen table, where her warm DDP still was, and she decided that she would think. Immediately she thought of Decker, and this made her stomach burn. It occurred to her that what she needed to think about were things that would take her mind off Decker. She decided to count up all the different important things that had occurred to her today—this one day that seemed to have lasted for six months. The electric clock on the wall near the fridge said two minutes to twelve. She could hardly believe it was only six and a half hours ago that she had made the bet with Decker about the baby. And that it was only four hours since she first met Short Bread. She felt as if she'd known Short Bread Marvin Kimberly all her life.

But she was getting off the track. She'd been about to count up the day's occurrences. She numbered them, of course, the way any scientist would.

Occurrence 1. In the parking lot at the track, waiting for the ninth to be over, it occurred to her why she was being so twerpy to Decker: because, even though she didn't want the baby, she was mad at Decker for not wanting her to want it.

Occurrence 2. Down by the barns with Blue Lady and Terry Blodgett, all those funny things to say occurred to her. About the Monsignor once was her lover and all.

Occurrence 3. It occurred to her to bet the baby on Blue Lady.

Occurrence 4. It occurred to her that Blue Lady couldn't lose, because of the law of averages. (If she was smarter, it occurred to her, this would have come before 3.)

Occurrence 5. It occurred to her why she'd said the Monsignor was once her lover. Because he had kissed her when she returned the virgin. No other man had kissed her until she was twenty-eight except her father, and he always smelled of liquor.

Occurrence 6. When Short Bread talked to her on the food line, it occurred to her to invite him to come watch, Zozobra burn.

Occurrence 7. It occurred to her to free the doomed horses.

Occurrence 8. This was not strictly an occurrence. Maybe half an occurrence. It was her speech to Short Bread about the genies. She had thought of this before, so it was not entirely new, but she had never said it to anyone before, and she was amazed at how clear and scientific and absolutely true it sounded.

So there it was. Seven and a half complete occurrences in seven hours. A world's record, certainly, for Midge B. A. Smith. She lifted her warm DDP, threw back her head, and shoved her Adam's apple in the air—feeling a little silly, as if maybe she had overdosed on Early Times—and gurgled down a toast to her new world's record. And then she had still another smart occurrence. It had occurred to her when Short Bread was there that she hadn't seen many fairies around lately. And now all of a sudden she knew why. Because the occurrences were taking their place! The fairies used to come around to explain things she didn't understand. Like when the soda-pop burst all over, it was because of the soda-pop fairy. Because she didn't know why else. Like when she got the idea to bet the baby, it came from the thinking-cap fairy. Because how else could someone so dumb get such a good idea? But if a person had occurrences, like she was having today, they didn't need too many fairies.

If she was really smart as a whip—the way Short Bread had said she was—she might never see another fairy again.

Tears were rolling down her cheeks. Because all this thinking was breaking her brain. Because she wanted Short Bread to still be there, to talk to. Because all she could think about was Decker. Underneath all this thinking, her stomach, with longing of its own, was reaching out for Decker. Calling him back.

She wiped her cheeks with the sleeve of her Fiesta dress. She didn't have to worry about one thing. There'd still be plenty of fairies around yet.

The love fairy, for instance.

The love fairy was still around, all right.

The only one missing was Decker.

The skin on her face seemed to hurt. She rubbed it with her hands. She got up from the kitchen chair and switched off the overhead light, went to the living room and switched off the light there, went into the bedroom and turned off that light too. Quickly she switched it back on, because the whole trailer had suddenly gone dark, as if her whole life had gone dark. She turned on the reading lamp on the night table by the bed before switching off the overhead again.

On the floor in a corner of the bedroom was Jack's phonograph set. Piled neatly beside it was her own record collection of seven LP albums. If she ever was rich, she liked to think, she would have nineteen records at least. She kneeled beside the records and pulled out the three Maria Muldaurs. She wasn't sure why Maria Muldaur was her favorite singer, except maybe because of the way her voice seemed to jump and crack all over the place when she sang. The same thing happened to Midge's voice whenever she tried to sing, but Maria Muldaur did it on purpose. Maria Muldaur made it sound pretty. She also liked Maria Muldaur because if you looked at the album covers she was the prettiest girl in the world. Inside the cover of *Maria Muldaur* was a close-up picture of her face and her long brown hair, and on the cover of *Waitress in a Donut Shop* was an even closer close-up, with her brown eyes and her smooth skin and a big red rose in her hair, and perfect lips so real they was ready to kiss. Midge had never seen anything so pretty. The closest she'd seen in real life was Kathee Praline. Kathee Praline was a blonde Maria Muldaur.

She switched on the phonograph and then plopped onto the bed and stretched out, her Fiesta skirt caught under her, pulling tight across her thighs. When she was feeling blue sometimes—though she didn't remember ever feeling *this* blue—she would stretch out on the bed like this and make believe she was Maria Muldaur, about to choose the songs for her next record. Only since she didn't know any new songs, she decided the record would be called *Maria Muldaur's*

Greatest Hits. Then she would listen to all the records, and choose which ones were the Greatest.

Lying on the bed now, she went over them in her head. She knew which ones were coming up even before the records played. "Don't You Feel My Leg" always headed her list. There was also "Anytime You Wanna Come Back Home," and "Sad Eyes," and "It Ain't the Meat It's the Motion," and "Three-Dollar Bill" and, "Honey Babe Blues."

She tried to listen but tears were wetting her ears. She had never noticed it before, but all the songs she liked were about Decker. It was hard to believe. Maria Muldaur had been her favorite singer long before she ever met Decker. But the songs were all about him. It was as if Maria Muldaur had known Decker back East, before Midge did, and then sent him west to meet her. As if Maria Muldaur was also the love fairy.

She wiped her ears with the pillow. She couldn't pick the Greatest Hits just now. All she could think of was Decker. Just lying there, in the bed where he used to lie, with her skirt pulled across her thighs, with the overhead light out and Maria Muldaur singing on the record, it made her sweat, it made her feel all itchy, just thinking of him.

"Do you love him?" Short Bread had said. Well, of course she loved him. Why else would he be around? But why did she love him? She thought and thought and didn't get an answer. No occurrences. It didn't seem to have to do with thinking at all.

She knew exactly which day she first knew. The day of Santa Claus Lake. *That* had not been a day for thinking. *That* had been a day for action. Catlike! Lionlike! It was funny, thinking back. But it didn't seem funny then. Probably everyone had a special memory of the first day they knew they was in love, she figured. But she was pretty sure not everyone's had a mermaid.

It was July twenty-third, a Thursday. Mrs. Gallegos had told her to take the day off because she had worked the Saturday before, an extra day, to trap rodents near one of the pueblos where a case of the plague had been found. It was a hot day, seventy-two when they woke up, going to ninety the radio said, and the trailer was awful warm. She didn't want to spend the day just hanging around, the way Decker usually did, and there wasn't any horse racing on Thursdays.

"You know what we should do," she said, as they sat at the kitchen table eating their cereal, "we should go swimming today."

"Swimming?" Decker said. "That's a good one. Where you gonna go swimming in a place like this? One of them fancy motels?"

"There's a lake," Midge said, licking the bottom of her spoon to capture a stubborn corn flake. "Santa Cruz Lake, it's called. It's only about seventeen miles."

"A lake? How big a lake?"

"I don't know. Maybe six hundred thirty-three feet. It's plenty big enough to swim in."

"I'd rather the ocean," Decker said. "In Jersey we had the ocean. You could dive into these waves, fifty feet high, and then swim out a mile or two and ride 'em in."

"You can swim like that? I didn't know you was a good swimmer."

"There's lots of things you don't know," Decker said, and he lifted his cereal bowl in his hands and slurped up the extra milk. "Naturally, that was a long time ago. A man naturally gets out of shape for swimming when he hasn't swam for a while."

"Naturally," Midge said. "So the lake'll be perfect to get back to shape just a little. We used to go there sometimes when I was a kid. It's real fun. I can make us some sandwiches and we can eat 'em by the lake and stretch out and get some sun, and then take a dip or two to cool off."

"Nah," Decker said. "Prob'ly there'll be a million kids there. I can't stand a beach with kids."

"Maybe there won't be anybody, you mean. It's not a big beach like at the ocean. It's just this little lake up in the mountains. Most people don't even know about it."

Decker shrugged.

"C'mon, Deck, it'll be fun. It's too hot to lay around here all day. Put on Jack's bathing suit from the dresser, under your pants, and go gas up the car. I'll make up some sandwiches. It'll be fun."

"Okay," Decker said. "But if there's a million kids there

we're gonna turn around and come right back. And no argument."

"No argument," Midge agreed, as Decker turned to go.

She made some peanut-butter-and-jellies, wrapping them in aluminum foil—she wondered whatever happened to wax paper, like her mother used to use—and put them in a paper bag along with some beers and some DDPs. In the bedroom she fished out her pink one-piece bathing suit. She couldn't remember the last time she had worn it, but it still fit. It didn't have much shape, she noticed, but then neither did she. Over the bathing suit she pulled on some old blue jeans she found in the back of the closet, and an old blue shirt. She tied her sneakers, pulled the blanket off the bed and tucked it in a ball under her arm, took the bag of sandwiches from the kitchen, and was waiting outside when Decker pulled up in the ratty-old.

"All gassed?" she said.

"Ten bucks worth. I took it from your bag."

"Let's go then," she said, and she shoved the blanket and the food in through the open window, uncoiled the wire on the passenger side, and climbed in.

The ride took half an hour, Decker driving, Midge navigating. When they rounded the last curve of the dirt road and drove up to the lake, Midge was ecstatic.

"What'd I tell you!" she said. "There's nobody here at all. We got it all to ourselves."

"No we don't. There's someone over there."

She looked where he was pointing, to the dirt where the lake curved about a hundred yards away. She didn't see anyone. Just a blanket with some stuff on it.

"It's just a blanket with some stuff on it," she said.

"Where there's blankets there's people," Decker said.

"Or person. Two or one at the most. We got half the lake anyway. It ain't a million kids."

Decker got out of the car and stretched. The lake looked almost black, without even a ripple, with small trees dotted all around it, and the sun shining straight overhead.

"Isn't it pretty?" Midge said, coming up beside him.

"It ain't the ocean," Decker said.

"I'll get the stuff," Midge said, and she pulled out the blanket and the food and her Instamatic, which she had put in the bag at the last minute. It still had half a roll of film in it, from before the summer. She didn't know if the film was good anymore. They walked down to the lake, picking their way among rocks, and she spread the blanket where the dirt became smooth, twenty-two feet from the edge of the water. She put down the bag and pulled off her sneakers, and then her jeans and her shirt. Decker pulled a beer from the bag, snapped off the top, and sat down on the blanket.

"Ain't you getting undressed?" she said.

"After a while. We got all day, don't we?"

"All day long," Midge said.

She pulled out a DDP and sat on the blanket beside him. She hoped he would say something nice about her bathing suit. But he didn't say anything about it, one way or the other.

She stretched out on the blanket and closed her eyes. The sun felt warm on her pale skin, warm and comforting. She could hear a light breeze rippling the lips of the trees. Between the sun and the lake and Decker there beside her, she had never felt so at ease with the world. This was the way rich people lived. She wished the moment would stay like that forever.

"Sure is quiet out here," Decker said.

"Mmmm," she agreed, dreamily, her eyes still closed.

"Wish we had a radio or something."

For a few moments she didn't say it. She just wanted to lie there in the quiet, with the sun kissing her eyes. But the moment was gone, she couldn't be at peace when she was holding out on him.

"We do," she said.

"What?"

"Got a radio. In the car."

"Good idea," Decker said. He got up and went to the ratty-old, about a hundred feet behind them, and switched on the radio and turned the dial till he found some rock and roll. He screwed the volume as high as it would go, then walked, backward, to the blanket, listening if he still could hear it. It wasn't loud by the blanket but they still could hear it, clear enough to blot out the quiet.

"There," he said. "That's better. Now we got everything."

She was sitting up again. She looked at his face when he said that. There was something emphatic, something definite, about his voice. And tender, too. It was the nicest thing he'd ever said to her. She reached out and squeezed his hand. She wanted to say, then, what people were always saying in her paperbacks, and in the movies and on TV. What she could never imagine herself saying in all her life. She wanted at that moment to say, "I love you." But she didn't say it. She was afraid. Her heart started pounding. She bit her lip instead.

"Hey," she said, because she had to say something, "let's take pictures." She picked up the Instamatic from the blanket. "We ain't got no pictures of each other."

Decker seemed to sour instantly.

"I don't like pictures," he said.

"How come?"

"Too many pictures around is asking for trouble."

She looked down at the blanket, quiet for a moment. The future spread suddenly before her in the weave: a lifetime of responding to such statements. The feeling was not all bad.

"That's prison talk," she said. Her voice was soft, disappointed almost. She was still looking down. "You're finished with all of that."

He was still for a time. When he spoke he wasn't angry. It was as if he had changed the subject, though he hadn't.

"I knew this guy in prison," he said. "He was an Indian. He used to go crazy whenever they took his picture. He said every time someone takes your picture, they take away part of your soul." He picked up a handful of sand and let it run through his fingers. "I don't got enough soul to spare."

The sadness, as it so often did, came into his eyes. Midge squeezed his hand again, pressing his fingers together.

"It don't matter," she said, brightly. "You take mine, then. I got soul to spare. Ain't nobody took my picture in twenty-three years. Besides, you need one for your wallet, don't you?"

She stood and pulled him up. "Down by the water," she said, giving him the camera, and she walked gingerly, barefoot on the rocky dirt, to the water's edge. She turned to face him, Decker standing fifteen feet away, holding the camera to his eye. He wiped it on his white shirt, then held it up again.

"Smile pretty," he said from behind it.

She smiled as pretty as she could, and she heard it click.

"One more," he said.

She turned a little sideways, sticking out her chest as far as it would go, and smiled over her shoulder, like a movie star, and heard the click.

"That should be a beauty," Decker called.

She walked on back to him and took the camera. Hand in hand they walked back to the blanket. The music from the car was drifting toward them in the breeze.

"How about let's go for a swim?" Midge said.

"Good idea," Decker said. He took off his shirt, exposing his pale chest to the sun. He sat on the blanket and pulled off his loafers, and his socks. He unbuckled his belt, and seemed to look down at the buckle. Then he said, "Shit!"

"What's the matter?"

"I forgot a bathing suit."

"Forgot? I thought you put on Jack's, under your pants."

"I was gonna. I went to gas up and I was gonna change when I got back. Then you was waiting outside and I forgot."

Midge felt disbelieving. Then disappointed. Then forgiving.

"You was gonna teach me how to swim across the lake. The way you used to do in the ocean in Jersey."

"Yeah. Hey, I'm sorry. Maybe next time. Why don't you go in anyhow."

"I think I will," she said.

She put the camera on the blanket and walked back down to the water. She went in up to her ankles. The water was very cold. She forced herself to go in farther, to her knees. It seemed even colder. She stood there till she got used to it, at one point turning and waving to Decker, who was watching her from the blanket. Then she took two more steps and spread flat out on her belly. She splashed about to warm up, swimming six feet before she had to put her toes on the bottom. The water was up to her waist.

"I can't swim too good," she yelled out in the direction of Decker. She splashed about for a few more minutes. Then, teeth chattering, she walked back out of the water, up to the blanket.

"Throw me a towel," she said.

Decker looked around on the blanket. "Where?"

"Oh, nerd! I forgot to bring a towel."

She was shivering all over, she couldn't stop.

"Use my shirt," he said.

She shook her head. "It's a good white shirt."

"Use it, I said! You'll freeze."

When she made no move to pick it up, Decker grabbed it and stood. Scrubbing her with the shirt he dried her arms, her back, her legs, though her bathing suit kept dripping. She felt herself warming from the inside out. It was six weeks ago he had knocked on the door. Something was coming full circle.

"Feel better?"

She nodded and sat on the blanket. Decker sat beside her, draping his shirt over her shoulders. It was wet now, she was better off without it. But she left it there.

"How's the water?" he said.

"Cold."

"Damn," he said. "That's the way I like it. That's the way the ocean is."

She didn't respond. Something had caught her eye, far out on the lake.

"Look," she said. "There's someone swimming, way out there."

Decker looked where she was pointing. He shaded his eyes with his hand, squinting. He glanced toward the empty blanket to their right, then back at the lake. "Must be that guy from the blanket," he said.

The bobbing head was far out in the middle of the lake. It seemed to be moving toward them, in toward shore.

"I think it's a girl," Midge said.

"Couldn't be, that far out."

The head drew closer. The hair was long. It looked like dark blonde.

"She's got long hair," Midge said. "I told you it's a girl."

"It could be a hippie," Decker said.

"A hippie girl," Midge said.

The swimmer was moving straight at them with long, powerful strokes.

"He swims pretty good," Decker said.

Twenty feet from shore the swimmer stopped. Again they saw only the head. The swimmer had touched bottom, was walking toward them out of the water.

"Oh, my God!" Midge said. "She lost the top of her bathing suit!"

The young woman, waist deep in water now, was walking toward them. She had large, upright breasts. She was making no attempt to cover them with her hands.

After a few more steps the water was at her knees.

"She ain't got no bottoms, neither!"

Decker wheezed when he tried to speak, his mouth dry. "It's a girl," he whispered.

The woman—she was twenty-two and a half, Midge decided—was out of the water now, was coming toward them. Her long blonde hair, dark from the wet, was dripping. Her private triangle—nicely shaped, Midge thought—was also dark from the wet, was also dripping. A curl of hair was hanging from the bottom of it.

"Hi," the girl said, and gave a small wave as she approached. She stopped five feet from their blanket, dripping, her large nipples blue from the cold. Midge and Decker were speechless. She was five foot seven, Midge decided. 39-24-36.

"Mind if I dry off here? It's kind of lonely over there."

Decker, with a struggle, found his voice. "Be my guest," he said, and he squeezed Midge over on the blanket. But the girl sat on the dirt instead.

"No need to get your blanket wet," she said.

She sat with her knees drawn up near her chin, her arms on her knees. Like a picture in a sunshine magazine. Midge, looking down the tunnel of her thighs—she couldn't help it —was enthralled.

"My name's Marilyn," the girl said. "Most people call me Mare. Because I love the water so much."

Midge and Decker, looking at her as she lifted her wet hair from her shoulders, were too astonished, too confused, to reply.

" 'Mare' means sea," the girl said. "In the Romance languages."

"Oh," Decker said. "Right."

"Oh," Midge said.

She never heard of a mare being romantic. Unless you was a horse.

"Who're you?" the girl said.

"I'm Decker. This here is Beatrice."

Midge looked at him, her head cocked, her brow furrowed. But Decker was busy ogling the girl. It would have been difficult not to.

"You from around here?" Mare said. "I'm from California. Surf country. I'm driving home from the East. I check out the local lakes whenever I can. Cute little town, Santa Fe."

"I'm from the ocean," Decker said. "I mean, New Jersey."

Midge's voice, when she found it, was small. "I'm from here," she said. But neither of them seemed to care.

"How come you're not swimming?"

"Forgot my suit," Decker said.

"You've got your born skin. That's all the Creative Force thought we needed. Look at me, I never wear a suit."

"On you it looks good," Decker said.

"Yours looks pretty good, too," the girl said. "I can tell."

Decker shifted his position on the blanket. Midge knew why. Because his pants were getting tight.

"C'mon," the girl said, "I'll race you across the lake."

"I don't think so," Decker said.

"We could rest for a while on the other side. Before we come back. There's a nice bed of leaves over there."

"Maybe later," Decker said.

The California girl stretched her legs, long and tanned, on the dirt in front of her, and leaned back on her elbows. Her full body was exposed to them, large breasts inviting and firm. Every part of her firm.

"That your car?" she said, and she began to beat one hand on the dirt in tune to the music in the background. "Makes me want to dance." And she shifted her blonde thighs back and forth on the dirt in time to the music.

Midge watched in fascination. She was almost hypnotized. She had never seen anyone so sexy in her life. Outside of her paperbacks.

"Where you staying?" Decker said.

The girl, still dancing on the ground, didn't miss a beat as she answered. "Wherever I'm invited. I'm traveling cheap."

"It's the only way," Decker said.

"You're not kidding. With the price of motels these days. You and your sister got room, by any chance? Just for tonight?"

"All we got's a trailer," Decker said. "It's pretty small."

"I don't need much room. I can squeeze in some tight places."

"I don't know," Decker said. He turned toward Midge. "I guess she could sleep on the couch for one night, huh?"

Midge didn't respond right away. She heard every word they were saying, but she was looking as through a telescope across the lake, beginning to turn silver now, and the dark trees and a cloud that was scudding toward the sun, blotting it out for a moment, sending a chill through them all, then passing on, leaving the sun to warm them again. More words telescoped, she couldn't make them out anymore, the girl, Decker, the girl, Decker. She didn't know how long this reverie lasted before she spoke, thirty seconds, or five minutes, or ten.

"Beat it," she said.

They had almost forgotten she was there.

"What?" Decker said.

"Not you. Her. Beat it!"

The girl stopped writhing to the music, but she still lay back, leaning on her elbows, basking in her nakedness. "You say something to me?"

Carefully, Midge took Decker's shirt off her shoulders. She uncrossed her thin legs and raised herself onto her knees. "I said beat it," she said.

The girl smiled, a glistening smile in her all-American face. "You got a problem, lady? You think you own this beach?"

"You got till two and a half," Midge said, "to scram."

The girl laughed, leaned her head back, closed her eyes to the sun, mocking the threat. Midge counted slowly, to herself. Decker wondered what Midge was going to do. Midge wondered, too. Then, almost without thinking, she sprang forward, throwing herself on the lean, naked body.

"Wha——" the girl said, opening her eyes, but Midge's knee had landed in her stomach, taking her breath away. Midge reached toward her hair with one hand, reached between her thrashing legs with the other. The girl convulsed under her and they rolled over, three times, the girl crying out once as a pointed rock pressed between her shoulder blades. They rolled over twice more and then came to a stop, both of them breathing hard. The girl was face down in the dirt now, Midge was sprawled across her back in her pink bathing suit, the neck-strap broken. Her left hand was gripping tight to the girl's tresses, close to her head. Her right hand disappeared between the girl's thighs from the rear, her fingers clenched tight to her private hair. The girl was trussed like a calf, and Midge was the rope.

"Hey!" the girl called with a grunt. "Get her off of me."

Decker, who had scrambled up to watch the fight, was jumping up and down without realizing it, making little hops two inches off the ground. He didn't answer.

"I'll make it worth your while," the girl said, struggling for breath.

Decker fell to his knees and placed his eye near the dirt, trying to get a better view, like a referee at a wrestling match. He scrabbled about that way like a crab.

The girl gasped again for breath. "Whatsa matter, you both crazy?" she said.

Midge held tight to the hair at both ends of the girl. Her back was to Decker now, she couldn't see what he was doing. Then she saw his toes, the bottoms of his pants. She looked up and saw the camera at his eye.

"Smile pretty," he said.

Midge smiled as best she could under the circumstances. She felt like a fisherperson showing off her catch. For a picture over the family mantelpiece.

Decker clicked the picture, clicked three more from different angles. Then the camera jammed as the film ended.

"No more film," he shouted.

The girl tried one more time to twist away. But her hair hurt at both ends.

"Now," Midge said from above her, "I'm gonna let you go. And you're gonna haul your California tail outta here. Right?"

The girl didn't answer. Midge yanked her hair.

"Right," the girl gasped.

"And your California orifice, too!"

With that Midge let her go and jumped away, so the girl couldn't grab her. But Mare just lay on the ground, not moving. Then, slowly, she rolled over, and sat up. Her wet skin was clotted with dirt. Midge walked over and stood near Decker.

The girl brushed the sand from her arms, from her breasts. Her nipples had turned from blue to red.

"Tell me something," she said, looking up at Decker. "Why didn't you pull her off?"

Decker looked around for his shirt. He picked it up from the blanket, and he put it around Midge's shoulders, the way it had been.

" 'Cause Midge here would have beat me up," he said.

The girl shook her head from side to side. She stood, began to brush off more sand, then thought better of it. "I've seen crazies," she said. She looked right at them from ten feet away, shook her head again, and strode off across the sand, toward her blanket a hundred yards away.

"Hey, Mare!" Midge called out when she was halfway across the beach.

The girl stopped and looked back.

"No hard feelings!"

The girl walked on without answering.

Decker laughed, then caught his breath up sharp. Midge's small hand was in the front of his pants, feeling something pretty hard.

They stood that way, nothing moving except Midge's fingers, as they watched the girl gather up her blanket and walk off to a car parked halfway around the lake. They waited till the car drove off. Then they undressed each other, without speaking, and splashed about in the shallow water. No one but the sun could see them.

As they drove home afterward, Decker seemed lost in his thoughts. Midge tried her best to keep still, but she was too puffed up with satisfaction.

"I really showed her, huh?" she said, as they curled from the dirt road onto the highway.

Decker winked at her, and smiled, and kept on driving.

"I nailed her in six seconds flat," she said five minutes later, as they sped over a hill toward the city.

Again Decker only smiled.

"Best fight I ever had," she said, as they waited in town at a light.

When they pulled into the Enchantment Trailer Park, and Decker switched off the engine, Midge tapped him playfully on the shoulder.

"How come you said that?" she said.

"Said what?"

"Back there. That if you pulled me off of her, I would have beat you up."

He touched the tip of his index finger to the tip of her nose, as if he were pushing a button. It was her favorite gesture of his, the one she trusted the most.

"Because prob'ly you would have," he said.

She took his finger from her nose and pressed it with her lips. This time she didn't think.

"I love you," she said.

She said it as if to his finger. She wasn't sure if he had heard. But she was pretty sure he had.

It was the first time in her life she'd said those words.

As if in answer, he squeezed the top of her hand.

They sat there a moment in silence. Then he went inside and took a shower.

Remembering it all, as she had many times before, lying on the bed now in her Fiesta dress, Maria Muldaur singing in a donut shop, Midge was breathing heavily. He had never said "I love you" back—not ever—but that was the day she knew he did. She remembered how when they got the snapshots back, that showed her and the naked girl, he put them proudly in his wallet, the way her father had done with the pictures from the paper of her and Father Brown. He took them out often to look at them, just as she took out the memory.

One time when he was looking at them she said, "You liked that Romantic-language horse, didn't you?"

"I've seen better," Decker said.

And they hugged and kissed and he touched his finger to her nose.

Remembering all this, lying on the bed with her records on, the Fiesta princess thought of a new song: "No California Girl Will Steal My Man." She knew just who should sing it, too. It would be her Greatest Hit.

She stretched as far as she could and switched off the reading lamp. Alone in the dark, waiting for sleep to come, she tried to think up words for the song. But all she knew was the returning pain in her belly. Neither words, nor sleep, would come. She decided to count something to help fall asleep, which she often did. She counted horses and jockeys jumping over a fence. But it didn't work, the jockeys kept falling off.

Just as she was certain that she wouldn't sleep at all, she slept. She dreamed that a handsome prince and a woolly brown bear were fighting a duel over who would marry Kathee Praline. The duel went on and on, and she couldn't tell who was ahead. Before it ended they all went home and ate Jesus-in-the-pot soup, which she had never heard of before. Which she figured must be new from Campbell's.

She slept for two hours. When she awoke it was still dark outside. She didn't remember where she was, or what day it was. Then in a rush she remembered all of it; Zozobra and Short Bread, the freed horses and becoming Fiesta princess. It all seemed part of the dream, one continuous story that some writer might make up, and then she felt the pain in her belly and she remembered that Decker was gone, that she had a baby growing up inside her, that it wasn't a dream at all. She thought of it all and again she couldn't sleep. She got up from the bed and went to the bathroom and tried to think of other things. Names for her baby, perhaps. She knew it was best to keep busy, to occupy herself, and then she got an idea: she would bake a cake. She would bake some shortbread for Short Bread, which he said he loved. Which she could give to him at the track tomorrow, to thank him for being so nice. She took down her checkered cookbook—*The Better Homes and Trailers Cook Book*, she called it—and looked up the recipe. All you had to do was mix up some flour, sugar, butter, and salt and bake it for fifty minutes.

"Easy as pie," she said.

She had all the ingredients around. She followed the recipe carefully, mixing the butter and flour till it was soft and creamy, biting her lip as she did; adding the sugar and salt and mixing it again; spreading it all in an aluminum pie tray. The book said cut into sixteen to twenty wedges, but she preferred fifteen herself. She put it in the oven to bake, set her little cooking timer, and stretched out on the couch in the living room to rest.

A minute later, it seemed, the ping-ping of the timer woke her up. She took the shortbread from the oven, warmed by the smell. Marvin would be pleased. She placed it on the table to cool, turned off the lights, and plopped back down on her bed, thoroughly exhausted now. She thought of two good names for her baby, one if it was a boy and one if it was a girl; but before she could make a note of remembering them, she fell asleep. Her Fiesta dress was speckled with flour. There was a smear of white across her face.

CHAPTER 12

The Machine Age

Midge had never been to the track in the early morning to watch the horses being worked. When she awoke at dawn and couldn't sleep anymore, her mind a tangle of the previous night's events, she decided that that's where she would go. The track seemed almost magnetic this day, drawing her toward the answers to questions that frightened her. As if it were the birthplace of some sacred new religion.

As she brushed her teeth and washed her face and took a shower, as she dressed and drank a glass of orange juice, the questions tumbled through her head. She had bet her baby on Blue Lady. With Decker gone did the bet still count? What if he showed up at the track, would the bet be on then? If Blue Lady won would she really have her baby? If Blue Lady lost would she really kill it?

She didn't want to think about it, or about Decker, or about life, or the future, at all. It was all too depressing, and she was not the type to get depressed, or to stay depressed very long. She had made herself feel better during the night by baking the shortbread for Short Bread. Now, she thought, she might feel better if she went on out to the track.

As she drove the ratty-old out of the trailer park, she said, "KRAP." Not the whole thing, not KRAP RELIART TNEMTNAHCNE, which had progressed in her mind in recent weeks from joke to superstition. Just KRAP, which summed up the way she was feeling. Superstition seemed

243

especially dumb on this particular morning, with Decker gone from her side. The enchanted arch was only a stupid sign.

But she was right about the track, the horses. As soon as she saw the empty grandstand brooding in the dawn light, as soon as she saw the horses on the back stretch, galloping, standing, snorting cold white breath, more horses than she had ever seen out there at one time, her spirits lifted. They lifted even more as she drove through the empty reaches of the parking lot, through general parking, through reserved parking, all the way to the front where she had never parked before. Where only the important people parked. You didn't have to pay in the morning. There were only six cars in the whole of the parking lot.

She climbed out of the car in her navy blue winter pea coat, which she had put on because it was very cold this time of the morning, no matter how hot it would get later on, and her white wool cap, which was pulled down over her ears. She walked through the open gate, to the front of the grandstand, and was amazed by the sound she heard: a steady high-pitched roar coming down from the roof in the quiet of the morning. She looked up. She could hardly see them but there were a million birds—fifteen thousand at least—tucked up under the roof, jabbering away about who was gonna win today's race. They sounded just like the people would sound later on, if all the people had very high voices like birds.

A splash of white splattered on the ground beside her. She looked up again, then changed her mind and hurried out from under the roof, glad that she had worn her white hat. She walked on down toward the rail, where half a dozen men—six at the most—were standing about watching the horses run by. It all sounded very different without any people in the stands. There was the chatter of the birds in the background, but down near the track the hooves of the horses were extra loud, the horses sounding like little trains as they sprinted by, blowing white smoke breath, toward the finish line and beyond. Even out of uniform, in blue windbreakers or just plain T-shirts in the cold, some of the jockeys were recognizable; others whom she had never seen before were exercise boys who only worked the horses in the morning. She felt as if she had entered a new world being here this early in the morning;

it was like seeing a rehearsal of a play, or being in a factory where cars and things were being put together bit by bit.

She was afraid to join the group of six men who were standing together near the winner's circle watching the horses run. Eighteen yards away she saw another man watching by himself, one foot up on the rail, a The Downs baseball cap on his head. She recognized him right away as her best friend at the track: Terry Blodgett. She wished she was wearing the thinking cap he gave her, but it was up there on the dashboard of the ratty-old and she was wearing her woolen hat instead. She took it off, because the rising sun was already warming things, and walked on over and sidled up, as best she could sidle, beside him.

"Howdy," she said, putting one foot on the rail in imitation.

"How you doin'?" Blodgett said. "It's Midge, isn't it?"

"Still Midge," she said. "Midge B. A. Smith."

"What brings you out here so early, Midge B. A. Smith?"

"Just thought I'd watch the horses run. See if Blue Lady's ready for the big race." She shaded her eyes from the low sun and peered across the infield. About fourteen horses were out on the back stretch. "Is Blue Lady out there?"

Blodgett shook his head and squirted some tobacco juice over the rail. "You don't work a horse the day she's gonna race."

"Oh," Midge said. "I guess they'd get tired out."

Blodgett didn't reply. His eyes were focused on a horse that was galloping at full speed from the top of the stretch, down the straightaway toward the finish line. As the horse raced by, Midge saw Kathee Praline's blonde curls shimmering under the edge of her helmet. Kathee stood in the stirrups as the horse crossed the finish line, slowing the horse's gait as it continued on around. Blodgett spit more juice. Midge said nothing, wondering what she was doing here at all, as Kathee walked the horse back along the outside rail and stopped beside them. She was wearing her regular jockey boots but they were mostly covered by blue jeans. On top she wore a pink warm-up jacket.

"She didn't run good," Blodgett said, looking up at the jockey astride the horse.

The jockey, breathless, shook her head.

"I guess she don't like the machine," Blodgett said.

The jockey's eyes darted from Blodgett's face to Midge. Then she seemed to decide that if Blodgett thought it was okay to talk in front of her, it must be okay. Maybe she owned the horse.

"The battery died," Kathee Praline said. "It wasn't working. We'll have to try it again next week." Her breath was coming quickly.

Blodgett crossed both arms on the top rail. "You got a fresh one for Blue?"

"Back at the motel," Kathee said.

"Okay. Better bring her down and let Fool cool her off. Bring Ajax up and we'll blow him out for Monday. That's all I'll need today."

Kathee nodded and tapped the horse with her heel. Horse and rider walked off along the rail, toward an opening near the paddock, while another horse raced by in the stretch.

The sun was getting warmer quickly. Midge unbuttoned the large buttons of her pea coat. It was interesting being among these track people, even if she didn't know what they were talking about.

"So," she said to Blodgett, "which Blue Lady you gonna use?"

Blodgett looked at her, rubbing his cheek with his hand, and grinned. "The real one, I think."

"That's what I figured," Midge said. "A big race like this, you got to use the real one."

Blodgett turned and walked ten steps to a stone bench where spectators could sit in the afternoons, and he sat on it, leaning his elbows back on a stone table. Midge followed and sat beside him and did the same.

"The Monsignor gonna come see the race?" she said.

Blodgett looked at her as if he were startled, then looked down at his knee. Carefully he brushed some mud off his jeans with his hand.

"The Monsignor's not gonna make it," he said.

"No kidding," Midge said. "If I owned a horse I'd sure wanna watch it run. Especially a big race like this."

Blodgett leaned back on his elbows, his eyes far across the track. "The Monsignor's dead," he said.

Midge turned and squinted into his face, to see if it was a joke. It didn't sound like a very funny joke.

"No he ain't," she said. "I saw him just last night."

"He died early this morning," Blodgett said. "Just after midnight. They called me." He crossed one booted leg over the other. "There was some big celebration downtown. Fiesta, or whatever. Somebody freed some horses from the slaughterhouse and they stampeded downtown. Lots of excitement. The Monsignor was crowning the Fiesta queen. The Fiesta princess. Something. They think he was stricken during the ceremony. He collapsed right after it, and they rushed him to the hospital. He died soon after."

Midge's eyes had never left his face. She saw that he wasn't joking. But it didn't seem possible. The way everyone was cheering him last night.

"The red lights," she remembered. "The ambulance by the church!"

"What?"

Midge didn't answer right away. She pressed her hands deep into the pockets of her coat. Her eyes were on the horses across the track. She felt sad, she felt as if she ought to cry for him. But she didn't.

"It was me," she said, quietly.

"What was you?" Blodgett said.

"Who freed the doomed horses."

Now it was Blodgett's turn to look at her. "Really? It was all over the radio this morning."

"It was me," Midge said, quiet as before.

Blodgett pushed his The Downs cap far back on his head, exposing his forehead and a lock of brown hair to the sun.

"You're the one they called up on the stage?"

Midge nodded and bit the base of her thumb.

"How come you did it?" Blodgett said.

"They was gonna kill them horses. It wasn't right."

"It's all part of the business," Blodgett said.

"Oh yeah? I bet there was none of your horses there."

Blodgett again brushed imaginary dirt from his knee. He spit tobacco juice off to the side. He turned the peak of his cap down straight.

"As a matter of fact, there were two."

Midge glanced at him quickly, and then she looked away. She thought she ought to be shocked, but things were happening too fast. She felt only a mild sadness instead.

"It don't matter," she said. "I suppose you could say it was me who killed the Monsignor."

"Now how do you figure that?"

"All the excitement, like you said."

"That's talking foolish. If he came to watch Blue today, that'd be excitement, too. You can't go through life avoiding excitement. When a man's time comes his time comes, excitement or not."

"Yeah," Midge said. "I suppose."

Her fingers in her pocket were playing with a stub of cardboard. She pulled it out and looked at it. It was a ticket stub from a movie. She tried to remember which one, but she couldn't. She hadn't worn the pea coat since last winter.

"Anyways," she said, "I think he died happy."

"How do you know?"

Midge shrugged her shoulders in the coat. "People didn't like him too much. He wasn't the favorite in the church, like the archbishop. Willie Cather didn't write nothing about him. He was more like a businessman, you know?"

"That's how he seemed to me," Blodgett said.

"But up there last night, on that stage, the people was cheering for him. They was cheering for me, 'cause I freed the doomed horses"—she glanced at him quickly and then away—"but they was cheering the Monsignor, too. Because he was being so funny about it. Because he made me a princess, too. I think the people liked him for that. I think he knew it. I could see it in his face."

"Then it may have been his perfect time to die."

Midge placed the balled-up movie stub on her bitten fingernail, and she flicked it straight out at the sun. It fell to the ground about sixteen inches from her feet.

"It may have been," she said.

Above and behind them the birds still were chattering under the roof, as if nothing bad had happened. As if all were right with the world. On the track horses and riders continued to run on by, one at a time. Other horses that didn't have riders trotted slowly alongside ones that did, one exercise boy holding two sets of reins. Midge imagined she was one of those horses without a rider. The thought led nowhere.

"You gonna cancel the race?" she said.

"Blue Lady?"

"Yeah."

"Why should I do that?"

"Because the Monsignor is dead."

Blodgett unzipped the zipper of his navy windbreaker. He was wearing a red-and-black-plaid flannel shirt underneath.

"What would that accomplish?"

"I ain't sure. Just to show respect, I guess. It's his horse, ain't it?"

"Blue don't know that. Blue thinks she's my horse. Blue don't know he's dead, either."

"So who'll get the money if she wins?"

"His estate. The church. Whoever. It doesn't make much difference."

"I suppose," Midge said. She wasn't sure why she'd asked about canceling the race. She had a feeling that she didn't want to part with, that somebody higher up ought to be in charge of things, somebody like the Monsignor, not just some guy named Blodgett. But maybe she was being selfish, she decided. With no race there would be no bet to worry about, one way or the other.

"Blue Lady gonna win?" she said.

"She'll try her best," Blodgett said. "She always does."

"Is Kathee Praline a good rider?"

"Kathee's one of the best. She's fearless. She goes all out to win, every time."

"She sure does," Midge said. "She's real pretty, too."

Blodgett didn't answer. His eyes were on the opening in the rail beyond the paddock, where Kathee Praline was walking another horse, a sleek black one, onto the track.

"Can I ask you something?" Midge said.

"Shoot."

"When you was talking to Kathee before, you said the horse don't like the machine. And Kathee said the battery was dead, but she's got a fresh one for Blue. I'm sorta new at racing, ya know? What did you mean by that?"

Blodgett spit tobacco juice between his legs. He pulled his

The Downs cap straight, though it was already straight. "I got to go now," he said. "That's Kathee out there with Ajax. Got to see how he runs." He stood from the stone bench and took two steps. "Nice talking to ya," he said, over his shoulder, and he touched his hand to the peak of his cap, as if she were a lady.

Midge stood and stuck out her hand. Blodgett reached over and shook it.

"Good luck in the race," she said. "Tell Kathee, too."

"I'll do that," Blodgett said. Then he walked off alone, down to the rail.

Midge looked across the track at Kathee Praline. She looked just as nice in her warm-up jacket as she did in her jockey silks. Midge wondered how she herself had looked on that horse in the Plaza last night. Sometimes she wished that life had instant replay, so you could see just how you looked doing this or that. But it would be just like pictures, she figured, and sometimes pictures lied. Like those pictures of her and the mermaid. She was the one who'd won, but the mermaid still looked better in the pictures. No matter what Decker said to be nice.

The thought of Decker depressed her. She'd forgot for a little while that he was gone. But it didn't make her stomach burn anymore. At least there was that.

She jammed her hands in the pockets of her coat and looked around. Behind her, row after row of the seats in front of the grandstand stretched up empty. The seats cost a dollar in the afternoon, and she and Decker couldn't afford to sit. She thought maybe she'd sit there now. Up above, the chorus of birds was still chattering away, but the first few rows of seats were safe, the first few rows were out from under the roof. She walked on over to them, her hat in her hand. Just as she was about to sit, she saw the unmistakable round figure of Short Bread waddling in through the open gate 102 yards away. Instead of sitting she climbed up on a bench in the second row and began to frantically wave her hat back and forth. Short Bread saw her and waved his stubby arm and began to waddle in her direction. It was not hard for him to see her, there was no one else in the grandstand, there was no

one else in the area except for the six men and Blodgett standing down by the rail and Midge on the bench waving her hat
back and forth.

"Hello, Little Lady," Short Bread said, which struck her as
funny because standing on the bench she was nine inches
taller than him. "What're you doing here? You should be
home getting your beauty sleep."

"I couldn't sleep," Midge said. She jumped down from the
bench. "I been watching the horses. Me and Blodgett there
has had a chat. What are you doing here?"

"I like to watch the workouts when I can. You pick up
information here and there. Try to get an edge."

"It's part of being a trout," Midge said.

"Right," Short Bread said, smiling his snowflake smile.
"It's all part of the game."

Midge sat on the bench. Short Bread sat beside her. Neither of them spoke. The question of Decker hung uncertainly
between them. Midge didn't want to ask if he had found him.
Short Bread hoped the subject wouldn't come up at all, after
what he'd done. He didn't know if Decker would show or not.
He didn't know which would be better for Midge. He felt
he'd made a mess of the whole thing. Marvin Kimberly God.

*"Midge wants that baby," him saying in the dark of the
Jockey Club, beneath the pink neon horse and rider. And
Decker asking, "She told you?" And him saying, "No, she's
afraid to admit it even to herself. But it's written all over her.
That's why she's getting smart all of a sudden. Because she
thinks you have to be smart to raise a baby. And you know
something? I don't think it's the baby you're afraid of. It's
her. You're afraid of this new Midge." And Decker saying,
"What's it to you? Besides, I owe this money." And him (pro-
tector of the innocent) saying, "I'll give you the thousand. I'll
give you a thousand bucks if you stay with Midge till after
the baby comes." And Decker, taking the money, leering, saying, "Who appointed you to play God?" And his own blas-
phemous reply: "Who appointed Him?"*

*It had seemed like the thing to do, in the bourbon-filled
night.*

"Your picture's in the paper," he said, and he took a newspaper from under his arm and handed it to her.

"My picture? Whaddaya mean, my picture?"

"Open it up," he said.

She unfolded the morning paper. Across the top a large black headline said: "Monsignor Brown Dead at 62." Halfway down, on the left side of the page, a smaller headline said: "Horses Spice Fiesta Crowning." Between the two headlines were two large pictures. One showed her, clear as could be, sitting in her Fiesta outfit atop the freed horse. Next to it another picture showed the Monsignor putting the crown on her head. Underneath the first picture it said: "Midge B. A. Smith sits atop one of the horses she claimed to have freed from Mountain Packing." Underneath the other picture it said: "Monsignor Joseph Brown crowns Ms. Smith the unofficial Fiesta princess moments before suffering a fatal heart attack."

There was a story next to the pictures about the Monsignor, another story under the pictures about the horses and Fiesta. She didn't feel like reading them now, but she looked at the pictures again. It was true, then. The Monsignor was dead. If they put it in the paper you knew it was true.

"They keep this up," she said, "I'll have no soul left at all."

Short Bread looked at her uncertainly, but she didn't bother to explain. Up above the sun had rolled behind a cloud, and a chill ran through her. She pulled her pea coat closed, though she didn't button it. She clenched the edges tight, as if she were fighting a fever. She forced herself to speak, and the shivering eased.

"So. You find old Decker last night?"

Short Bread put his hands on his fat knees. He was looking down at the ground. He saw an ant struggling along under a mighty burden of crumb. He let his eyes absently follow the ant.

"I did. I found him in a bar. Like I thought."

The ant crossed over in front of Midge, between her legs. She was watching it too. She leaned over to drop some spit on it to see what would happen. But her spit sprayed out like a shower. The ant continued on, undisturbed.

"So. Is he leaving town, or coming back, or what?"

Short Bread dropped some spit in a large round glob. It clung like jelly to the pavement. But the ant was long gone, under Midge's dangling sneaker and out the other side. He pulled out a handkerchief and wiped his mouth.

"He's thinking it over," he said. "He said he needs to think it over."

Midge nodded her head several times. She put her sneakers up on the back of the seat in front. The sun was out again and she let the front of her coat fall open.

"A man needs to think. I guess he's entitled to think," she said. But she didn't sound very convincing, even to herself. She leaned her head on Short Bread's shoulder. "Still, he didn't have to disappear like that."

Short Bread didn't answer. With her head against his shoulder, he started to lift his hand, to touch her cheek. But he hesitated in mid-course, and he pulled at his ear instead.

Midge closed her eyes to the sun. "Can I ask you something?" she said.

"What?"

Her eyes still were closed, her voice was dreamy as she spoke. "Can I see your daughter sometime?"

"See my daughter?"

"Mm-hmm. Some Sunday, when you go to visit her. I'd like to go too."

This time he did touch her cheek, lightly, as if he were brushing away a crumb. Midge didn't move for another moment. Then she opened her eyes, slowly, and sat up straight.

"I could teach her to color inside the lines. I used to be pretty good at coloring books."

"That would be very nice," Short Bread said. "Clarissa would like that a lot."

"Then it's a deal," Midge said.

"It's a deal," Short Bread said.

Out on the track a black horse was streaking toward the finish line, Kathee Praline aboard. Midge could tell by her pink jacket. They watched as Kathee stood in the stirrups and eased the horse to a walk around the turn, bringing him on back.

"Ajax is looking good," Short Bread said.

"How do you know it's Ajax?"

"Just by his looks. That right front leg got a white sock, for instance. Horses are individuals, like people."

They watched Kathee talk to Blodgett by the rail, then walk Ajax back toward the paddock. Short Bread started to stand.

"What's a machine?" Midge said.

"A machine? How do you mean, a machine?"

"I heard Kathee and Blodgett talking before. She said her machine didn't work, that the battery was dead. But she's got a new one to use for Blue Lady."

"What is it you want to know?"

"What were they talking about? What's a machine got to do with horses? With Blue Lady?"

Short Bread rubbed his mouth with his hand, as if he didn't want to speak. As if he was formulating his answer. For the first time, he heard all the birds, singing above.

"It's not really a machine," he said. "They just call it that. Other places they call it a buzzer. It's just a little flashlight battery. With two metal prongs attached. You touch both prongs at the same time, you get a shock."

"Why would anyone want a shock?"

"It's not for people. It's for the horses. Sometimes a jockey will carry one in a race. He'll touch it to the horse's neck as he rides. To make him run faster."

Midge looked at him, squinting, her mouth open.

"That's allowed?"

"It's not legal," Short Bread said. "But it's done."

"Come on," Midge said. "Tell me the truth. No joking."

"That's the plain truth. Scout's honor."

Midge looked at the newspaper in her lap, then up at Short Bread again. "But what if they got caught?"

"It's a felony. They could get kicked out of racing."

"Well, that proves it, then. Nobody is that stupid."

"It may be stupid, but they do it all the time. Nobody checks much. The last thing a track wants is a scandal."

"Maybe those Mexican boys do it," Midge said. "But not Kathee. She wouldn't do something like that."

Short Bread looked out across the infield and said nothing.

"She wouldn't," Midge insisted. "I know it!"

Short Bread kept his gaze averted. He didn't reply. Midge

looked at his belly under his brown shirt, and with her right hand clenched in a fist she punched it.

"Hey!" Short Bread said, more startled than hurt, and he grabbed her fist. Quickly Midge pulled it away. She turned her head away, wanting to cry, and saw Kathee Praline on Ajax walking down the slope behind the paddock, toward the barns.

"You wait here!" she said, and she shoved the newspaper into Short Bread's belly and jumped out of the seat.

"Where you going?" Short Bread said, but she was already five steps away, running past the empty seats toward the paddock. She ran as fast as she could, her wool cap clenched in one hand, her pea coat flapping, across the empty pavement where she usually picked up tickets among the taller people's feet, down the six stone steps to the paddock, almost falling on the last step but catching herself on the fence. She squirted through the opening and ran across the grass of the paddock, and through the rear gate, and started down the long dirt embankment, stumbling on rocks, catching her balance, running as fast as she could. Suddenly she was face to face with a large brown horse. She changed direction to avoid crashing into it and lost her balance and skidded to the dirt, throwing her hands out in front. She slid along the ground, scraping the base of her thumb before she managed to stop. She looked at her hand and saw it was raw with blood, but she didn't care. She jumped up and looked around, in the direction of Blodgett's barn, and saw Kathee's pink jacket still atop the horse. She hurled herself in that direction again, running full speed down the embankment, down the dirt road between the rows of barns, past another horse walking up, past two pickups stopped in the road, their drivers talking to each other, watching her running by. She kept going till she caught up with Kathee and Ajax outside Blodgett's barn, Kathee still aboard the horse, preparing to dismount.

"Hey!" Midge called as she came running up to her, breathing heavily, her heart pounding inside her.

Kathee looked down quizzically from the saddle. "You want me?"

Midge nodded but couldn't speak from running so fast. She tried to talk but found herself only coughing, and feeling slightly sick to her stomach. From down along the barn she saw Fool, the deaf and dumb boy, come out of a horse's stall with a pitchfork full of straw. She wanted to wave to him, but the pea coat was feeling heavy on her shoulders, and she didn't have the strength. She realized also that she no longer had her woolen hat. She must have dropped it while she was running, or when she fell.

Kathee, seeing that Midge couldn't speak, slid out of the saddle to the ground, holding the horse's reins in her hand. She patted his neck, and waited. Midge was surprised to discover that standing on the ground like this Kathee was not much taller than she was. An inch and a quarter at the most. She had never been this close to the jockey and was also surprised to see that she had on a lot of makeup, thick pancake makeup to cover up blotches in her skin. From ten feet away she looked all peaches and cream, the face of an angel, but up close there were sprinkles of pimples. From eating too much chocolate, she supposed.

Kathee waited till Midge caught her breath and stuck out her hand. "My name's Midge," she said, and Kathee, looking puzzled, shook it. "I got to ask you something."

"What do you want to know?" Kathee said.

Midge took more deep breaths, till her breathing slowed down. She was perspiring from running so fast, from the pea coat, from the sun, from being face to face with Kathee Praline. She didn't know how to ask.

"The machine," she said. "Is it true?"

The jockey frowned at the question. "Is what true?"

Midge looked around to see if anybody was near. The closest people were the two men in the pickups forty-nine yards away and Fool who had gone back into a stall and who couldn't hear anyway.

"This is private," Midge said. "I won't tell a soul. I just need to know. For myself."

"To know what?"

"If it's true you use a machine. Them buzzer things."

Kathee turned away. She reached under the belly of the black horse and uncinched her saddle and slid it off the horse's back. With both arms she carried it to a railing beside the barn and set the saddle there. Then she came back to the horse, with Midge standing beside it.

"I'd rather not talk about it."

Midge looked at her with pleading eyes. "I won't tell a soul. I swear. You're my favorite jockey, I root for you every race. I'm a friend of Blodgett's, and Short Bread, too."

"Yeah, I seen you with them," Kathee said.

"I won't say a word. I just need to know the truth. For myself."

The jockey took off her hard rubber helmet. She wiped her forehead with the arm of her warm-up jacket, and she shook out her curls.

"Everybody uses them," she said.

"Everybody? In every race?"

"Not every race. Some horses quit if you use it. Others run better. You got to know your horse?"

"How do you find out?"

"You test it. In the morning."

Midge felt as if she were dreaming. Standing here in the sun, face to face with Kathee Praline, having this impossible conversation.

"And Blue Lady? You use it with Blue Lady?"

"Have to," Kathee said. She lifted her right leg, scraped some mud from the bottom of her boot. "She's lazy, she's a pig. She won't run worth a damn without it. You give her the machine, she's a dream. It keeps her honest."

Midge looked down at the ground. She pressed her lips together. "It don't seem honest to me."

"Hey, lady," Kathee said, banging her helmet against her thigh. "I don't know why I'm talking to you. I really don't. But you said you want the truth, so I'm giving you the truth. There's a lot of crap that goes on at a race track. Everyone knows that. There's trainers that dope horses so they don't win. There's trainers that pay you extra to hold their horses back. There's jocks who rig races every week. I won't do any of that shit. I go all out to win, every time."

Midge licked the scar on her lip, heartened somewhat by the outburst.

"I knew it! But . . . Why do you use the machine, then?"

"Because it helps me win. That's what this business is about. Winning. That's what they pay me for."

"What if you get caught?"

"I see to it that I don't."

The jockey lifted her other boot to remove more mud. "Any more questions?"

"No," Midge said to the ground.

The jockey took the horse's reins and prepared to lead it away. Fool came over, waiting to cool down the horse.

"Yeah," Midge said. "One more question. Today. Blue Lady?"

"I told you," the jockey said. "She won't run worth a damn without it."

"Right," Midge said. "You told me."

Kathee waited several more seconds. When Midge didn't speak again she led the horse over to Fool, who took it from her. Then she came back and took her saddle from the rail and put it in the front seat of a pickup that was parked nearby. She closed the door and went around the front and climbed in behind the wheel. Midge walked over to the truck as the engine started.

"Good luck in the race," she said.

Kathee threw the floor shift into gear. "Right," she said to Midge out the window, and then she drove off, Midge watching a trail of dust rising on the dirt road. SPITFIRE, the license plate said.

She felt very warm in her pea coat now, she was wet all over. She took off the coat and put it under her arm. In front of the barn, Fool was attaching Ajax to one of the metal machines that let the horses walk round and round in a circle without getting anywhere. Everything else seemed peaceful down here. Peaceful and hand-made. The walking machines seemed out of place. She watched for two minutes as Fool disappeared into another stall and the horse walked around in circles by itself. Then she turned, the pea coat under her arm, and walked slowly along the dirt road, back up toward the embankment and the track.

Short Bread was down by the rail, talking to Blodgett. She walked over to the empty benches and sat alone in the second row, where they'd been before. She put her pea coat on the seat beside her, put her sneakered feet on the back of the seat in front. Horses were still being worked on the track. On the highway behind it the morning traffic was increasing. But those were the only signs of life. The tote board wasn't lit. There was no flag on top of the flagpole. The only building she could see was the penitentiary, 1.8 miles away. Behind the city, which she couldn't see from here, the mountains looked pale in the morning light. In a few weeks, she knew, the aspen leaves would be turning, turning the whole mountains golden. Up above, the singing birds had lost their voice.

For twenty minutes she sat that way, alone, looking out beyond the track at the pale morning mountains. Much of the time, unconsciously, her tongue was licking her lip. When, at last, her reverie was broken by footsteps, when she saw Short Bread walking toward her, she knew what she had to do. She had not so much made a decision as rummaged around inside herself, inside the jumble in her head, and seen with sudden clarity what had been there, veiled by doubts and uncertainty, all along.

Short Bread eased himself onto the bench beside her. "Why'd you go running off like that?" he said.

Midge clasped her hands on her knees, her sneakers still up on the back of the bench in front. "I had to talk to Kathee. To ask about the machine."

"What did she say?"

"She said it was true. Like you said."

"That get you upset?"

"Yeah."

"Me, too," Short Bread said. "The first time I heard of it, years ago. But it's the way of the world. Everybody looking for an edge."

"Yeah," Midge said.

"There ain't no saints among us. And very few has got the mark of innocence."

"What about Clarissa?"

"Maybe," Short Bread said. "Maybe."

Out on the track the horses were thinning out. They watched together in silence for a time. Then Midge spoke.

"I'm gonna have my baby."

Short Bread nodded his head, as if he had known it all along. "What made you decide?" he said.

Midge squeezed her lips together with her hand, then bit her fingernail. She looked at Short Bread's face, then out at the track as she spoke.

"The machine. The buzzer. It's bad enough betting your baby on a horse. That was me and Decker. One of our things, you know. The way we used to be. Then it turns out the horse don't run without no machine. And the machine don't run without no battery. And the battery could die in the middle." She looked at Short Bread's face. "I was betting my baby on an Eveready. And I didn't even know it."

Short Bread blew breath into his fist. "I guess you could look at it like that."

"It ain't just that," Midge said. "I mean, it's not the machine that decided me. The machine just made me see the truth. Ain't nobody outside can decide things for you. You got to decide things for yourself. No horse race can do it, no Terry Blodgett or Kathee Praline or Blue Lady. No Monsignor, even. The Monsignor dropped dead last night, for Chrissake. I got this baby inside me, and I want it, and I don't care what anybody says, not Decker or anybody or Decker. If Decker wants to come back and be its daddy, well, maybe he can. And if Decker don't come back, I'll be its mommy and its daddy too. Maybe that ain't the best arrangement, but I'll do the best I can. You do the best you can, right? Heck, little Cynomys loved me a lot."

Short Bread's face seemed to glow as he turned to her. He took both of her hands in his.

"Congratulations," he said. And he leaned over and kissed her cheek.

"Congratulations for what?" Midge said. "For not being dumb no more?"

"For your intended," Short Bread said. "For your intended little one."

"Oh," Midge said. She held herself very still, trying to be a lady. But she couldn't. She threw her arms around Short Bread, and she pressed her face into his soft, fat shirt, and she cried.

It lasted less than a minute. She pulled herself away, sniffled, smiled, wiped her eyes with her coat.

"When you just talked to Blodgett," she said, still sniffling, "did he say Blue Lady's gonna win?"

"He's not sure. It's gonna be very close, either way."

"Oh, yeah? Well, Blue Lady better not lose," Midge said, wiping her nose with her fist. "It won't be no way to start off a baby."

They sat a few minutes longer in the sun, then walked together to the parking lot, to the Futura and the ratty-old parked side by side.

"Where you heading?" Short Bread said. "You like to get some breakfast?"

"I got to go home," Midge said. "I didn't sleep too good. I got to take a nap before the races." She climbed in behind the wheel and closed the door, then stuck her head out the window. "I'm sleeping for two now, ya know."

CHAPTER 13

The Unicorn Handicap

For the big race she put on her best pink pants, her sneakers, her best yellow blouse, the one that had soaked up Decker's beer that first night. Looking in the mirror behind the door, she felt that she looked the same. It was everything else that had changed. If she felt taller it was because everything else had shrunk since yesterday. The trailer had shrunk, where could you keep a baby in the trailer? The trailer park had shrunk, old pervert Peters was certainly no match for the Fiesta princess. The distance to the track had shrunk as Midge the Liberator of Doomed Horses drove toward it in the ratty-old in no time at all. Even the track itself had shrunk as she parked in general parking, paid to get in like everyone else, for the first time ever, and inched her way among the biggest crowd in the history of The Downs.

But if the world had shrunk down in size, if she was the only Sanforized thing in the lot, which felt pretty good, there had been another change also, which didn't. The world seemed to have tarnished at the edges. The magic with which she had always imbued it was gone. Until today there had always been magic in the endless blue of the sky—what made it blue up there when it was colorless down here? There had been magic in the clouds—what held them up?—and in the rain—who spilled it down? There had been magic in the beauty of horses, so strong and proud, and in the antics of prayer dogs, so small and funny. There had even been magic in being Beatrice, or Midge, in being the smallest person you knew, in being the only one you knew with a harelip. It was the magic of being special. That was the difference between her and Decker from the beginning. She knew always, deep down inside, that she was special. Decker didn't know that he was special too. A shortage of genies, like she said.

As she moved through the crowd, as she looked at the American flag atop the pole, as she watched the horses being saddled for the first race, she did not feel bad. She felt quite good, in fact. She'd had a good nap, with pleasant dreams. She had a bag of shortbread in the car for Short Bread. She was going to have a baby, and it was right. It was just what she wanted all along. She'd even had a new thought, a kind of ambitious thought, that she had never had before: that even though her job was supposed to end next week, and she was supposed to go back on Welfare, that maybe, with her picture on the front page of the paper for freeing the doomed horses, which showed how much she loved all animals, that maybe, because of this, they would keep her on at the department full time, that she could work there all year round, at least till the baby came. She wasn't sure if they had a job full time, but it wouldn't hurt to go see Dr. W. Manheim and ask. She even thought of something she could tell him: that it wouldn't be such good publicity if they let her go.

These were big thoughts, she felt. Smart thoughts. Adult thoughts. It was as if, at thirty and a quarter, she had become a grown-up at last, something she had thought would never happen. It was a good feeling, but also it wasn't. She would miss the magic. Numbers, even, seemed somehow less special, as if things that measured magic were magic themselves, but things that measured the ordinary were only ordinary. She kept thinking of what had happened to her father. When she was a little girl she had thought her father was the handsomest man in the world. Years later, many years after he died, when she had taken out his picture to look at it, he didn't seem so handsome anymore. He just looked like a man, like any other. That was how the world looked today. It didn't look so handsome anymore. It just looked like a world. Like any other.

She watched the first race being run, and the second, but she couldn't get too excited. In this machine age some of the magic was missing even from the races. This made her sad for a time, everyone yelling and screaming for their horses, not knowing they had bet on Evereadys. Then she had another adult thought. It occurred to her that maybe they really did know. Maybe they knew and decided not to care. Maybe they purposely put the truth out of their minds for a few hours, so they could have some fun at the track playing make-believe, so they could have a few hours' pleasant escape from the real machine age that was waiting back in town, that was waiting all around.

This was dumb, she decided. It was dumb to make believe that you didn't know the truth. And then she thought: maybe that's what I been doing all these years.

The thought made her ill. She quickly rejected it. It wasn't so. She hadn't known anything. She hadn't known at all.

The third race was run, and the fourth. She didn't see Short Bread in the crowd, but she didn't go out of her way to look for him. Not yet. She was enjoying being alone in the crowd. She was enjoying thinking all these thoughts. She'd been alone in many crowds before, it occurred to her, usually with a wide circle of space. But never quite like this. Never, before, by choice.

She had half a thought that people might recognize her from the night before, from her picture in the paper. That they might come up to her to shake her hand, to thank her for freeing the doomed horses. But nobody did, nobody seemed to notice her. They were too busy reading the racing forms, making their bets, watching the horses being saddled, watching the races on the track. Maybe they didn't care about the doomed horses at all. Maybe they had their own problems, maybe all that cheering for her last night was only beer and Fiesta, nothing more. Nothing to do with the horses at all. If that cop was right the doomed horses was probably all rounded up by now anyway, all taken back to be killed by Mountain Packing.

Then she remembered the boys taking the horse, to hide it. Maybe that one horse, at least, was safe. If that was so then it had all been worth it after all.

The fifth race passed, and the sixth. Her thoughts grew bigger and bigger, like a great balloon filling up. It was good being a large adult, even at four feet eleven. But she also felt dirty somehow, her hands felt sticky. She felt as if she was bad. If not all of her then part of her at least, though she didn't know what she had done. It was as if learning about the bad things in the world made you yourself bad. She couldn't figure out why this should be. What if she learned of more and more bad things? Would she herself begin to be worse and worse? If this was so then being grown-up might not be so nice at all.

Her brain was beginning to burst with all this thinking. It wasn't making sense anymore. She would have to discuss things with people. With persons.

The eighth race was coming up. The ninth would be Blue Lady. It was time to enjoy herself. To stop thinking. She thought she'd look for Short Bread Marvin Kimberly and watch the race with him. He wasn't by the paddock where she was—at least she didn't see him in the crowds—so he must be down by the rail. As she started to move in that direction, she felt a tap on her shoulder. Short Bread had found her, she figured, and she turned around. But it wasn't Short Bread at all who was standing there. It was Decker.

For half an instant they looked at each other's eyes.

"Hi," Decker said. He said it in a small voice, and then he looked away, sheepishly.

"Hi," Midge said. She felt embarrassed. They both felt embarrassed. They hadn't felt embarrassed like this since the first night. The night of the peeping Tom.

"How you been?" Decker said.

"Pretty good, if I say so myself."

They were speaking as if they hadn't seen each other for fourteen years, instead of fourteen hours. As if they couldn't help themselves.

"You're looking good," Decker said.

"You too."

Decker's cheek muscle began throbbing. Midge looked down at her sneakers.

"I ain't been picking up tickets," she said. "I didn't know if you was coming."

"That's okay," Decker said.

All around them people began moving away as the horses

left the paddock and moved up onto the track. Where a minute ago they were in the middle of a crowd, now they were all alone. They walked together to the paddock rail. Inside the paddock the last of the trainers were moving out, leaving it empty in the afternoon sun.

"I got to talk to you," Decker said.

"Why'd you run out on me?"

Decker turned away from her and looked across the paddock, beyond the shed with its colored, numbered stalls, to the faded mountains in the distance. His hand gripped tight to the rail.

"I was scared," he said.

"Scared?" She put her hand on his shoulder. "What was you scared of?"

"Everything. I was scared of you."

"Me? How could you be scared of me?"

"Up on that stage last night. You looked so pretty. I always been kinda scared of pretty things."

"Why would you be that? You take me, I love pretty things. Flowers and prayer dogs and such."

"I don' know. You got something pretty, you worry all the time about losing it."

"But while you got it, you got it."

"Yeah, that's what I been thinking. While you got it you got it.'

"You can't be a getaway in everything."

"That's another thing," Decker said. His face looked pained beneath his close-cropped hair. "I ain't never been a professional getaway. Not really."

"Oh, yeah? What do you call last night?"

"I don't mean that. I mean twenty-eight robberies and stuff. I made them up. Two jobs was all I pulled."

"I know," Midge said.

"Whattaya mean, you know?" He looked at her with needle eyes.

"Jack told me. One visiting day."

"You mean you knew all along? Then how could you let me pretend like that? Like a first-class jerk."

"You let me pretend I was a scientist, right? Everyone pretends about something."

269

Decker pulled his Camels from his shirt pocket, but he couldn't find his matches. He put the cigarettes away. He puckered his mouth and blew a smoke ring in the air, without any smoke.

"Anyway, I'm sorry I run out last night."

Midge looked again at her sneakers, but didn't answer. It occurred to her that loafers might look more ladylike than sneakers. She would have to get herself a pair of loafers. She tried to think of what to say, but instead heard her name being called. Her old name.

"Beatrice!"

It was Mrs. Gallegos from work, coming up behind them. Mrs. Gallegos looked from one to the other, waiting to be introduced.

"Hi. This is Mrs. Gallegos, from the plague. This here is my friend, H. Decker." She wasn't very enthusiastic at the moment.

"Nice to meet you," Mrs. Gallegos said. "You here for the big race?"

"Wouldn't miss it," Decker said.

The big race? For a minute Midge had forgot what they were talking about.

"Who do you think will win?" Mrs. Gallegos said.

"Blue Lady," Midge said.

"Not me," Mrs. Gallegos said. "I'm betting Thunderbolt. How about you, Mr. Decker."

"I'm with Midge," Decker said. "Blue Lady all the way."

Midge looked at his face, at his crazy eyes. They didn't seem crazy just now. They seemed to be almost smiling. She'd never seen his eyes smiling before.

"Well, that's what makes horse races," Mrs. Gallegos said. "You heard about the Monsignor? Poor devil. I guess the Lord gave him his comeuppance."

"Everybody dies," Midge said.

Mrs. Gallegos ignored the statement. "You were wonderful last night, Beatrice. Up there on the stage. You'll be the hit of the department come Tuesday. With your picture in the paper and all."

Midge and Decker didn't know what to say. They stood in

silence, until Mrs. Gallegos spoke. "I have to find my husband. See you later," she said, and she turned and left.

"See you later," Midge called out, afraid that she had acted rude. But when she turned back to Decker, things had changed. Before Mrs. Gallegos had showed up, they were stiff and different with each other. After she left it felt like yesterday. As if nothing had happened at all. Their assumed pretensions were gone. Their old, comfortable pretends were back. Once more they were alone together.

"One thing I got to tell you," Midge said, "the better the sooner than later."

"What's that?"

"The bet's off."

"What bet's off?"

"Betting the baby on Blue Lady. The bet's off."

"Well of course the bet's off," Decker said, "seeing as how we're both for Blue Lady."

"How come you're for Blue Lady now?"

"I got some information. From a trout."

Midge punched his arm with her pointy elbow. "The word is 'tout,' she said. "Unless it's me who says it."

Decker found her hand at her side and threaded his fingers through hers.

"Don't get fresh," she said. "I got something else to say."

"What's that?"

"I'm gonna have my baby."

Decker placed the flat of his palm on her head.

"I know."

"I got to, Deck. I want it more than anything."

"I know," he said again.

He leaned over and kissed her, softly, on the lips. He started to pull away, then put his arms around her and pulled her close and kissed her again. Midge was blushing when they pulled apart.

"Deck! Why'd you do that? People will see!"

"So who the hell cares? H. Decker don't care what nobody thinks. Never did, never will."

"Oh, yeah? Since when?"

"Since now."

Midge looked up at his tall form. She put her arms around him, tightly, and hugged him. She didn't know when she had felt so happy in her life.

They stayed that way for a moment, feeling each other's warmth, and then the gesture, her head against his chest, reminded her of Short Bread, whom she hadn't seen since the morning.

"Let's go find Short Bread," she said. "Let's go tell Short Bread Marvin Kimberly!"

"Let's go find who?" Decker said.

"Short Bread."

"Short Bread? Who the hell is Short Bread?"

"You remember Short Bread. He's the round fat black man who . . ." She stopped in mid-sentence as she looked at his face and saw it turning red from holding in his laughter. "Nerd!" she said, and she punched him hard in the shoulder.

"Gotcha that time," Decker said.

She tried to be mad, but she couldn't. Her whole plan was out the window, and there was nothing she could do about it. She'd made up a whole plan when she woke from her nap and ate a peanut butter sandwich for lunch, about what she would say and do if Decker showed up at the track. Half of her felt sure that he was halfway to California by now and that she would never see him again. The other half of her felt sure that he would show up at the track, that he would get down on his hands and knees and beg her to take him back. And she knew what she was going to say then. She was going to say, first of all, that even if she was the Fiesta princess he was still a man, and that he should get up off his hands and knees, because it wasn't very manly to beg. She was going to say, second of all, that she was going to have her baby, take it or leave it. And if he made the slightest objection to that she was going to spin on the heel of her sneaker and walk away. The next thing she was going to say, third of all, was that he had been both cowardly and rude to disappear like that last night, right in the middle of her world's greatest triumph, and that this sort of behavior had to give a woman pause as to what sort of a man she was involved with. The fourth thing she was going to say, fourth of all, was that if he really wanted to come back for good, she would have to think it over. The fifth thing was that if they were going to get married they ought to do it soon, so the baby would be born in bedlock. The sixth thing was that a married man with a baby on the way should certainly get a job, washing dishes or whatever it took.

All these things she was going to say to him. All these things she would make him promise before she took him back. And here he was, and though she had said what needed to be said about the baby, that was all she had said. And all the rest didn't matter, all the rest was out the window. Because she wanted him back, one way or the other, him and the baby too. The rest would happen in time, she could tell. He would get a job and she would be at home in the trailer with the baby, giving him a bath so he would be nice and clean when her daddy came home from work—him or her, that is—and then Deck would come home with his newspaper and kiss her cheek, and bounce the baby in his arms, and she would ask him how was things at the office, and they would sit down and eat their hamburger sandwiches, and later on, when he was making more money and they could afford it, they would go out back and barbecue some steaks. That was how the world was gonna be. She had some names picked out for the baby, too. She could hardly wait to tell them to Short Bread.

But they couldn't seem to find him anywhere.

"I wonder where he is," Midge said. "He said he'd be here. I hope nothing's wrong."

"He was here before," Decker said. "I saw him."

"You did? Where?"

"Down by the winner's circle."

"Let's go look there now," she said, and she took his hand and led him toward the rail, easing their way among the thick-packed crowd. But Short Bread wasn't there.

"Where'd you see him?" she said.

"Right about here."

"How long ago was that?"

"Two races ago. We had a talk."

"I wonder where he went," Midge said. "Maybe something's wrong. Maybe he got a call from Albuquerque, that something's wrong with his daughter. Maybe he had to leave in a hurry."

"There ain't no telephones at the track," Decker said.

"There must be somewheres, for emergencies."

"I guess in the office somewhere. Maybe he went upstairs, to watch with the rich jerks."

"He wouldn't do that," Midge said. "We was gonna watch Blue Lady together."

They went back to the paddock, and then up and down through the grandstand, and then by the betting windows. They couldn't find him anywhere.

"I sure hope nothing's wrong," Midge said.

"It's the biggest crowd ever. They announced it. Prob'ly we just can't find him, is all."

"Yeah," Midge agreed, uncertainly. "Prob'ly, I guess."

She looked around again but there was 2.7 jillion people in every direction. It was hopeless to look. She decided they should wait by the paddock. That's where he would show if he was here.

The eighth race was over, the horses weren't up yet for the ninth. As they got to the paddock rail half the people at the track seemed to be following them, pressing close to await the arrival of the two horses for the big match race. To the left beyond the paddock Midge saw pale dirt swirling in the wind, and then over the embankment they came at a slow walk: first a man on a pony leading a big bay horse, which must be Thunderbolt. Then Blodgett on a pony leading the little gray. Blue Lady.

The horses were led by handlers into the first two stalls, Thunderbolt into number one, Blue Lady to number two. As the horses were being saddled a bunch of jockeys came down the ramp, some in silks, some in undershirts, and walked out to a slope of grass beyond the paddock, and lounged in the sun. They were riders who weren't in the race but wanted to watch it from there. A few minutes later two other jockeys came down the ramp and sat on the bench at the bottom. The first was Bobby Juarez, the Mexican apprentice, the leading rider at the track this year. He was wearing the special black silks with gold stars of Thunderbolt's owner. The second, dressed all in white except for her brown boots, was Kathee Praline. Blue Lady's owner—the late Monsignor, or Danny Roybal of Chimayo, or whomever—did not have special silks, even for the big race. Kathee was wearing the ordinary whites of number two.

Midge peered hard at Kathee Praline. She knew now that the jockey had blotches on her face, and pimples. But from here she couldn't see them. Kathee always looked her best in the whites of number two, and from here, nineteen feet away, she looked as beautiful as ever.

In the middle of the paddock the starter looked at his watch. "Okay, riders," he said, and Bobby Juarez and Kathee got up, talking and laughing together, and walked toward the horses. Bobby was boosted onto Thunderbolt, Kathee onto Blue Lady, and while the crowd stirred with excitment the shortest post parade in the history of The Downs at Santa Fe made its way onto the track. Midge looked intently as they passed, staring at the hands, first at the hands of Bobby Juarez, then at the hands of Kathee. They were holding the reins but that was all she could see. There weren't any machines that she could see.

"Maybe they ain't gonna use them," she said.

"What?"

"Nothing, Deck. I'll tell ya later. I ain't supposed to say in public." Her staring eyes were on the rumps of the horses now, but her thoughts were on the jockeys' hands. "Maybe she took to heart what I said. Maybe they ain't gonna use them after all!"

The horses were up on the track, parading in front of the stands. From high above, the track announcer was talking down.

"And now ladies and gentlemen the horses are on the track for the running of today's ninth and feature race, the Unicorn Handicap, a $25,000 match race, winner take all. This is a first annual invitational race between the leading two-year-old at The Downs and the leading two-year-old at Tucson Park in Arizona. The race is six furlongs. Number one is Thunderbolt, unbeaten in six starts this year at Tucson. Thunderbolt is owned by C. J. Forman of Phoenix, trained by Walter Larkin. He'll be ridden by the leading rider of the season here at The Downs, Bobby Juarez. Number two is Blue Lady, unbeaten in eight starts here since May. Blue Lady, a filly, is owned by Danny Roybal of Chimayo, and trained by Terry

Blodgett. She'll be ridden by her regular rider, number two in the standings this year, Kathee Praline. In this two-horse race there will be only Win betting. Post time in nine minutes."

As the announcer talked, the people melted away from the paddock, swarming toward the rail to give the horses another look, or up toward the grandstand to bet. Like waters parting they flowed away, Midge and Decker standing their ground, waiting, and then through the ebbing throng they saw Short Bread pushing his way upstream to meet them.

"He's here!" Midge said, happily. "Here he comes!" She took Decker's hand and they hurried over.

"Howdy," Short Bread said.

"Howdy," Midge echoed. "Where you been? We been looking all over."

"You have? Sorry about that. I thought we were supposed to meet before the ninth. I've been keeping busy, meeting folks, greeting folks. Big crowd today. Lots of action."

"Oh," Midge said.

"He means he's been working," Decker said, seeing her disappointment, "It's his job."

"I know it's his job," Midge said, irritated. She felt hurt without knowing why, and then she told herself that wasn't true, she knew exactly why. Short Bread was so special to her. She'd rescued him from loneliness on the food line last night, they'd watched Zozobra together, they freed the horses, he'd helped her when Decker left, they'd had the best talk she'd ever had with anyone. About a shortage of genies and all. She thought he liked her, too, that she was special to him, that prob'ly they'd be friends all the time. And here he was, showing up only for the ninth, when they could have watched every race together. She'd forgot that this whole daytime world out here was different. That this was Short Bread's game. That he had a million people out here to see. Then she remembered that the first few races, caught up in her own big thoughts, she hadn't looked for him, either. It was terrible, but she hadn't. She had no right to feel hurt. Even if she did anyway.

"Well, here we are," Midge said, because nobody else was talking. "Midge and Decker, together again!"

"So I see," Short Bread said. "That's good. That's real good."

"And baby makes three," she said, patting her belly.

"Be just about Kentucky Derby time," Decker said. "That's what I figured out. The foal should drop maybe right on Derby day."

"Be a good omen," Short Bread said.

"I got the names all picked out, too," Midge said. "If it's a boy we're gonna name it after Decker."

"We are?" Decker said.

"Well of course we are. We'll call it Decker Junior."

"That ain't a name," Decker said, but he seemed to be pleased anyway.

"Well, you don't like Horace, so you'll have to pick another one. Larry Decker Junior, or Richard Decker Junior. Whatever you like."

"And if it's a girl?" Short Bread said.

"I had one name picked out yesterday for a girl. Kathee Blue. Kathee Blue Decker. That's what I picked out yesterday, when the bet was on. Also, I figured that with me and Decker being both kinda short, we might raise ourselves a jockey. And that would be a pretty good name. Kathee Blue. But I'm not sure if that's such a good idea, cause riding gives you pimples."

"It does?" Short Bread said.

"Sure it does. To ladies. But anyway, since the bet's off, I thought of another name."

She waited. She waited for them to ask her. But they didn't.

"Well, ain't you gonna ask me?" she said.

"He already asked you," Decker said.

"Ask me again. Ask me what it's gonna be if it's a girl."

"Jesus H. Christ!" Decker said. "What's it gonna be if it's a girl?"

Shyness came over her as she looked at Short Bread's face.

"Clarissa," she said. "Clarissa Kimberly Decker."

"That's pretty," Decker said.

He waited for somebody else to say something, but they didn't. Short Bread and Midge were staring at each other's face. Finally Short Bread spoke. "That's real pretty," he said

Midge and Short Bread both discovered embarassing things to look at on the pavement, till Decker couldn't stand it anymore.

"Enough of this baby talk. Who's gonna win this here race?"

"Blue Lady," Short Bread said.

They all looked out at the track. The horses were walking in a circle behind the starting gate.

"How do you know?" Midge said. "You said it was gonna be close."

"I been nosing around. Thunderbolt don't like the altitude. He's gonna fade in the stretch."

"You sure of that?" Decker said.

Short Bread, still looking across the track, nodded.

"Then maybe I should go bet," Decker said.

"All you'll win is ten cents on a dollar."

"That's a hundred bucks, if I bet a thousand."

"That's a good one," Midge said. "I think I'll bet a million. A million on Blue Lady."

"What do you think?" Decker said to Short Bread.

"All I said was that Thunderbolt's gonna tire in the stretch. That don't mean Blue Lady can't break a leg."

"Like Ruffian?" Midge said.

"Precisely."

"Blue Lady won't break no leg. I'm putting my million on Blue Lady. How about you, Deck?"

"I think I'll hold onto my thousand," Decker said.

"Yeah, I guess that makes sense," Midge said, all bubbly. "If I win my million it's half of it yours anyway. So you hold onto your thousand just in case."

She took his hand and threaded her fingers through his. She loved it when he would kid with her like this.

A moment later it was post time. They stood that way, Midge and Decker holding hands, Short Bread beside them, as first Thunderbolt and then Blue Lady were led into the starting gate far across the track.

"Maybe they won't use no machines," Midge said. "When they came out I didn't see them holding no machines."

"They don't hold them where you can see them," Short Bread said.

The crowd was tense, expectant, as an assistant starter fussed with the gate. On the highway beyond the track there was no traffic at all. Up above, the sky was a deep blue, and cloudless. A question flashed through Midge's mind: would she rather have Blue Lady win with a machine, or lose without it? It was fifty-fifty, she told herself, she didn't know the answer. But she knew that wasn't true.

Her hand felt very sticky. She rubbed it on her pants. Just as the gate sprang open, she crossed her fingers.

"They're off," the announcer said, and by that time the horses were already five lengths out of the gate, running side by side, appearing from the grandstand as if they were one horse.

Down the backstretch they sped, or rather it sped, because that was all she could see, this one brown horse, Thunderbolt, this one jockey in black and gold silks leaning over it, legs stretching, hooves flashing, the crowd roaring now, the two horses so perfectly synchronized that the gray on the outside had become invisible, the female jockey invisible; they had disappeared so completely that in momentary panic Midge flashed her eyes back toward the starting gate, to see if something was wrong, to see if Blue Lady had fallen, had not gotten out of the gate. But no, the gate was empty, she must be out there, filly beside colt, jockey beside jockey, one beautiful creature in lockstep—they must be together, you had to take it on faith—as if it were not a race at all but some timeless exhibition, until, going into the turn suddenly there was a double image, Thunderbolt on the rail with a neck in front, Blue Lady, with more ground to cover, trailing slightly, eight legs visible now instead of four, brown horse, black rider trailed ever so slightly now by their paler gray and white shadows. Around the turn they raced that way, the brown with a neck in front, holding its edge, the crowd on its feet now, bettors and fans screaming for their favorites—"Come on, Blue, catch him, catch him!" Midge screaming in wild abandon, Decker squeezing her hand, Short Bread watching, outwardly calm, his heart pounding in spite of himself, the two horses side by side now coming out of the turn, the riders low over their necks, holding nothing back, going to the whip now, Juarez first so that Thunderbolt seemed to leap forward, to gain a few more feet, to lead by half a length, ready to draw away, then Kathee going to the whip, just twice, Blue Lady fighting back, the smaller horse seeming to lengthen its stride, beginning to gain, a foot, two feet, the two of them roaring down the stretch, Blue and Kathee on the grandstand side now, Bobby Juarez whipping non-stop with his left hand, Kathee not using the whip but leaning low over the horse, neck-riding, neck-riding, gaining with every stride, inches behind now, then even, the two of them straining toward the finish side by side, dead even, one horse again, the crowd in a frenzy, and then, ten feet from the wire, Thunderbolt seeming to falter, Blue Lady to leap forward, whichever, Blue Lady pulling away in the last two strides, flashing across the finish line in front by a head. The two jockeys standing in the irons, the horses continuing on around the far turn, unable to slow down even, the roaring crowd a thunderstorm of noise—"She did it, she did it, she did it!" Midge screaming at the top of her lungs, jumping up and down, Decker still squeezing her hand—the horses slowing finally far out in the backstretch, Midge running out of voice, out of strength, collapsing, almost, into Decker's arms, Decker holding her up. The noise beginning to taper off, then exploding into a roar again as the tote board lit up in red—PHOTO—the grandstand abuzz like a nest of bees, she won it, she won it, Midge saying, I swear it; Short Bread saying they just want to be sure, but she won it all right, and then the PHOTO sign going out, the numbers up on the board in order, first 2, then 1; the crowd roaring again. Midge limp from the excitement looking at Decker, putting her arms round his neck, oblivious to everything around her, saying softly, despite the noise: "I guess we can have our baby now, huh?"

They didn't stay to see the rest of the races. They waited till the horses came back, they pressed into the crowd near the winner's circle, they watched as pictures were taken of Blue Lady, Kathee Praline up. Midge peered as best she could over the taller people, looking at Kathee's hands as she held the reins, as she uncinched her saddle, as she got on the scale and weighed in. Hard as she looked she didn't see a machine. But that didn't mean much, she knew. What you could see meant hardly nothing. Prob'ly she'd never know, one way or the other. She liked it better that way.

When the jockeys disappeared and the crowd broke up they walked on out of the track, out to the parking lot. Midge pulled Short Bread along with them, to the ratty-old, and she reached in and pulled out a brown paper bag and gave it to him, the shortbread that she had baked.

"It's delicious," Short Bread said, taking a bite, but he didn't take another bite, he put the piece back in the bag, saying he would save it till after dinner. "Thanks a lot," he said.

"Thanks for nothing," she said. "It's me who got to thank you." And she put her arms around his bulk as best she could, and she kissed him on the cheek.

"Give a kiss to Clarissa, too," she said, and then they were inside the ratty-old, Decker at the wheel, driving off, Short Bread watching them go, his round bulk receding behind them.

Decker drove slowly through the parking lot, then faster on the access road. "Son of a goddamn fuckin' bitch!" he said.

"What's the matter?" Midge said, startled.

"I coulda won a hundred bucks," he said. And he reached into his side pocket and tossed a handful of money on the seat between them.

"Where'd you get this?" Midge said, wide-eyed. She gathered up the bills and counted them. There were ten one-hundred dollar bills. "A thousand dollars. You really had a thousand real dollars!"

" 'Course I did," Decker said. "Horace Decker don't mess around."

Midge watched his face as he swung the car from the access road onto the highway, heading back toward town. She had never seen that much money before.

"I ain't supposed to ask, huh?" she said. "Your business."

Decker peered through the spotty windshield at the traffic ahead. On the left, the horse and rider above the Jockey Club were not yet lighted. He seemed to be measuring his words.

"It ain't really mine," he said "It's a loan. I owe this guy some money. Short Bread give me a loan, to pay him back. I'm gonna pay Short Bread back, little by little. When I get a job."

"Oh," Midge said. She wasn't entirely sure she understood. She would figure it out later.

"I got one thing to say, though" Decker said.

"What?"

"If we're gonna stay together—if we're gonna get married, or whatever—I don't want you kissing no more niggers."

"What? Who? Kissing nig——? What are you talking about? You mean Short Bread? That ain't no nig——." She was livid as she looked at his face, she was ready to scream at him to stop the car. Then she saw his face turning red, saw him bursting to keep from laughing.

"Oooooh!" she said, letting out her breath, and she punched his knee as hard as she could.

"Ouch!" he said. "I gotcha again, didn't I?"

"You just wait," she said. "You wait till I get you."

"I'll be waitin'," Decker said.

Her fist hurt from hitting his knee. In her other hand was a thousand real dollars. She started to put it in her pocket, for safekeeping. Then she got an idea.

"I think I'll throw this money out the window," she said, "since it ain't yours anyway." And she threw her hand holding the money out past where the wire was tied, and the wind ripped greedily at her fist.

"Wha!" Decker said, grabbing for her, and then he had to grab the wheel again as the car swerved almost off the road.

Midge pulled her hand back in, still holding the money.

"I think the score is tied," she said. "One-one."

She folded the money and put it in her pocket. On the dashboard in front of her was her cap that said The Downs. She put it on her head, then pulled it over her face, till the dark peak covered her eyes, her nose, her lips. She rode that way, happy and silly both, all the way home.